THE DEVIL
AND THE
DEEP BLUE
SEA

A JERSEY SHORE MYSTERY

BETH SHERMAN

AVON BOOKS
An Imprint of HarperCollinsPublishers

AVON BOOKS
An Imprint of HarperCollins*Publishers*
10 East 53rd Street
New York, New York 10022-5299

Copyright © 2001 by Beth Sherman
ISBN: 0-380-81605-9
www.avonbooks.com

First Avon Books paperback printing: May 2001

Avon Trademark Reg. U.S. Pat. Off. and in Other Countries, Marca Registrada, Hecho en U.S.A.
HarperCollins ® is a trademark of HarperCollins Publishers Inc.

Printed in the U.S.A.

10 9 8 7 6 5 4 3 2 1

*For Sam,
with love*

Acknowledgments

My novels need lots of TLC, not just from me, but from people who provide me with esoteric information free of charge, people who read my work and offer suggestions on how to improve it, and most importantly, people who help me find time to write. Thanks to Andy Edelstein, Jessie Rose Edelstein, Dominick Abel, Trish Grader, Johanna Keller, Lindsey Murphy, Harriet Ellner, Luci Zahray, Cyndi Raftus, and Maryellen Rowley, R.N. I'd also like to thank the following law-enforcement officials for their help and expertise: Neptune Police Chief James A. Ward and Mauro V. Corvasce and Joseph R. Paglino, detectives with the Monmouth County Prosecutor's Office in New Jersey. Any mistakes, intentional or otherwise, are mine.

Chapter 1

*Raising children is
one of life's greatest
challenges. Nobody tells
you how hard it is until
after it's too late to send
the kids back.*

Dr. Arlene Handelman,
*From Diapers to Dating:
Becoming the Perfect Parent*

The body lay at an angle about forty yards from the ocean, surrounded by tall dune grass that rippled softly in the early-morning breeze. Around it an imperfect circle had been traced in the sand in such a way that each limb was carefully circumscribed within the circle's confines. It was the body of a girl, a teenager with a deep tan and curly black ringlets fanning out from her face like dark tendrils. Her eyes were closed, her head

1

tilted to the side, her chin jutting skyward. She wore short denim cutoffs and a tight black top with a plunging neckline. Around her throat, choker-style, she wore a rectangular piece of amber fastened with a black velvet ribbon. On her feet were black sandals with lots of crisscrossing straps and chunky three-inch heels.

They were the type of shoe favored by Jersey girls that summer, along with butterfly-shaped hair clips, tie-dyed tank tops, and violet-pink lipstick. This girl was wearing the lipstick and had painted her nails and toes the same color. She wasn't especially pretty. Her nose was too big for her narrow face. Her mouth, which hung open, revealed a prominent overbite and slightly crooked teeth. She would have looked vulnerable lying motionless in the sand had there not been a certain toughness about her features, a hard, brittle aspect, as though somewhere during her adolescence she'd learned life would kick her in the face if she didn't kick hard first.

It was just after dawn on a hot August morning, the kind of day when the heat started building early and got more and more oppressive as the hours wore on. But now the sun was partially hidden by a strand of clouds, and a fine layer of mist hung over the beach, obscuring part of the water and the entire horizon.

Anne Hardaway had been out for her usual morning three-mile run and was heading home along the boardwalk. She had her Walkman tuned to a jazz station and was in what she called the "zone," an endorphin-induced state in which the pounding of her feet, the pumping of her arms and the steady melodious flow of the music made it feel like she was gliding over the gray wooden planks. When she caught sight of the girl she pulled up short and stopped, instinctively flicking the radio off.

The body lay fairly close to the boardwalk, facing the ocean. Anne approached the railing, swung herself over it, and dropped down onto the sand. She knew the girl was dead. She knew by the way the body was sprawled on the beach, legs askew, absolutely still. But it was the last thing she expected to see on a morning jog through Oceanside Heights, and her brain was having trouble processing the information. The mist that hung over the beach seemed to bathe the air in white gauze. Anne was aware that her heart was flapping noisily in her chest, that all her senses were keyed up. Colors had become sharper, the pounding of the surf and the keening of the gulls throbbed in her ears.

She stepped closer, moving carefully through the dune grass. The girl was a local. Anne had seen her around before, hanging out on the beach, maybe working behind the counter at one of the inns that served the tourist trade. A friend of Tracy's, that was it. Anne had seen them both on Main Street last week, their heads bent close together, talking loudly and steadily the way teenagers do, lost in their own private world, as if nobody else existed.

She noticed the circle traced around the body and, taking care not to disturb it, knelt beside the dead girl. A faint unpleasant dusky odor rose from the body. The girl's right hand was curled into a fist, and there were a couple of empty Heineken bottles by her feet. Anne gazed at the body. No surface wound or any sign of blood. The only visible mark on the girl's tanned skin was a tattoo of a black, fanged snake, near her left ankle.

Anne stared at the tattoo, at the amber choker around the girl's throat. She shivered suddenly, although the morning air was warm. Something had gone very wrong here. Out of the corner of her eye, she caught sight of a scrap of white fluttering in the grass. Rising, she walked nearer and came upon a dirty piece of paper. She held the paper up to the light. There were three strange marks written on the paper in faint black ink.

They looked like ancient hieroglyphic symbols. Anne studied the paper for some time. When she looked up, the mist seemed to have thickened. The water fanned out before her and abruptly stopped, swallowed up by a curtain of white. She put the paper back where she found it.

Then, heart pounding, she turned from the body, sprinted home, and phoned the police.

In the summertime, the population of Oceanside Heights swelled to three times its original size. Tourists from as far away as Australia and Alaska descended upon the tiny town on the Jersey shore known as "God's own acre" for a glimpse of the historic Victorian architecture and the chance to attend one of the gospel sings, sermons and concerts at the Church by the Sea, the largest Methodist church on the entire Eastern seaboard.

The Heights had been founded in 1896 by a Methodist minister who organized fervent camp meetings by the ocean. That tradition had grown and flourished over the years until there were more than a hundred tents surrounding the church each summer and a long waiting list of people who wanted nothing more than to spend three months in the Heights soaking up the spirit of Christianity.

Up until about twenty years ago, blue laws were in place, forbidding a variety of activities on Sunday. You couldn't ride a bike, swim at the beach, hang wash, or play in the streets. You couldn't do home repairs or order ice cream unless you ordered a meal first. You had to park in Neptune and wait until Sunday at midnight to retrieve your car. Today all that survived was the ban on alcohol, which stores and restaurants were prohibited from selling. It served to make the Heights more family-oriented than some of the surrounding towns.

Of course, not everyone came for religious reasons. The town was picturesque, the beach was clean and pristine, and the accommodations much cheaper than in Cape May, its sister Victorian city to the south.

A dead body definitely disrupted the normal flow of events, especially on a hot Saturday morning when tourists and townspeople alike would normally have flocked to the narrow strip of beach and the sand would have been peppered with striped umbrellas and brightly colored towels.

Anne's yellow Victorian cottage was at the south end of town, directly across the street from the beach and about four blocks from where she'd spotted the body. From her front porch she could see police cars parked by the boardwalk and uniformed officers patrolling the sand. Two of the cops had questioned Anne for about twenty minutes. Then the girl's body had been taken to the Medical Examiner's Office in Freehold, and a section of beach had been cordoned off.

Anne had taken a quick shower, changed clothes, and was eating a breakfast of coconut donuts and mint iced tea on the porch. The mist was beginning to burn off, leaving the sun to fry everything it touched. The air felt heavy and thick. It was even hot in the shade.

Anne mopped her face with a napkin and pulled her curly red hair back into a ponytail. She loved living by the beach, but her skin was fair and if she sat in the sun for very long, she wound up looking like a boiled lobster.

In a couple of months, she'd be turning forty. Hard to believe. Each year, the summer seemed to get shorter and shorter. Maybe she needed a vacation. Or a lighter workload. Or a winning lottery ticket. Maybe if you had a lot of money, you could stretch the hours out like saltwater taffy. Then again, maybe not. The rich are different from you and me, F. Scott Fitzgerald once said. Yes, they had more problems.

Right now Anne's biggest problem was Dr. Arlene Handelman, who was upstairs in the guest bathroom singing an off-key rendition of "Love to Love You, Baby." Dr. Arlene, or Dr. A., as she was known to her fans across the country, was a radio psychologist. She was also the houseguest from hell.

It had all started ten days ago when Dr. Arlene showed up on Anne's doorstep unannounced and uninvited.

"Did you know," Dr. Arlene had said, sweeping into the living room with a suitcase, a bulging leather briefcase, and a black Prada bag, "that the Jersey Turnpike is one of the ten worst highways in America? Forget the rotten drivers, forget the fact that the whole damn road is one gigantic parking lot after five o'clock. You know what the worst thing is? The rest stops. You can't even get a decent cup of coffee at any of them and believe me, I've been trying. I stopped at the Vince Lombardi, the Thomas Edison, the Grover Cleveland." She paused for a split second to snap her gum, before barreling on. "Why do they all have such peculiar names? Whatever happened to Food/Gas/Lodging?"

Anne had watched Dr. Arlene with a sinking feeling in her heart. The suitcase looked awfully heavy. "What are you doing here?"

"On-site interaction. We're not making much progress,

as you must have noticed." Dr. Arlene had taken a silver compact out of the Prada bag and checked her face. The perm had fallen out of her dyed brown hair, which rested limply on her shoulders, windswept and disheveled, as if she'd been doing eighty on the Turnpike with the top down. Bright red lipstick was smeared on one of her front teeth, and two of the buttons had popped off the jacket on her too-tight flesh-colored gabardine pants suit. "God, I'm a wreck. I need a hot shower, a foot massage, and coffee that doesn't suck."

"You're not planning on . . ."

". . . staying with you? Just for tonight, Anne. Tomorrow, I'll check out some inns. See if any of 'em have a room that isn't falling apart at the seams and reeking of mildew."

Anne had sunk into a chair, trying to process the fact that Dr. Arlene was in the Heights, that they were going to have to work together, face-to-face, *mano a mano*. This was not supposed to be happening. When she'd signed on to be the ghostwriter for *From Diapers to Dating: Becoming the Perfect Parent*, it was with the usual understanding. She'd work from home, translating Dr. A.'s parenting advice into a coherent, easy-to-read manuscript, and the radio shrink would stay in Manhattan, hosting a radio show, running workshops on becoming a perfect parent, and sending Anne copious notes, via fax, phone, and e-mail. Yes, the book was due to Triple Star Publishing in seven weeks and yes, they weren't even close to putting together a first draft, but this was an outrage.

"You should have called first," Anne had protested, as Dr. A. headed back to the car and began removing what looked like copious amounts of food from her black Grand Cherokee sport utility vehicle. "We should have talked this over."

"Not necessary," Dr. A. had said, carrying several grocery bags into the house. "We're running behind schedule. We're not going to make our deadline unless we take drastic action."

How drastic, Anne had wondered grimly, watching Harry glare at the intruder. Harry was an old one-eyed black-and-white cat. He didn't care for strangers. To be perfectly honest, he didn't like many people, including most of Anne's friends. He watched with disdain as Dr. A. unpacked bag loads of food. She'd brought enough provisions for a month. And whose fault was it anyway that they were behind?

Despite the take-charge image she projected on her show, Dr. Arlene was indecisive when it came to the book. Each time she sent Anne a new batch of notes, she changed her mind about what she wanted to say or how she wanted to say it, which slowed their collaboration down considerably.

It was the exact opposite of what Dr. Arlene preached to parents across the country: Take charge. Take command. Take control of the situation. Her message had been enthusiastically received. Dr. Arlene charged parents $1,200 per workshop, and there was a six-month waiting list to sign up. Anne had sat in on one a couple of months ago and observed twelve insecure mothers fret about potty training and tantrums and whether it was okay to feed kids canned veggies instead of fresh ones. She wondered what her mother's generation would have made of it. Those women hadn't relied on books or radio shrinks for advice. She doubted whether her mother had even read Dr. Spock.

"This is going to work out great, you'll see," Dr. Arlene had said cheerily, opening the refrigerator and sticking goat cheese and radicchio next to Anne's leftover chili.

No, it's not, Anne had wanted to shout. But she knew she couldn't. And Dr. A. knew she knew. Dr. A was the "expert," Dr. A. had the clout. The terms of Anne's contract clearly stated that if Dr. Arlene Handelman was unhappy with their working relationship, she could find herself another ghost writer. Which wouldn't be a problem if Anne hadn't already spent the first half of her advance money. She couldn't afford to get fired.

She had watched in silent fury while Dr. Arlene opened a kitchen cabinet, extracted a glass, and poured herself mineral water exported from New York. "Someone told me," Dr. A. had said, "that there's a Howard Stern rest stop on the turnpike. Is that true?"

"I take it you're not a fan of the Jersey shore," Anne had said, trying in vain to stem her sarcasm.

"Anyplace that's not Manhattan is bound to be deadly dull," Dr. A. had said, pouring a second glass for Anne. "If I have to leave the city, I prefer the Hamptons or the Vineyard. But I'm willing to sacrifice big for this book. You and I have got to be on the same page from now on. No more delays. No more setbacks. We start working on how to survive your child's high school years tonight."

Anne had groaned inwardly. The survival notes Dr. Arlene had faxed her were an incoherent mess. The radio shrink tended to hopscotch from one topic to the next, jotting down random bits of advice without any thought to how they should be organized and presented.

"Here are some more ideas I scribbled down this morning," Dr. Arlene had said, dumping a sheaf of papers on the coffee table.

Scribbled was the operative word. Dr. Arlene's handwriting left a lot to be desired.

"I'm hungry and bone tired, in need of some small town hospitality. Where can I get an edible meal and a good, hot cup of Joe?" Dr. Arlene had said, slipping off one of her high-heeled pumps and rubbing a bunion on her left foot.

"There's Quilters. Or the Pelican Café. They're both on Main Street. If you like Italian food, Vic's in Bradley Beach is good. It's right in the center of town."

"I guess it's next to impossible to mess up spaghetti, right?" Dr. Arlene had said, slipping her shoe back on.

"Try the veal piccata. It's heavenly," Anne had said. "About tonight, I already have plans. But we can start tomorrow morning."

"I'm up at six. And I'll need a key, in case you're not home when I get back."

Anne had gotten her spare key and reluctantly handed it over. The only thing worse than an uninvited houseguest was an uninvited houseguest you had to humor and cater to. As she'd watched Dr. Arlene climb into the Grand Cherokee, she wondered how soon the radio shrink would be leaving.

Not soon enough, as it turned out. Dr. A. pretended she didn't see the colorful brochures for inns that Anne left in conspicuous places around the house. And to make matters worse, they'd hardly worked on the book at all. Each morning the radio shrink left the house and didn't come back until almost nightfall. A few evenings ago, she'd done her weekly live radio broadcast, via telephone, from Anne's office. Anne felt like she was running a bed-and-breakfast for one. And it was really starting to get on her nerves.

The cat raised his head to watch a butterfly dancing overhead, then settled down for a morning snooze on the porch as if chasing it weren't worth the effort. Harry wasn't crazy about the heat either. It made him lethargic and slow. Normally, he'd be prowling around the garden. But it was just as well he wasn't. The garden was a disaster area this summer. It was tough having a black thumb, especially when it hadn't rained in weeks and you kept forgetting to water the lawn. The grass grew tall and wild. The geraniums and impatiens looked half-dead. The tomatoes refused to ripen, and the peas had withered. So much for fresh flowers and vegetables. The lawn was an eyesore.

Anne took another bite of her donut and tried not to listen to Dr. A's singing. Anne was crazy about donuts, especially fresh-baked Jersey donuts, but this morning she was feeling slightly queasy. She couldn't get the dead girl out of her mind. How had the girl died? What had she been doing on the beach? Who had drawn the circle around her? Anne thought back to the jewel glistening at her throat, the strange symbols in the sand.

She took a small notebook off the table in front of her and started sketching the symbols from memory. The first one looked like three-quarters of a bow tie. The second one resembled an elaborate F. The third looked like two flags touching. Anne wondered if the writing could be Arabic or Greek.

What a bizarre scene to come upon in the Heights. Other towns on the Jersey shore attracted teenagers who drank beer like it was water, had delicate parts of their bodies pierced, and flocked to wet T-shirt contests held in dark, smoky bars. But Oceanside Heights was different. After all, it was a dry town. No liquor sold anywhere. The religious aspect tended to appeal to churchgoers, not kids who partied hearty. There was a wholesomeness about the Heights, a family atmosphere.

But there had been strange goings-on this summer at night: mysterious bonfires burning on the beach. Strange, primitive-looking tools littering the boardwalk. Weird chanting and drumming. Twice during the past month Anne had been jolted awake by the noise. But when she'd gone to investigate, she'd found nothing.

Several people who lived opposite the beach claimed they'd seen a horrible-looking black figure dancing above the waves at night. Anne didn't know what to make of it. Some of her neighbors might have been a little close-minded and uptight, but they weren't prone to hallucinations. Nor did they give much credence to supernatural phenomena.

"Annie," a familiar voice called out.

"Delia, hi."

Delia Graustark was the town librarian, resident gossip, and one of Anne's best friends. She was in her mid-seventies, but that didn't stop her from working six days a week. In fact, she usually had more energy than most people half her age. But not today. Now Delia walked shakily up the porch steps as if her bones were brittle. Wisps of white hair had escaped her bun and stuck out from her head like frayed cotton threads. Her wire-framed eyeglasses had slipped halfway down her long, aquiline nose. She looked more upset than Anne had ever seen her. In fact, she looked panicked.

"I need your help," Delia said weakly, reaching into her pocket and producing an embroidered linen handkerchief, which she used to dab her face.

"Sure."

Delia was usually the one helping Anne out. As a ghostwriter who'd written books on everything from astrology to wind surfing, Anne had to do a fair amount of research. And the library was the perfect place for it. Delia had spent countless hours tracking down out-of-print reference books, wading through microfiche, and poring over old newspaper clips to help Anne get a handle on dead celebrities or organic gardening or whatever her latest assignment was.

"It's Tracy," Delia said grimly.

"What about Tracy?"

Delia was gazing intently down the beach toward where the cops were stationed. "I think my grandniece is in serious trouble."

Anne leaned back in her chair and waited. The thing about Tracy Graustark was she was usually in some kind of trouble. Oh, nothing major for a sixteen-year-old with a wild streak. Cheating on tests. Shoplifting lipstick from Stern's. Driving without a license. Tracy's parents had died in a car accident three years earlier, and Delia had volunteered to raise the girl herself, a task that had caused her no small amount of aggravation.

"I don't know how to say this without sounding ridiculous," Delia continued, in a high-pitched, anxious voice. "But here it is. Tracy thinks she's a witch."

Anne resisted the impulse to smile. "A what?"

"A witch. Not the cute kind like in *Bewitched* or *Casper*." Delia twisted the handkerchief into a ball. "The evil kind."

Anne looked over to see if Delia was serious. Apparently she was.

"Go on," Anne said.

"It all started two months ago. Tracy was taking an English class in summer school and the teacher had them read *The Crucible*. Next thing you know Tracy and some of the girls she goes around with decide they want to be witches. Tracy bought a book of spells, and she set up an altar in her room with incense and candles and strange pictures. I didn't pay much attention at first. I figured it was just a phase, like last summer when she wanted to learn to parasail." Delia paused. Her gray eyes were fearful.

"That girl they carted away." Delia jerked her hand toward the far end of the beach. "Her name's Abby Podowski. She was one of Tracy's closest friends. It's a tragedy. But I can't say I'm all that surprised. She was a hellcat, that Abby. An unhappy girl growing up much too fast."

Delia paused and peered down the beach to where the cops were gathered. A crowd of curious onlookers buzzed about the boardwalk, adding to the commotion. "Now this," Delia said. "Witches. Spells. Abby's dead."

"I'd like to help," Anne said slowly. "But I'm not sure what I can do exactly."

"Find out why Abby Podowski died. And find my grandniece. She's missing."

Chapter 2

Signs that your child is considering running away: He feels neglected, guilty, ashamed, or embarrassed. He's been spending more and more time away from home. He engages in "secret" phone conversations, correspondence, and meetings.

 "Missing since when?"

Delia took a deep breath. "I'm not sure. The last time I saw Tracy was at dinnertime last night.

15

She picked at her food. Ever since this witch business, she has no appetite at all."

"What time was dinner?"

"About six. Six-thirty."

"And then?"

"I watched a little TV. Did the crossword puzzle. And went to sleep at ten. I thought Tracy was in her room, listening to music or praying at that altar of hers. This morning, I went to wake her up and saw that her bed hasn't been slept in. She's gone."

"I think you need to call the police."

"No." Delia shook her head vehemently, and Anne looked at her in surprise. "She's probably gotten herself into a scrape, and I'd just as soon the police not know about it, whatever *it* happens to be. Besides, Tracy's run off a couple of times before. She always comes home the next day. But this time, with that poor girl dead . . ."

Anne gazed out at the ocean, which was a deep royal blue tinged with flecks of white foam. Devoid of sun-worshippers, the sand beckoned invitingly, like a soft tawny carpet. Farther down the beach, the officers were still clustered on the sand. One of them was taking pictures of the scene.

"Do you think Tracy's mixed up somehow in Abby Podowski's death?" Anne said.

"I don't know," Delia said, with a worried frown. "The witchcraft was harmless enough, at first. But I found something this morning that . . . well, it troubled me a great deal."

Anne waited, studying her friend. Delia's voice was trembling. Her eyes scanned the beach restlessly, and the wrinkles in her broad, kindly face seemed to have deepened overnight. She was clutching the handkerchief so tightly her knuckles had turned white.

"I went through Tracy's dresser, trying to find her address book so I could start calling some of her friends. I wasn't prying," Delia added hurriedly. "I've never done anything like it before."

"Of course not," Anne said in a reassuring tone.

"Anyway, I found a notebook with a scarlet cover. It wasn't a diary exactly. More like a spell book, if you can believe it. Tracy and her friends have been casting spells on people here in town. It actually lists names and dates and . . ." Here she paused, her lips pursing in disgust. "Recipes. Anne, I don't know how they did it, but they got hold of people's nail clippings and hair, bits of clothing, personal articles." Delia's mouth trembled, her expression was horrified. "They were trying to break up the Trimbles' marriage and give your next-door neighbor, that Cox woman, migraines, and there was something about how to harm girls who got in their way." Delia's hand fluttered to her heart. "I realize it sounds ridiculous. But when you see the elaborate planning that went into it, the ingredients they used, you'll understand why I don't want the police involved."

"But Delia, what can I do? How can I possibly help?"

Delia turned her troubled gray eyes on Anne. "In case you haven't noticed, you've gotten quite good at solving murders. I don't know how you manage it, but you've definitely got the knack."

Anne smiled grimly. It was true. These past couple of years she'd encountered more than her share of dead bodies. Through luck, persistence, and a penchant for tracking down facts, she'd managed to solve the crimes. Delia and Helen Passelbessy were always saying how she should give up writing and become a cop or a private detective.

Aloud, she said, "Then you think Abby Podowski was murdered?"

"I want you to find out what happened to Abby. Please, Anne. Tracy probably had nothing to do with it, but I don't want her mixed up in this."

Anne took another sip of iced tea and thought it over. She was so behind on the parenting book that even if Dr. Arlene finally decided to start spouting advice and they worked round the clock, they wouldn't be able to make the deadline. Plus, she wanted to help Delia out. If only to pay her friend back for all those late nights and weekends the librarian had worked overtime to aid a struggling, overworked ghostwriter with no money to hire a research assistant. But she couldn't just barrel right into a police investigation and start asking questions. She wasn't an acquaintance or a relative of the dead girl. And she certainly didn't know the first thing about witchcraft.

Still, Delia was a good friend, and after finding the body in the first place, Anne was more than a little curious about how it came to be there. There was something about the girl that touched a chord in Anne. It wasn't right that someone so young should unexpectedly die. It wasn't fair. Maybe understanding why Abby had died would make the death less awful, so that the body sprawled on the sand and Abby's sad, hardened demeanor, would stop haunting Anne's thoughts.

"I'll see what I can do," she said, and was instantly gratified to see Delia relax ever so slightly.

"Thanks, Annie. I knew I could count on you."

"Was anything missing from Tracy's room or from her closet?"

"Not that I could tell."

"So you don't think she packed a bag?"

"Not a suitcase, no. Only her khaki knapsack's gone. She carries it everywhere with her."

"What was she wearing when she disappeared?"

Delia thought a moment. "White shorts. Sneakers. A navy T-shirt, I think." Delia leaned back in her chair and dabbed at her face with the balled-up handkerchief. "About the spell book. There's something else."

"What?" Anne said, almost dreading the reply.

"Several times in the book Tracy referred to a certain person the girls saw on the beach. It was during the witches' Sabbath when they gathered to practice black magic or whatever fool thing they were doing down here at night."

"Did Tracy say who this person was?"

"She wrote he had 'incredible powers.' Apparently persuasion was one of them because all the girls seemed anxious to do his bidding."

"Could you tell if it was someone from town or from their school?"

Delia grimaced. Her nose twitched as if she smelled a distinctly unpleasant odor and was too polite to comment on it. "Tracy hasn't been herself lately," Delia began. "The witchcraft is making her confused."

Anne had known her friend long enough to recognize when the librarian was stalling. "Delia? What's going on?"

A small sigh escaped Delia's lips. "I don't know what's gotten into that girl. She's convinced the person they met with on the beach is the Devil himself."

*   *   *

Detective Mark Trasker rang the doorbell and strode briskly into Anne's living room when she answered the door.

"I heard you're the one who found the body," he said. "You better watch it, Hardaway. This is getting to be a habit."

She was just about to rattle off a comeback when she noticed the playful expression in his eyes and the smile on his lips. Trasker liked to tease her, but he also took her ideas and opinions seriously and had solicited her advice on a number of cases.

The first time they'd met he'd pegged her as a suspect in a murder investigation. The second time he'd nearly thrown her in jail. Since then, things had definitely been on the upswing.

Every so often, they went out to dinner. Or he took her out on his boat. Or they caught a movie together. It was strictly platonic, although sometimes Anne found herself wishing for more. Since she'd broken up with Jack Mills nearly a year ago, her dating life had undergone a serious dry spell. More like a drought, actually. Oh, there'd been a few dates: a colleague of Helen's from the bank. Her mother's cousin's neighbor's son. A guy she'd met at a four-mile summer fun race. But nothing to get excited about. That left Trasker. She liked him. She was attracted to him. She had fun with him. But he didn't seem interested in dating her or anyone else, for that matter. His work kept him busy round the clock, and as far as she knew his social life consisted of an occasional drink with a fellow cop.

Lately, she'd found herself fantasizing about meeting someone new, taking long moonlit walks on the beach or biking along the boardwalk from Bradley Beach to

Spring Lake. Unfortunately, the Heights wasn't exactly overflowing with available men. The tourists were either married or gay, and she could count the number of single guys who lived in town on one hand. So much for summertime romance.

"It's going to be a long day," Trasker said, sitting down on the faded chintz couch in the living room.

He was wearing a tailored gray suit, black leather shoes, and a striped tie. As a concession to the weather, he'd slung his suit jacket over his arm and rolled up the sleeves of his crisp sky-blue shirt. None of the other detectives in the Neptune Township Sheriff's Office dressed as well as Trasker did. But then none of the other detectives were black. Anne wondered if Trasker put such a premium on his appearance in order to gain respect on the job. He'd once told her how early in his career, the owner of a nearby 7-Eleven had reached under the counter and pulled out a gun when Trasker approached him to talk about a string of robberies that had occurred in the area.

Anne figured it must be tough being a black cop in a predominantly white county. But then Trasker always struck her as someone who liked a challenge. He was a good-looking man, with skin the color of cocoa beans, deep penetrating brown eyes, and a toothpaste-perfect smile. He had a way of listening to you when you talked—and remembering everything you'd ever said— that Anne found especially appealing.

She sank into an armchair and fanned herself with a magazine. She'd opened every window in the house as wide as she could, but the heat seemed to cancel out the breeze blowing off the ocean. It was stiflingly, oppressively hot, and not even noon.

"What's up?" she said to Trasker. "Aren't you supposed to be on vacation?"

"Change of plans. Cooperman's wife had a baby yesterday and Wells has a broken ankle. So I had to postpone
my fishing trip for two more weeks. Can you believe it?
You know where I should be right this minute? In the
Thousand Islands, where it's probably thirty degrees
cooler than it is here, and the bass are jumping."

Anne nodded sympathetically. "Tough break."

"Not as tough as what happened to that poor girl on the
beach."

"It's awful, isn't it? Do you know how she died?"

"Looks like suicide. She had some pills in her hand
and she'd apparently been drinking."

"Could it have been an accident?"

Trasker shook his head. "She left a note."

"Where?"

"In her pocket."

"What'd it say?"

"The usual: She was unhappy. She couldn't take it anymore." He sank back against the sofa cushions. "It's so
sad. She was just a kid, with her whole life ahead of her."

Anne looked out the bay window. The portion of beach
that hadn't been blocked off was jammed with sun worshippers, many of them teenage girls. A giant wave
crested about twenty feet from shore. She imagined what
it would be like to dive underneath it and feel cold water
explode around her.

Trasker said, "How are you holding up? It must have
been tough to come upon the body like that."

"It was quite a shock."

"I know you talked to the patrolmen already. You have
anything else to add to what you told them?"

Anne debated whether she should tell him about Tracy. But Delia had been adamant about not contacting the police. Maybe Tracy had already come home. Maybe she was sitting at Delia's kitchen table right this minute.

"I found some weird-looking symbols on a scrap of paper near the body."

Trasker looked puzzled. "The cops didn't see anything like that at the scene."

"The wind must have blown it away. I could make you a copy of the way I remember them." Inwardly she was kicking herself for not keeping the symbols. Maybe they had something to do with witchcraft and Tracy.

"That'd be great," Trasker said. "By the way, how's the book coming?"

Anne rolled her eyes. "Don't ask."

"I heard Dr. Arlene on the radio once. You think people are actually helped by her advice?"

"I suppose. According to Dr. A., today's parents are incredibly insecure. They can't discipline their kids or choose a preschool without first consulting her."

Which was ironic, come to think of it. Before Anne had signed on for the project she'd visited Dr. Arlene in her three-bedroom, prewar apartment overlooking Central Park West and had immediately noticed that Arlene's three sons hated her. Dr. A. had seemed to shift between wanting to be their best friend and forgetting they existed. The oldest kid, a defiant seventeen-year-old with dyed orange hair and a nose ring, had wandered in and out of the den, smoking marijuana, and the two younger ones had taken turns throwing water balloons out the window and making up nasty rhyming songs about their mother, which they then proceeded to sing at the top of their lungs.

Trasker said, "She's pretty difficult, huh?"

"That's putting it mildly."

"Maybe you need a break. Are you free for dinner tonight? My treat. I took out all this money for the trip, and I feel like blowing some of it."

Anne felt a surge of happiness. Even if it wasn't an official date, dinner with Mark Trasker was bound to be fun.

"Sure. Count me in."

She went into her office and made a copy of the symbols for him.

"Thanks," he said, taking the piece of paper. "I'll be by to pick you up around seven."

After he'd left, Anne got out a few transcripts of Dr. A.'s radio broadcasts and took them into her office. Maybe she could cull advice from here. She was just about to get to work when Abby Podowski's face came back to her. *Suicide*. It was practically a teenage epidemic from everything she'd read. She wondered if Delia knew anything about Tracy's state of mind these days. Sometimes girls copied everything their friends did, the hair, the makeup, the walk. And suicide could sound so romantic, from Romeo and Juliet to Kurt Cobain.

She thought back to the body on the beach. The clothes. The nails. The defiant, tough girl expression. There was nothing romantic about Abby. Nothing at all.

Chapter 3

It's perfectly natural for teenagers to rebel against their parents. But you should be alarmed if this form of acting out includes harming themselves or harming others.

Oceanside Heights was laid out on a rectangular grid. Each home on streets running east to west was set back slightly from its neighbor to allow partial views of the Atlantic Ocean. Situated on thirty-foot-by-sixty-foot lots, the Victorian-style houses were packed together so tightly there was barely three feet of space between them. The density was deliberate. The Methodist ministers who founded the town wanted to promote a sense of community and interaction. There was little room for lawns or other private spaces, so the front porch wound up serving as a meeting and greeting spot where neighbors gathered to chat, eat, and watch their children play.

It made for a friendly, close-knit community. The downside was that everyone in the Heights knew everybody else's business. You could barely have an argument or make a phone call without the entire block hearing it, especially in the summertime, when windows were thrown open and front doors stood ajar except for their screens.

When she was half a block away from Delia Graustark's house, Anne heard the strains of a Mozart symphony and knew immediately that Delia was home. Delia lived on McClintock Street in a style of house known as Victorian Eclectic. It was a two-story putty-colored dwelling, with Italianate, Gothic, and Queen Anne elements tossed together willy-nilly in an architectural salad. Slender white columns punctuated the front porch, and each window was ornamented with white lace curtains. With its narrow gable roof, shingle facade, and double-leaf door, the house looked like a contemporary gingerbread cottage—tidy, quaint, and inviting.

Sunflowers and marigolds bloomed in the tiny front yard. Anne couldn't help noticing that they looked a whole lot healthier than the flowers in her own garden. After knocking on the screen door and waiting a few seconds, she heard Delia call, "Come on in."

Delia was seated at the kitchen table poring through a stack of old magazines. Over the years, she'd assembled hundreds of clip-and-save folders. There were folders devoted to decorating and movie stars and music and recipes and countless other topics, both weighty and ar-

cane. Brandishing a pair of sewing scissors, Delia was
working her way through a copy of *Time* magazine that
was so dated it had a picture of the original Charlie's An-
gels on the cover. The early-afternoon sun streamed
through the window, bathing Delia in a circle of white
light.

Usually, Delia liked to spend time trading gossip, but
Anne could tell that today there was only one thing on
her mind.

"Did you manage to find anything out?" she said, looking up. Her face sagged with worry. The lines around her
eyes appeared etched into her skin.

Anne quickly related what Trasker had said about
Abby Podowski's suicide.

"I don't know whether to be worried or relieved,"
Delia said, when Anne had finished. "I still haven't heard
from Tracy, and none of her friends have seen her."

"Could I see Tracy's room?"

"Is that really necessary?"

"It might be helpful."

"All right," Delia said reluctantly, putting down the
scissors. "Follow me."

She led the way upstairs to a small back room decorated in Early American Witch. The walls and ceiling
were painted black and plastered with drawings of
medieval-looking women who were undergoing various
forms of torture—stretched on racks, burned alive,
drowned, flogged, pierced with needles. Opposite the
narrow bed was a makeshift altar set up on a black, brass-
bound trunk.

On either end stood two thick tapered candles, dripping with dried wax. There was an iron cauldron, a dead
stuffed snake, a silver chalice, a steak knife, a pack of

cigarettes, an array of ointments and potions in small colored vials, a stale-looking cupcake, and a pile of silver coins in a foreign denomination Anne didn't recognize. A framed picture of a naked and grinning Devil, sporting horns and a long hairy tail, stood in the middle of the altar. Against the wall, in the far corner of the room, was a worn-looking straw broom with a long black handle.

Anne didn't know what to say. The best she could come up with was "wow."

"It's a little over the top," Delia said with embarrassment. "But she's sixteen. I couldn't exactly force her to have a canopy bed with ruffles and cute stuffed animals."

Anne nodded. When she was in her early teens, she had forsaken the dotted Swiss decor of her bedroom for Indian prints and had tacked posters of Black Sabbath and Grand Funk Railroad onto the walls. It was her first taste of teenage rebellion, but it looked like amateur hour compared to this. She could see why Delia hadn't wanted to call the police. The whole witch identity crisis thing wouldn't go over well in the Heights. Methodists worshipped Jesus, the Devil be damned, and Anne suspected Delia's neighbors would be profoundly offended.

What, she wondered, had Tracy Graustark been going through to embrace witchcraft? Sure, the room was scary. But it also struck Anne as sad. It was as though Tracy were trying too hard, as though the evil-looking objects were props in a play.

Anne's mind flew to the body on the beach, inscribed in the carefully drawn circle on the sand. The tableau, she realized now, also struck her as staged: Cue the lights, raise the curtain. Death by design. But why would Abby bother?

Anne touched the top of the trunk, which was tinged

with a thin film of dust and faint coppery red streaks. "Delia," she said slowly. "This looks like blood."

"What?" Delia exclaimed. She hurried over and stared down at the trunk.

"Have these marks been here a while or do they seem fresh to you?"

"I don't know," Delia stammered. "I refuse to come in here most of the time. Tracy's responsible for cleaning it herself."

"Delia . . ." Anne began.

"No."

"We have to tell the police Tracy's missing. They'll be able to help us find her."

"No," Delia repeated. "She'll be back. I know she will."

Anne studied her friend. Delia was either in serious denial, or she was being incredibly naïve. Maybe both.

"Besides," Delia said testily, "the police were already here."

Anne threw her a questioning glance.

"They wanted to talk to each of Abby's friends. I told them Tracy was away, visiting relatives."

"You did *what*?" Anne asked.

She was beyond stunned. In all the years she'd known Delia, the librarian had never so much as told a white lie. This was a whopper.

"Do you know what Tracy and her friends do in this room?" Anne asked.

"I don't want to know," Delia said defensively.

For the first time, Anne heard the guilty tone in Delia's voice. Well, of course she feels guilty, Anne reasoned. Delia is Tracy's legal guardian. She's responsible for Tracy's well-being. And judging from this room, Tracy wasn't at all well.

Delia said, "It's just a phase Tracy's going through. She'll snap out of it and get into country music or take up jewelry design or something."

Anne wasn't so sure. It looked like a lot of time and attention had been lavished on the room. Where was the kid buying all this stuff? Through mail-order catalogs? A witch superstore at the mall?

"During the last few weeks, did you hear the girls talking about anything in particular? Did you see them perform ceremonies or special rites?"

Delia sat down gingerly on the edge of the bed, which had sheets decorated with skulls and bones. "I heard chanting sometimes and smelled incense burning. They called it a coven and gave themselves code names: Lilith, Pandora, Zoroaster. Tracy's is Hecate. And then there's somebody called 'the Nameless One.' I don't know who the heck that is."

Anne thought of the "devil" Tracy referred to in her book.

"What other girls are in on this?" she asked.

Delia smoothed the wrinkles from the black cotton coverlet on the bed. "Abby." Delia's face registered pain at the name. "And Pam Whitehouse. And Lauren Jensen. And Melissa Baker."

The last name surprised Anne. She knew Melissa Baker slightly. Melissa was pretty and popular and didn't seem the type to dabble in witchcraft.

"What about Tracy's other friends?"

"She doesn't have any."

"Classmates, then. Girls she studies with or speaks to on the phone occasionally."

Delia let out a sigh. "Tracy keeps to herself. She doesn't have any other girlfriends, as far as I know."

"What about boyfriends?"

"There aren't any."

"How about boys she likes? Crushes, that sort of thing."

Delia drew herself up stiffly. "Tracy doesn't confide in me, Annie. We aren't very close."

Anne was beginning to think that was a huge understatement.

Delia looked around the room as if seeing it for the first time. "The thing is," she said quietly. "Tracy's done this before."

"Done what?"

"Run off without telling me. The first time she did it she'd only been here a few months. I was frantic, as you can imagine. I thought about calling the authorities. Believe me, I did. But in the end, I waited up all night, and, at nine in the morning, Tracy breezed through the door, pretty as you please. After that, it happened fairly regularly, always at night. Her night flights, I call them. I go in to wake her up in the morning and her bed hasn't been slept in. When she comes back, she refuses to tell me where she's been or what she's been doing."

"Do you have any idea where Tracy goes?" Anne said.

"In the beginning, she lied to me. She'd say she slept over at Abby's or Lauren's house. But when I checked with their parents, I found it wasn't so. Once I tried following her. I trailed her to Ocean Avenue, but then she just seemed to disappear.

"I asked her about it, and she got furious with me. Said I was spying on her. That she liked to take long walks at night, to clear her head. That she'd gone to get ice cream. That she was out with friends, on a study break, at the diner. She's even tried to convince me she'd been home the whole time and was simply an early riser. The problem is this: Lying comes as easily as breathing to Tracy. Sometimes I think she's incapable of telling the truth. It isn't in her nature."

"And the witchcraft?"

"She lied about that, too. Told me it was only a school project, a way to get extra credit in English."

"Was she good friends with Abby?"

Delia hesitated, and Anne found herself wondering why. "Abby was Tracy's closest friend," Delia said carefully. "Which is not to say they were peas in a pod. Tracy goes her own way. She keeps herself apart from people. Maybe it has something to do with her parents' deaths. I don't know."

"You mentioned something about a spell book."

"It's right here." From the top of the dresser Delia took a scarlet-colored notebook. On the cover, in black marker, it said *My Book of Shadows*. "I didn't read all of it," Delia explained. "Actually, I had to stop about halfway through. It was starting to make me ill."

"Do you think I could borrow the book for a little while?"

"Take it."

Anne tucked the book into her handbag. "Do you have a recent picture of Tracy?"

"Just a sec." Delia left the room and came back a minute later carrying a snapshot.

In it, Tracy was standing by the ocean in a black one-piece bathing suit. She had plain, dark features but she'd done everything possible to change them. Her jet-black hair was saturated with blond streaks. Her heart-shaped face was heavily made up, so much so that the skin tone above her neck looked several shades lighter than that below. It was a cheesecake pose, probably done as a lark—with her chest thrust forward, one hand on her hip, the other angled behind her head. But Tracy couldn't quite pull it off. She didn't have a bad figure, but the pose made her look self-conscious. The sun was in her eyes, and she squinted uncertainly into the camera. Her smile seemed forced.

"If Tracy's not back by tonight," Anne said, pocketing the snapshot, "you really have to call the police. They'll initiate a search and have far better luck than I will, believe me. And while they're at it, they can analyze the blood."

Delia fixed her gray eyes on Anne. She looked tired and old. Her mouth sagged. "I know you'll find her. I'm counting on you."

Don't, Anne felt like saying, as Delia headed toward the door. For starters, she hadn't the faintest idea where Tracy Graustark was. If Tracy had run away, she was probably miles from the Heights by now. She could be practically anywhere.

Anne glanced around the room again. What was it about witches that appealed to teenage girls? The power aspect, probably. She remembered feeling out of control during her teenage years, lost and alone and helpless. How wonderful it must be to believe you had magic powers, the ability to cast spells and cause everyone around you to do exactly what you wanted.

Her gaze fell on one of the pictures tacked to the wall: Two hooded, cloaked figures on a beach lifting a middle-aged woman in a bonnet and long dress over a bonfire. The woman's feet dangled in the flames, yet she appeared to howl with laughter.

Anne drew closer and looked at the caption underneath

the image. *Witch-hammerers attempt to elicit a confession.* What on earth were witch-hammerers? Did they have anything to do with the coven of teens? With whatever ritual Abby Podowski had been performing on the beach? It was too bizarre for words—this tricked-out room, the "spell book," the blood caked on the altar. She shuddered. Maybe Tracy wasn't coming back after all.

In the early afternoon, Main Street was bustling with tourists cruising in and out of the shops. The Antique Boutique was hopping, and people streamed in and out of the handful of stores that sold postcards, newspapers, and assorted beach-related souvenirs. There were long lines at the Mini-Mart and a forty-five-minute wait for a table at the Pelican Café. A typical summer day in the Heights, which was a mixed blessing. The tourists infused the town with money in the summer, but it was a pain in the neck to look for a parking space or shop or eat out.

Anne bought an iced coffee at Elizabeth's, where people talked of nothing but what had driven poor Abby Podowski to her death. After paying for the coffee, Anne stepped back outside into the broiling heat, ducking under awnings to avoid the sun's glare. She'd dropped the spell book off at home, grabbed a quick sandwich, refilled Harry's water dish, then headed out, ignoring the urgent phone message from Phil Smedley on her machine.

He wanted the first five chapters of *From Diapers to Dating* on his desk *yesterday.* He needed to give the designer something to work with. What was going on up there? At this rate, they'd never make the deadline, he'd yelled, rattling off production costs. She'd erased the message just as he was threatening to ask for her advance back and reassign the project to another writer.

The thought of it made her stop in the middle of the sidewalk and wait for the sick feeling in her stomach to pass. She was practically broke. She needed this gig.

Okay, she told herself. There had to be a way to get Dr. Arlene to spend less time shopping and more time spouting advice. She'd talk to Dr. A. when she got home. She'd make the radio shrink understand.

In the meantime, she wanted to talk to some of Tracy's friends. Cutting down Pilgrim Pathway, Anne headed north, toward the Church by the Sea. She rarely went to church anymore, but not a day went by that she didn't see, hear, or read something about it. The massive stained glass building was a tourist attraction, a concert hall, and the spiritual hub of the Heights, especially in summertime when camp meetings were held. There was a Back to Holiness Drive going on, which as far as Anne could tell meant an influx of gospel sings, Bible study groups, and a drive to raise money to build a new youth center.

Gathered around the church like sheep around a shepherd were over a hundred gaily colored tents. Standing arm's length apart they were cabinlike structures measuring about twelve-by-twenty-six feet, made of canvas and wood with tiny front porches and wooden floors. Most were equipped with all the comforts of home—TVs, VCRs, microwaves, major appliances. And each tent had its own distinctive decor, whether it be wind chimes, flags, lawn ornaments, or flowers. Each year, families came from as far as California and Texas to tent in the Heights, joining townspeople who "roughed it" in the summer and moved into tents they'd been renting for generations.

The Jensens were in the latter group. Their tent featured a green-and-white-striped awning and a porch festooned with baskets of pink and purple petunias. A child's red bike lay on its side in the grass, near a couple of battered plastic lawn chairs. Anne smelled incense burning. She was just about to announce her presence when she heard voices coming from the rear of the tent. Teenage girls, from the sound of it. Sliding soundlessly around the side of the tent, she positioned herself under one of the windows.

"Let me do it," one of the voices commanded.

"No way," a second voice countered. "If I'm ever going to get the hang of this, I have to do it myself."

The canvas flap covering the screen was partially open, but the window was too high off the ground for Anne to see inside. She crept to the back of the tent, took a quick look around, and noticed a wooden orange crate with some paperback books inside. Removing the paperbacks, she dragged the crate over to the window, climbed up on it, and peeked inside.

Two girls, one with long dark hair and the other with auburn curls, were huddled in front of a small object. Flanking them were two lit candles. The incense smelled sweet, almost sickly.

The girls straightened up and Anne saw they had been leaning over a foot-long rag doll. The doll wore jeans and a blue-and-yellow-flowered top. She had a heart-shaped face, black marbles for eyes, and black and yellow hair that looked human. But the most disturbing touch were the long straight pins that pierced the doll's stomach and chest.

The girl with auburn hair picked up another pin and jabbed it roughly into the doll's stomach. "O mighty one," she intoned, in a low, cracked voice, "hear my prayer. Let she who has betrayed us feel the sting of our wrath."

The girl took a red scarf from her pocket, held it up by the corners, and dropped it directly over the doll. "Cause us to rejoice amid suffering, to . . ."

"You forgot the best part," her friend interrupted.

"Oh, right." The girl tossed the scarf aside and picked up the doll again. "Creature of darkness, creature of fire," she recited, "work thy will by my desire." She dangled the doll over one of the candles, where it hung limply in the air. "Cloth will now give way to flame. What remains is ours to claim."

The girl dipped the doll toward the candle, and flames shot up its leg, tearing hungrily at the cloth. In the sudden burst of light that followed, Anne caught sight of the girls' faces. Their eyes shone with a passion and devotion that was nearly rapturous. Their expressions were similar to the way people sometimes looked in church when they were convinced they had just been saved by Jesus. *Possessed* was the word that came to mind.

Where were these girls' parents? Did they know their daughters were dabbling in witchcraft?

Climbing down from the crate, Anne went back around the tent and knocked on the front door. From inside, she heard muffled voices and scuffling.

"Who is it?" one of the girls called out.

"Anne Hardaway. A friend of Tracy's."

More whispering from inside the tent. Anne heard clattering, then a shushing sound, and the door was yanked open. The dark-haired girl stood before her, staring at her with large cat-shaped almond-colored eyes. She took a drag from what looked and smelled like a hand-rolled cigarette, then threw the butt on the grass and stubbed it out with her shoe. A lemony scent emanated from the tent, mixing with the incense. They must have sprayed something in the air to cover up the burning smell.

"Tracy Graustark is missing," Anne said. "Can I come in?"

Alarm flickered in the girl's eyes.

"It's hot inside. We'll come out. Pam," she called over her shoulder. "Somebody's here."

The girl with auburn curls came to the door and glanced apprehensively at her friend. She was chunky and short with a round, doughy face. "What's going on?"

"This lady wants to talk to us about Tracy. Seems she's missing."

The short girl sucked in her breath. "Oh," she gasped. "Oh, God."

The dark-haired girl slunk out the door and sat cross-legged on the grass. The other one followed. They had on short skirts and solid-colored shirts and sneakers without socks. Around their necks were amber pendants similar to the one Abby Podowski had worn that morning.

"I know I've seen you around town," Anne said to the auburn-haired girl. "You work at Nagle's, don't you?"

"Yup. I'm Pam."

"And I'm Lauren," the other girl said. "Lauren Jensen."

Anne recognized Lauren, too. She worked at one of the restaurants in town. The Pelican Café or Quilters. Anne couldn't remember which.

"Nice to meet you." Anne sat down facing the girls. "Tracy's been missing since last night. Her great-aunt is very worried about her."

Lauren plucked a piece of grass from the ground and twisted it around her index finger. She'd regained her composure and had adopted the bored-looking, vacant demeanor many teenage girls seemed to affect. Apart from her eyes, which were strikingly beautiful, her features were quite ordinary. Turned-up nose, a smattering of pimples, black hair cut shoulder length, with a layer of bangs feathered across her forehead. "I haven't seen Tracy since early yesterday. How about you, Pammy?"

"No," Pam stammered. "I mean I was with *you* then. Hanging out. So no. I haven't seen her since then."

"Do either of you have any idea where she might be?"

"Uhn uhn," Pam said loudly.

She was studying her fingernails as if she'd never seen them before, and Anne had the feeling she was lying. And scared. Pam Whitehouse was definitely scared.

"You might try the mall," Lauren said. "Or the beach." She looked up and smiled, and for a moment she looked almost pretty. "I'm sure she'll be back soon. She probably just lost track of time."

"I understand you both were friends of Abby Podowski," Anne said, changing course.

Pam gave a startled little jump. Her eyes darted toward Lauren. Then she shrank back, as if she were afraid of her friend.

"We've already talked to the police," she said hurriedly. "They came by both our houses this morning."

"It's awful, what Abby did to herself," Lauren said.

"We had no idea she was so unhappy," Pam added, still focused on Lauren, as though everything she said and did was subject to the other girl's approval.

"She hadn't mentioned anything about harming herself?"

Anne saw the two girls exchange a sideways glance.

"No," Lauren said. "Abby was always full of life. You know, I hate to be rude, but we were right in the middle of something. A school project."

"School?"

"Summer school. We're taking a few classes over at Neptune High. You know how teachers are." Lauren rolled her eyes. "They pour on the homework even in August. If we see Tracy at school, we'll tell her to call her aunt right away."

Lauren scrambled to her feet, and Pam followed, rising awkwardly off the grass like a plump turkey struggling to fly. As she got up, Anne noticed a small tattoo below Pam's left ankle, a unicorn rearing up on its hind legs.

"Nice tattoo. Where'd you have it done?"

Instead of answering, Pam backed away, toward the house.

"Belmar," Lauren spoke up. She rolled up the sleeve on her left arm to display a tattoo of a black crow with sharp, pointy teeth. "There's a place on the boardwalk. A bunch of us got them."

"Abby had a tattoo of a snake on her ankle," Anne said. "I saw it this morning when I found her body on the beach." She looked up at the girls and noticed that the color had drained from Pam's face. "You know, it was the strangest thing. Someone had drawn a circle around Abby's body, and I found this nearby on the dunes."

Anne pulled the weird symbols she'd drawn from her pocket.

"Oh," Pam exclaimed. Her hands fluttered in the air like errant moths. Her eyes were glazed with fear. "Oh, no."

Anne started to go toward her, but the next thing she knew Pam Whitehouse had collapsed, falling on the grass in a dead faint.

Chapter 4

If your child is overeating, examine her home life, school life, and social life for signs of stress. Also, try to avoid linking love with food, for example by saying, "I baked this cake especially for you" or "I know how much you like macaroni and cheese."

Anne knelt over Pam's body, picked up her wrist, and felt for a pulse. It was weak, but steady.

"She's been dieting like crazy," Lauren said, staring down at her friend. "It must be making her light-

41

headed. And it's so hot. God, I wish these tents had air-conditioning."

"Could you go inside, and get a cold washcloth?" Anne said. "I think that'll help."

"Um. Okay."

Lauren trotted inside, and Anne began rapidly rubbing Pam's hands and arms. After a few seconds, Pam's eyelids fluttered and the girl blinked.

"What happened?" she asked wanly.

"You fainted. How are you feeling?"

"A little dizzy."

"Let's get you out of the sun."

Helping Pam to her feet, Anne steered her gently into the shade of a nearby pear blossom tree. It was slightly more bearable out of the sun, but the heat still rose up in saunalike waves. Pam's skin was pale, and Anne noticed there were circles under her eyes.

"Have you eaten today?" she asked.

"I had half a grapefruit for breakfast and three Melba toasts about an hour ago."

Anne signaled to Lauren, who was emerging from the tent with a damp cloth. "We don't need that anymore," she called out. "But could you fix Pam a sandwich? And a glass of ice water? She might be dehydrated."

The girl hesitated, then ducked back inside.

"Lauren mentioned you were dieting," Anne said to Pam.

"I have to lose sixty pounds."

Anne studied Pam carefully. The teenager had thick, chunky legs and a wide rear end, but that kind of weight loss seemed excessive. She felt sorry for Pam suddenly. It must be tough to live up to the standards set by willow-thin models in fashion magazines and TV actresses who appeared to survive on lettuce and tofu.

"It looked like the strange symbols I found on the beach upset you. Do you know what they stand for?"

Pam's gaze veered off, toward the white Victorian gazebo near the church, which fairly glittered in the afternoon sun. "Uhn uhn. I've never seen them before."

"Listen, Pam. I'll be honest with you. I know about the witchcraft." The girl's eyes widened. She shifted uncomfortably and stared up at the branches of the tree, which formed a leafy canopy. "I saw you set the doll on fire. Was that human hair on its head?"

Pam's mouth dropped open. Her chest heaved with the effort it took to breathe, reminding Anne of the way a bunny freezes in its tracks once it knows it's being observed. "You were spying on us?" Pam whispered.

A fair question. "I heard voices inside the tent and looked through the window. Where'd you get the hair?"

"I . . . don't know what you're talking about. I've had that doll since I was a little kid."

Right, Anne thought. *And I'm the Tooth Fairy.*

"Actually, I'm fascinated by witchcraft myself," Anne lied. "In fact, I could use a love spell right about now. There aren't too many eligible guys in the Heights, and I can't stand the singles scene. Think you girls could whip something up for me? Something that doesn't involve burning effigies."

Pam smiled weakly.

Anne decided to take a different tack. "It was awful, finding Abby's body this morning," she said. "It must be really hard for you because she was your friend."

Pam swallowed hard. "It's such a terrible thing," she whispered. "I still can't believe she's dead."

"Were you girls with her last night, on the beach?"

Pam shook her head vigorously, but couldn't look

Anne in the eyes, and again Anne got the feeling she was being lied to.

"Did you have any idea Abby was contemplating suicide?"

Pam thought a moment. "She was upset. She cried a lot, but wouldn't tell us why. And she was giving stuff away. Isn't that what people who are thinking about suicide do? Give stuff away?"

"What kind of stuff?"

"Oh, she'd go to the mall and buy all these clothes and give half of what she bought to us. The day before she died she gave me a pair of Calvin Klein sunglasses that cost, like, four hundred bucks." Tears welled up in Pam's eyes. "I'd have helped her if I'd known she was going to off herself, I swear."

"Do you have any idea what was making her so upset?"

Before Pam had a chance to answer, Lauren bounded from the tent with a sandwich and a glass of water. She must have set the land speed record for making peanut butter and jelly.

"Here," Lauren said, thrusting the food at Pam. "Are you better?"

Pam took a reluctant bite of the sandwich, then gulped down some water. "I'm fine," she said nervously.

"I don't suppose you know what the letters on the paper stand for?" Anne said to Lauren.

"Maybe it's Greek."

"I don't think so," Anne said ruefully. "Anyhow, getting back to Tracy, do either of you know why she would take off so suddenly?"

No answer from either girl. Pam's head had dropped,

so Anne couldn't see her face. Lauren's expression was stony.

"Were Abby and Tracy close?" Anne asked.

"You ask more questions than Abby's old man," Lauren said.

"You mean her stepfather," Pam corrected.

"Whatever," Lauren snapped. "All I know is he was badgering us for like, an hour, this morning: What had Abby said to us? What was she so upset about? What was the deal with her? On and on and on. That guy gives me the creeps."

Anne had a sudden image of Rich Podowski's leering face. She had to agree with Lauren on this one. Podowski was pretty creepy.

The girls had stopped talking, and the silence felt uncomfortable. Overhead, cottony clouds drifted across a sky the color of a swimming pool. There was no breeze at all. Flags hung limply from the tents and none of the wind chimes made a sound. The Heights looked more deserted than usual, maybe because the heat had forced people inside. Anne scanned the green. Empty, except for a gray-haired man with a mustache who was reading a newspaper, and two teenage boys.

Anne saw the boys cross the grassy expanse where a statue of the town's founder stood. One of the boys raised his arm and waved. The girls, noticing, looked momentarily self-conscious.

"Hey," said Lauren, glancing up when the boys had drawn closer.

"How you doing?" said the taller of the two boys, who was slender and dark with sharply chiseled features and hair that looked soft as down.

"We're okay," Lauren replied.

There was an awkward silence. Pam played with her sandwich. Lauren twisted another blade of grass around her finger. Anne thought it was a good time to introduce herself.

The taller boy nodded a greeting. "I'm Leo Farnsworth," he said. "And this is my friend, Brian Miller."

Anne took a good look at Brian. Brown curly hair, blue eyes, a smattering of freckles. He had the thick, muscular build of an athlete and what seemed like no neck. The way he walked, kind of bounding across the grass, made Anne think of a frisky puppy.

She tried to recall what she'd read about him in the *Oceanside Heights Press*. But all she could remember was that he'd set some kind of record last season on the field. High school sports weren't her thing.

Nor Leo's from the looks of it. Although he was tall, his delicate cheeks and wide, full lips looked like they belonged on a pre-Raphaelite painting. She was sure she'd never seen him before.

As if reading her mind, Leo said: "I'm from California. My parents finally got off the waiting list for a tent this summer. So I came out to join them."

"How do you like it so far?" Anne asked him.

"Nice town. Kinda quiet. Right, girls?"

Pam giggled. Anne could tell she liked Leo by the way she was staring up at him, as if she wanted to drink him in. But then Leo Farnsworth probably had girls mooning over him wherever he went. He had gorgeous green eyes and a certain charm that went beyond looks, a relaxed, engaging manner that projected confidence and ease.

"Summer's always slow around here," said Lauren.

"We heard about Abby," Leo said slowly. "We just

wanted to stop by and see how you girls are holding up."

"Thanks," Lauren said. "That's really nice of you."

Anne could see Lauren was attracted to Leo, too. She kept stealing quick glances at him, then looking away, like a thief who'd stumbled upon a precious jewel and was covertly plotting how to steal it.

"Do you guys know Tracy Graustark?" Anne asked.

"Sure," Brian spoke up. "Is she in some kind of trouble?"

"Have you seen her lately?" Anne said.

Brian thought a moment. "I ran into her yesterday morning in town."

"What's going on?" Leo said. "What's up with Tracy?"

"She didn't come home last night. Her great-aunt is worried."

"Wow," Brian said. "I hope she's okay."

"Do you have any idea where she might be?" Anne said.

Brian's brow furrowed. "Not really. But I could check out a few spots, see if anyone's spotted her."

"We'll all help," Lauren said quickly.

Anne thought she saw Pam shoot Lauren a frightened look. Lauren smiled at her friend. It was a chilly smile, and Pam shrank from it.

"How about you?" Anne said to Leo. "Did you know Tracy?"

"Not really," he replied. "But I hope you find her. Anything I can do to help, just let me know. Anyhow," he said, turning back to the girls, "we came by to see if you wanted to get some ice cream or something. You up for it?"

Lauren got to her feet. "Sure."

Pam stood too, still holding the sandwich. "I just need

to get rid of this. They have low-fat yogurt at the ice cream place, right?"

"Yeah," Brian said. "The strawberry's not bad."

"Nice meeting you," Lauren said to Anne. "We'll call if we hear from Tracy."

"There's one more thing," Anne said. "I'm writing a book. A parenting book, on how parents and kids relate to one another. I was wondering if the four of you would be interested in being part of a focus group I'm setting up."

"What's a focus group?" Brian asked.

"You just have to show up and answer some questions."

"Do we get paid?" Brian asked.

"No. But I could ask Dr. Handelman to credit you in the acknowledgments of the book. I'm sure it won't be a problem."

"You mean Dr. Arlene Handelman?" Lauren said with interest. "Wow, she's awesome."

"She doesn't think it's wrong for teenagers to have sex—if you're in love, of course," Pam added. "I wish my parents felt that way. They're so straitlaced."

"Like you're going to be having sex anytime soon," Lauren said sarcastically, with an eye roll.

Pam's cheeks reddened. "Well, I could be," she protested. "I mean, someday I will be. When I have a boyfriend."

"What's the point in rushing things?" Leo asked. "I think you should get to know somebody really well before you fall into bed with them."

"That's what I meant," Pam said, throwing him a grateful look.

"Sure," Brian added. "Relationships last longer when you take it slow."

"You should talk, Mr. Football Star," said Lauren sarcastically. "Girls throw themselves at you every day."

"That doesn't mean I take them up on it," Brian shot back.

"So are any of you interested in being part of the focus group?" Anne said.

"Okay," Lauren said.

"Sounds like fun," said Brian.

"Sure," Pam added.

Leo just shrugged.

"It's at my house, tomorrow at five-thirty. Eleven Ocean Avenue. Okay? And girls? About the witchcraft. I'd love to hear more."

Brian stared at Anne with interest, and Leo raised a quizzical eyebrow. Lauren opened her mouth as if to speak, but didn't. She glared at Pam, who seemed to want the ground to open and swallow her up. *If looks could kill.*

Walking around the Freehold Mall, Anne kept an eye out for Tracy Graustark. But locating a teenage girl in the mall was about as easy as finding a pearl earring on a sandy stretch of beach. There were hundreds of girls wandering through the mall. And they all looked exactly the same: long hair parted in the middle. Tight clothes. Makeup. Platform sandals. Bursting into fits of giggles every few feet. Constantly on the lookout for cute boys. In fact, there was a veritable army of girls, shopping and smoking and hanging out in packs.

Earlier Anne had made several color Xeroxes of Tracy's photo and left them with supervisors at the Landsdown Park train and bus stations, which were the nearest ones to the Heights. None of the ticket takers on duty had recognized Tracy's picture when Anne stopped by.

After leaving the mall, Anne took a quick drive to Barnes & Noble. Oceanside Heights didn't have a bookstore. Or any chain stores, for that matter. It would ruin the quaint quotient of Main Street, with its old-fashioned hardware shop and luncheonette. People in the Heights weren't especially fond of change.

The biggest controversy of the summer had to do with whether or not to allow rolling chairs on the boardwalk. There was no objection to the chairs themselves—old-time relics of a more glamorous age. But it would pave the way for commercialization of the boardwalk. With citified yuppies invading Spring Lake and the beer-and-big-hair set ensconced in Avalon, the Heights provided a respite from loud music, cheap thrills, and the raucous good-time flavor of other shore towns.

Still, it would have been nice to have a bookstore closer to home. After checking with a salesperson, Anne headed to the New Age section, where she found more books on witchcraft than she had time to pore over. Modern witchcraft, she quickly gathered, was called Wicca and involved positive or white magic, used for healing and spiritual growth. "First, do no harm" was the main philosophy. It didn't seem like a message that would appeal to the wanna-be teen witches of the Heights.

She opened *The Modern Witch's Spellbook* and flipped through it. Talk about your up-to-the-minute spells. There were incantations to get child support money, ease suicidal thoughts, become pregnant, avoid office romance, stop drinking, lose weight, and avoid getting sexually transmitted diseases. To catch a lover admired from afar, you'd need to collect dust from a tombstone while

chanting bad poetry. Sounded positively yucky. She pe-
rused a few more pages of love spells, then impulsively
pulled pen and paper from her handbag and jotted down a
spell "to attract an interesting man." It looked fairly easy
to execute and besides, she could use a little assistance,
otherworldly or not.

She put the book back and pulled out another, called
The Whole Witch Encyclopedia. Under the A's she found
amber, a yellow gold fossilized resin worn as jewelry to
protect against sorcery and poison. Interesting. Anne
wouldn't have thought witches needed to worry much
about their safety. Weren't they supposed to be all-
powerful and invincible? Not really, she discovered, as
she paged through the book. Witch-hunting had resulted
in an estimated hundred thousand executions in western
Europe between the mid fifteenth and early eighteenth
centuries. And that didn't even cover Salem, Massachusetts.

She looked up D for devil. *Witches summon the Devil
with precious stones, vials of treated water or a mirror of
quicksilver*, she read. *When he arrives, the Devil may appear in the shape of a man dressed in black, a ghost, a
dog, cat, wolf, or bird. Sometimes the Devil's appearance
is accompanied by chanting and the lighting of bonfires.
When the Devil inhabits a witch she falls senseless to the
ground as though cold and dead. She becomes the Devil's
handmaiden, acquiring magical powers, and can kill and
destroy by supernatural means. The bargain is sealed
with a pact, which is always signed with her own blood.*

Wow, Anne thought. To think that thousands of women
summoned the devil and later died at the hands of their
torturers. The most bizarre part was that some of them
had believed they were witches, believed in the magic.

How was that possible, even hundreds of years ago? On the other hand, who was she to scoff? She'd just written down a love spell, for heaven's sake.

She shut the book and put it back on the shelf. There was probably a huge market for a teen witch book. She could find one of the women involved in Wicca, maybe somebody local, and interview her. Include spells on how to get better grades, how to get asked to the prom, how to get the cute guy in your algebra class to notice you, how to get into the college of your choice. Or maybe she could research and write the book herself. Now there was a concept. No know-it-all expert making unreasonable demands, no pulling information from prima donna "experts." No letting somebody else get all the glory and take all the credit. A break from ghostwriting. It just might work.

Meandering over to the parenting section, she took a quick look at the competition for her current project. There was tons of it. Books on disciplining your toddler, making your child more creative, less dependent, able to manage money, boost self-esteem, become more assertive, overcome shyness, avoid sibling rivalry and on and on. What if after they got it written, *From Diapers to Dating* didn't sell?

Leaving the store, Anne passed a sign that said a psychic named Dr. Amelia Richardson, author of *I See the Future . . . And It's Not All Bad*, would be giving a lecture that evening. Maybe someday Anne herself would be speaking at Barnes & Noble. But first she needed a book proposal. And of course, a catchy title. *The Magical Teen? Witchcraft for Tenth Graders? Broomsticks, High School, and You*? The possibilities seemed endless.

Chapter 5

Respond to temperamental toddlers in a consistent manner. Set out the rules and stick by them, whether it's teaching them to clean up their rooms or not to play with their food at dinnertime. Always reward good behavior, even if it's only with verbal praise, such as "good job."

Landsdown Park was situated right next door to Oceanside Heights, but the two towns couldn't have been more different. In the 1920s, Landsdown was a picturesque seaside resort, with a world-renowned Convention Hall that drew top performers from around the country. But by the sixties, the malls had killed the downtown shopping district, the amusement arcades had closed down, and the beach was deserted. Housing projects replaced the grand hotels near the ocean. Storefronts were boarded up. And the very air seemed to reek of neglect and decay.

Anne drove slowly through the main thoroughfare, past sullen-looking teenage boys sitting on stoops getting high and young women still in their teens trailed by crying toddlers. The street was littered with vacant lots and torn-up buildings with missing windows, their skeletal frames scarred by graffiti. The prostitutes hadn't ventured out yet, but the drug dealers were in evidence, standing on street corners, brazenly hawking pills and pot. Anne drove past shuttered dry cleaners, clothing stores, stationery shops, antique boutiques, that had all closed their doors for good. The drug trade looked to be the only business in Landsdown that was flourishing these days. That and the bars.

She turned down side streets, searching for Tracy, hoping to spot the girl in the long shadows cast by the trees, or huddled in a deserted alleyway, trying to stay clear of the riffraff that had laid claim to the town. Why come to Landsdown, the armpit of the Jersey Shore? What better place to get lost, Anne thought, than in a town full of drifters, druggies, and people so down on their luck that scratching their way back up seemed next to impossible.

From time to time, newspapers ran articles outlining how Landsdown could bounce back. But corrupt government officials, unrelenting poverty, and a steadily declining tax base made the possibility no more real than a politician's pipe dream.

Anne drove east, toward the ocean. The boardwalk looked like something out of a Fellini film. It was eerily empty, as was the beach, quiet save for the keening of gulls. The only building was a blocky shack belonging to a fortune-teller named Madame Marie, who was practically an institution in Landsdown. On the outside of the shack a gigantic purple eye with long spiky eyelashes advertised the seer within. The all-seeing eye seemed to mock Anne's search. She swept her own eyes up and down the boardwalk. There were no houses. No hot dog stands. No sunbathers. No sign of Tracy.

She turned the car around and headed home.

"Does Tracy have a tattoo?" she asked Delia.

There was silence on the other end of the phone. Then, "Yes. How did you know?"

"The other girls involved in witchcraft have them. I thought Tracy might, too. What does it look like?"

"A small wolf, near her left ankle. She had it done a couple of weeks ago."

"Where?"

"Someplace down the shore. I don't know exactly where." Delia sighed. "I told her she could just as easily have gotten one that washes off after a few days, but she'd already had the blasted thing put on. It's permanent, you know. When she's sixty-five, wearing support hose, she'll have to look at that wolf with its great big pointed teeth."

"In the meantime, it's a good identifying mark."

"You're right. I hadn't thought of that."

"One more thing," Anne said, trying her best to sound casual. "Does Tracy own a blue-and-yellow-flowered shirt?"

"Yes." Delia hesitated a moment. "Why?"

Anne decided to lie. "I spoke to someone who thought they saw a girl matching Tracy's description on the beach in Belmar. Could you check if the shirt's in her closet?"

"I'll go see." After about a minute, Delia got back on the line. "It's not in her closet or in any of her drawers. And I couldn't see anything else that was missing." Delia's voice was hopeful. "Oh, Anne, do you think Tracy's in Belmar?"

"I'll go down there and check it out," Anne said, feeling badly about the deception she was perpetuating. But the truth was even weirder. What were Tracy's friends doing with a piece of her clothing? What spell were they casting on that doll?

"Delia, I think you should bring the police in on this."

"No," Delia said sharply. "Not yet. You'll find her. Or she'll come back on her own."

Now it was Anne's turn to sigh. She'd feel a whole lot better if the cops were involved. But it was clear Delia wouldn't budge. After she hung up, she got out the phone book and looked up Pam Whitehouse's phone number. She got the machine and left a message asking Pam to call her as soon as possible. It might be easier to wheedle the truth out of Pam than Lauren. Then she'd see about the third girl in the coven, Melissa Baker.

Anne took a shower, washed her hair, and tidied up the downstairs part of the house. She was straightening up the kitchen when the phone rang.

"Hello," she said, picking up on the first ring and hoping it would be Pam.

"Hi, Annie," said Dr. Arlene. "Just wanted to let you know I won't be home for dinner."

What are we, Anne thought. *A married couple?*

Aloud, she said, "Okay. I'm going out myself tonight."

The connection was laced with static. Anne heard the

low rush and hum of traffic in the background. Dr. A. was probably calling from her car again.

"Listen," Anne said. "Can we sit down tomorrow morning and go over the temperamental toddler material? I really need your input."

"Tomorrow's no good. Maybe later in the week."

"But if you could just . . ."

"Gotta go," Dr. Arlene interrupted. "Have a good evening."

Then she hung up.

The nerve of that woman, Anne thought to herself. *This is ridiculous.* They were getting no work done at all. Dr. A. might as well have been living on a houseboat in the San Francisco Bay.

Anne opened a cabinet and spread out a bunch of stuff on the counter. She'd had to make an extra trip to the Mini-Mart (and wait on line behind a half-dozen cheerful, badly sunburned tourists), but she'd gotten nearly everything the spell at the bookstore required.

She measured out the ingredients: one teaspoon crushed basil, one teaspoon dried sage, three pinches ground nutmeg, and the teaspoon of honey she'd substituted for European vervain, whatever that was. She poured the mixture into a half a cup of red wine and stirred. This was nuts. Really nuts. As if drinking this stuff and reciting some stupid words could make Bachelor Number One suddenly materialize out of thin air. The cat stared up at her from his wicker basket near the window and appeared to smirk. She could swear Harry was mocking her with his one good eye.

If anybody ever found out she was doing this, she'd never be able to live it down. It was almost as embarrassing as placing a personal ad. No, she amended. Nothing could be as bad as that. Her one foray into the wonderful world of the personals had resulted in a handful of dates with men who were either losers, painfully shy, or severely strange. She wondered about the spell's choice of words. An interesting man. Not an attractive, brilliant, funny man. But an interesting man. Well, she already knew Trasker. He was interesting. At times, she felt an electricity between them. She thought he felt it, too. But he wasn't exactly falling all over himself to be anything more than her friend and drinking buddy.

She tied a pink ribbon around the glass of wine.

Next—and this was the silliest part—she turned around three times and recited the words she'd copied down in Barnes & Noble. *Come to me, my hidden love. Shining like a light above. Fate be gentle, fate be kind. Darkness cannot make me blind. Before too long he will appear. Before the waning moon draws near.*

Anne poured some of the concoction into a tall glass. *Here goes nothing. Down the hatch.* She drank quickly. It didn't taste half-bad.

The dining room of the Molly Pitcher Inn in Red Bank was fancy enough to require that men wear jackets and ties at dinner. The tables were set with starched pink tablecloths, the rolls were piping hot, and the flowers serving as centerpieces looked positively exquisite. Anne was a little surprised that's where she and Trasker were eating dinner. She'd expected they'd go to one of their usual haunts: the Windmill in Long Branch where the burgers were juicy and smothered in onion rings or the Parker House in Sea Girt, for a mess of fried clams and oysters, topped off with Watermelon Italian Ices at Ralph's in Lavallette.

But here they were at the pricey-but-worth-it Molly Pitcher, at a candlelit table overlooking the Navesink River. She was glad she'd worn her navy sleeveless sundress, instead of the slacks and shirt she'd first tried on. Her hair was pulled back from her face with two small tortoiseshell barrettes, and she'd even managed to put on some makeup without getting lipstick on her teeth. If she didn't know better, she could almost believe she and Trasker were on a date. Even though he'd made a point of telling her not once, but twice, that the reason he'd chosen the inn was that he wanted to make himself feel better about having to miss his vacation.

Still, it was a gorgeous night, the sky tinged a delicate ballet slipper pink as the sun slipped toward the water. Anne had ordered grilled salmon with new potatoes and a medley of peas and carrots. But she was eyeing Trasker's filet mignon with shiitake-mushroom demiglace enviously. She didn't eat in fancy restaurants often. Okay, practically never. She definitely should have treated herself to the steak, which Trasker was attacking with gusto.

Apart from one of the busboys, he was the only black man in the room. It was usually the case when they went out. She wondered if it made Trasker uncomfortable, or if he was so used to it he barely noticed. She always noticed. She wished things weren't so segregated. In this part of the Jersey shore, blacks tended to live in Landsdown Park. If you did well for yourself, you moved away, moved up and out.

Trasker was born and raised in Trenton and lived in a condo in Avon. He'd told her that when he moved in it took four months before he encountered another person of color—a middle-aged Hispanic woman who came once a week to clean his downstairs neighbor's apartment.

"More wine?" he said, tapping the bottle.

"Sure."

He refilled her glass as well as his own. "You were telling me about the book."

"Like I said, it's not going very well."

She didn't want to talk about Dr. Arlene or the parenting stuff, not while she was in such luxuriant surroundings, overlooking a gorgeous sunset. Out the plate-glass window, the sky was a deep, surreal blue, laced with orange and pink smudges.

"You know, this day has been truly bizarre. I start out finding a body on the beach and wind up at the glamorous Molly Pitcher. Kind of a striking contrast. By the way," she asked, trying to sound casual. "Is the autopsy report back?"

"The lab's so backed up that it's not going to be performed until late tomorrow afternoon. By the way, the girl's parents almost forbid us to do the autopsy, on the grounds that it would be sacrilegious."

"They're not Catholic."

"Methodist. They said it went against their religious beliefs. The mother finally agreed, but the stepfather was dead set against it."

"That's strange. Rich Podowski never struck me as the religious type."

"You know him?"

"Not really. He owns the doll shop in town. I've been in a couple of times, and he waited on me. He struck me as a little strange because he seems so into the dolls. Changing their clothes, brushing their hair, shifting the displays around. He treats them like they're people."

"When I talked to him this morning he seemed angry."

"That's understandable, isn't it? He'd just found out his stepdaughter had died."

Trasker pushed the remaining pieces of steak around on his plate. "Not angry about Abby's death. Angry at me, at the questions I was asking. At one point, he told me to mind my own damn business. The wife was sitting there sobbing, and he was blowing his stack. If we were looking at a homicide investigation, I'd say that man is hiding something."

"Could it have been homicide?"

"We still think the Podowski girl killed herself. We analyzed the note. It's in her handwriting. And we interviewed the family and a few of her friends. They all said she'd been depressed for weeks, not eating, not sleeping, having crying jags. Classic stuff. Although her mother refuses to believe the girl was troubled."

"Did anyone know what was wrong?"

"Nope. She was pretty close-mouthed. Didn't share the specifics of her problems, according to friends. We analyzed the pills in her hand. They turned out to be Ecstasy."

"What's Ecstasy?"

"It started showing up in the eighties. Gives a wild high, like taking an amusement park ride. You hallucinate, flip out. Abby was holding four of them."

"Where would she have gotten them?"

"Who knows? There are plenty of drugs coming into the area from New York and Philly."

"Not in the Heights."

Trasker smiled ruefully. "Probably not. But certainly in Landsdown, which is right next door."

That was true. Landsdown Park was probably the drug capital of the Jersey Shore.

"Did you find out what the symbols stand for?" Anne asked.

"Not yet. They're not in any language we know. Listen, why the interest in Abby's death?"

Anne thought of the blood on the trunk in Tracy's room. She'd called Delia right before Trasker arrived. Still no sign of Tracy.

"I need a favor, if you can swing it."

Trasker put down his fork and studied her. "Uh oh. I recognize the signs. You're working on something, right? What's going on, Hardaway?"

"It's probably nothing. But Abby Powdowki was friends with a girl named Tracy Graustark, who's the great-niece of my friend, Delia. You've met Delia, right?"

Trasker nodded. "The librarian."

"Right." Anne hesitated, feeling twinges of guilt. She disliked going against Delia's wishes, but this was too important to ignore. "Delia told me that Tracy disappeared sometime last night. She doesn't want to file a missing persons report or bring the cops in at all. Tracy's a wild child. I think Delia's worried she's mixed up in something stupid, and she doesn't want to make matters worse."

Something shifted in Trasker's face.

"What?" Anne said, picking up on the change.

"Abby's mother believes Tracy is responsible for her daughter's death."

Anne felt a tremor of alarm. "How?"

"She says Tracy's been badgering Abby the last few days. Trying to make Abby do something she didn't want to do."

"Did she get any more specific?"

"That's as far as we got. But it's Suzanne Podowski's contention that Tracy urged Abby to take her own life."

Anne suddenly got a sick feeling in her stomach.

Teenagers were immensely susceptible to peer pressure. Had there been a suicide pact between the two girls? Was Tracy Graustark dead?

"Is there anything you can do to find Tracy, unofficially?"

"It'd be easier if her aunt reported her missing. That way, I could get the FBI and some other agencies involved. Right now, we're really shorthanded in the department."

"I understand. But I'd appreciate anything you could do to help."

"You think Tracy may have known about the suicide? She was with her friend at the time or she was so shook up by the whole thing that she ran away?"

"I'm not sure. But something strange is definitely going on with those girls."

She told him everything—about the witchcraft, the burning doll, and the state of Tracy's bedroom, including the dried blood she'd seen on the trunk.

When she'd finished, Trasker threw down his napkin and leaned back in his chair. "I don't like the sound of this. And I don't like the fact that your friend Delia lied to us this morning."

"I know."

"She needn't have been so protective. We did manage to see Pam Whitehouse's bedroom. And Abby's, of course. They're mirror images of Tracy's room."

"What about Lauren?"

"Her room looked okay. I guess there's not much privacy in those tents. The witchcraft paraphernalia would be harder to keep under wraps."

"So what now?"

"We look for Tracy. I don't like that business about the blood in her room."

Anne took another sip of wine. For the first time all day, she felt cold. "I did some reading on witchcraft today. Sometimes, when the coven meets, they offer sacrifices to the Devil."

Trasker signaled the waiter to clear away their plates. They both seemed to have lost their appetites. "Sacrifices, huh? And here I thought the biggest thing a Jersey girl had to worry about was her tan."

Chapter 6

No matter how many times you say, "There are no monsters hiding in the closet," your child is unlikely to believe you.

When they returned to her house, Anne invited Trasker in for a nightcap. They'd taken his car to the restaurant, and now he let the motor of the Camry idle. He'd rolled down the windows, and the sea air drifted into the car. Etta James was crooning a slow, sad version of "At Last." Clouds skated across the surface of the moon.

Anne hoped he was going to come inside. She felt happy, energized. She didn't want the evening to end.

"I envy you, being so close to the beach," he said.

"I don't think I could live anyplace else. After a while,

you get spoiled. The view. The air. Falling asleep to the sound of the waves."

He nodded. "That's what I like about fishing. Being out on the water. The vastness of it. The tranquillity."

In the half-dark, his skin looked almost coppery. His eyes were the deepest shade of brown she'd ever seen.

The breeze through the open windows lifted her hair in front of her face. He reached out and leaned toward her, tucking her hair back behind her ear. Her insides melted at his touch and for a delicious moment, she thought he was going to kiss her, and she felt her body tremble in anticipation, felt that old unspoken connection between them, taut and fragile as a spider's thread.

Then he abruptly pulled back and the moment was gone.

"I have some paperwork to catch up on," he said, not looking at her, staring straight ahead out the windshield.

"Okay. Sure," she said offhandedly, trying to mask her disappointment.

"I'll do what I can to find Tracy."

"Thanks."

She opened the car door and got out with a backward wave, running lightly up the front steps, pretending it didn't matter, that she didn't care.

So much for love potions, she thought wryly, fumbling with her key. Maybe she should have searched harder for the missing ingredient. Nah. Who was she kidding? It would take more than European vervaine for an interesting, available man to materialize in the Heights and ask her out. She had a better chance of bumping into old Beelzebub on the beach than of meeting Mr. Right.

It was probably just as well Trasker hadn't made a move. Getting involved with a cop wouldn't be good.

Long hours, risky job, work that was often frustrating and slow-going. Besides, police officers seemed to belong to a closed, mostly male club. The fact that Trasker was planning on vacationing alone, in a remote part of the country, with only a fishing pole and camping equipment for company should have told her something.

She went upstairs and heard loud snores emanating from the guest bedroom. There would be no confab with Dr. A. tonight. After changing into an oversize T-shirt that served as pajamas, Anne settled down in front of the TV. She flipped from channel to channel, then turned the set off. Fifty-six channels, nothing to watch. Go figure.

Harry curled up on her lap. She stroked the fur between his ears, and he purred contentedly. Cats were supposed to be mixed up with witchcraft, that much she knew. It was almost a cliché: the black cat sitting beside the cauldron as the witch stirred her noxious brew. She wondered whether she should keep him inside the house from now on. Harry was black and white, but she wasn't taking any chances. She got up, locked the doors, and decided the great outdoors was officially off-limits to the cat.

Taking Tracy's spell book out, she began to read through it again. On the very first page was a list labeled Tools: knife, sword, wand (ash, willow, or hazel), bell, cord, scourge. Scourge? Anne had no idea what that meant. Apparently all the tools had to be ritually cleansed and purified before they could be used, to remove any negative vibrations. Then they were supposed to be wrapped in a piece of clean, white linen and safely stored away until the "consecration."

The next page talked about names. "To know a person's name is to have power over them," Tracy had written. "If you know the name of your enemy, you can conjure with it."

Anne leafed through the book. It seemed to be part instructional and part motivational, filled with drawings, charts, recipes, and pithy sayings, like: "My goal is to build up my power and then to release it for the magick to work. If I can focus and keep a picture in my mind of what I want to happen, it will!"

Leafing through the rest of the book, Anne was struck not so much by the information as by the way in which it was presented. It was almost as if Tracy were taking notes, copying down information she learned from a book or in a classroom.

One page showed a drawing of a doll (or a "poppet," as Tracy called it), which seemed to be a rough figure cut from two pieces of cloth. Tracy had made a detailed diagram linking parts of the doll's body with a corresponding symptom that could be produced. If you stuck a pin into the doll's right palm, it would affect the heart. A pin in the ear would cause memory loss. Anne's mind flew to the doll that Pam and Lauren had set on fire. Was it possible that they'd hurt Tracy before tormenting the doll? Was the poppet a ritualistic symbol for unspeakable acts? But it wasn't supposed to work that way. First, you hurt the effigy. Then the real person suffered.

Anne turned the page to find another drawing outlining something called a "witches' cradle," where a female figure was tightly bound in order to separate the conscious mind from the body and allow the witch to roam beyond the physical horizon. You could achieve the same effect, Anne learned, through meditation and chanting.

"I flew high above the ocean last night without ever leaving the beach," Tracy had written. "It was wild! At first I was scared, but the Devil held my hand and guided me through the darkened skies. He is amazing!!!!"

Who was this guy, Anne wondered. Was someone really playing Prince of Darkness for a bunch of impressionable teenage girls? Or was he a figment of their overactive imaginations?

She turned her attention back to the book. Under a section called Rites of Passage, Tracy had listed about a dozen herbs, opposite their "magickal" names. Foxglove was called "witches' bells." Heather was "witches' broom." Ginseng was "wizard root." Mandrake was called the "Devil's candle." Anne skimmed through the list: Nightshade, henbane, belladonna, thornapple, jimsonweed. Not exactly your garden-variety herbs.

Underneath, Tracy had drawn a picture of the initiation ceremony, with the initiate blindfolded, bound, and led into a circle to face a large stick figure called the Nameless One. "It was exhilarating and terrifying," Tracy had written. "I knew I was turning a corner and would never go back to the life I've left behind. Long live Hecate! May she always triumph!"

Two pages later, in large capital letters, Tracy had written: AM I A TRAITOR? And then, on the facing page, WHAT IF ABBY TELLS????"

Tells what, Anne wondered. About the secret rites and rituals these girls were performing?

Anne skimmed through the rest of the book. At the top of several pages was a person's name, followed by spells outlining what was about to befall them or what already had. To bring on Martha Cox's migraines, there was a recipe featuring a mixture of clove buds, catnip, and something called black cohosh. Anne wondered if certain herbs could bring on physical symptoms, like headaches or stomach pains. It seemed entirely possible. But how had the girls planned on feeding Martha the concoction? Martha had lunch every day at Quilters, which served coffee, tea, lemonade, and various fruit juices. If Lauren worked there, she could be tampering with the drinks. But it would be tough to slip black cohosh in Martha's cranberry juice and have it remain undetected.

Another spell was intended for "People Who Get In Our Way." Tracy had made a list of items they needed for the spell to work: articles of clothing, nail clippings, strands of hair, eyelashes, a lipstick print. The spell was supposed to make the offending person disappear. Anne thought about that one for a while. Disappear as in getting out of the wanna-be witches' way or a more permanent disappearance, the kind that ended in death? It was ironic, in light of Tracy's own disappearance.

Anne closed the notebook. She was tired. She'd had enough witchcraft to last a lifetime. As she switched off the lights her thoughts returned to Trasker. For a split second, she'd been sure he was going to kiss her. She'd seen it in his eyes. So why had he pulled away? If she was braver or more confident, she would have said something; she would have put an end to this strange wordless back-and-forth dance they did. But what if she was just imagining he had feelings for her? What if she'd been wrong?

On her way up to bed, she took the romance spell and tossed it in the trash.

The music woke her out of a dream. It was soft, muted, barely audible above the crash of the waves, but loud enough to break the chain of sleep. She rolled over groggily and looked at the clock on her bedside table—3:20 A.M. Her bedroom overlooked the beach, and the music, a steady, low-pitched beat, drifted in through the open window.

Anne got out of bed. She'd been dreaming she was swimming underwater. Brightly striped fish glided by her, seaweed grew in wavy green clumps on the ocean floor. She'd swum to the surface and looked toward land. There were no houses, no town, nothing but sand dunes as far as the eye could see. A large black bird had swooped low over the dunes. She heard the crow screech, heard the soft steady hum of music, then woken up with a start.

Before the last couple of weeks, she almost never was disturbed by noises outside her window. Oceanside Heights was quiet at night, even on weekends. Hardly any cars drove down Ocean Avenue in the early hours of the morning. And the ocean always lulled her to sleep, with its lovely ceaseless crashing. But lately, Anne had heard strange sounds coming from the beach at night: chanting, drumming, fragments of song. She'd gone out to investigate a couple of times, but the minute she'd crossed the street the noises had stopped.

Now, she threw on a pair of shorts and her running shoes and crept downstairs. Dr. A. was still asleep. Harry was curled in a ball in his basket, probably dreaming of Purina. Instead of going out the front, Anne exited through the kitchen, skirting the side of the house. When she reached the yard, she ducked down behind her car and peeked over the hood.

The beach looked completely deserted. The only light came from the curved streetlamps on the boardwalk, which cast spidery shadows down the lifeguard stand. She glanced up and down the street. There was no one in sight. The houses on either side of her were completely dark. But still the music played. Softly, steadily, with an almost monotone beat. She thought she heard faint singing, but couldn't make out the words.

It sounded like it was coming from under the board-walk. She darted forward, staying low to the ground, try-ing to keep behind trees and bushes. When she reached the street, she quickly scrambled across it and hid behind a row of cars. During the off-season, none of the spaces would be taken. But on weekends in August, finding a parking space in the Heights, especially along the beach, was a major coup.

Above the ocean, a crescent moon hung like a white sickle slicing the sky in half. Anne smelled salt and sand and beneath that the faint scent of incense drifting over the dunes. It was different from the incense that had em-anated from the tent. Deeper, woodier, not as sweet.

There were steps leading from the boardwalk down to the beach. But Anne knew if she took them, she'd be more visible. Instead, she crawled over the gray wooden planks to the railing and dropped noiselessly to the sand below.

She could hear them now. No more than fifty feet away. Girlish voices. Giggling, whispering. The music had grown louder. Someone singing in a foreign lan-guage, the words nearly indistinguishable. Then a low steady ringing. Anne peered into the darkness. She saw the white foamy spray of the waves, the metal garbage cans, the sea grass rippling in the wind. From underneath the boardwalk came a faint bluish light. She moved for-ward, toward the light.

Suddenly, the music stopped, and she heard a faint ring-ing sound. The tinkle of a bell. Or wind chimes. A sudden movement by the ocean caught her eye. A dark form rose out of the sea, towering above the waves. What on earth, Anne thought. The thing was seven or eight feet tall, with long arms and curved ears like ram's horns stuck on either side of its head. She stood up and took a few steps toward the water, no longer caring if she was spotted.

All at once, she saw a blinding flash of red light and then a face so horrible it would haunt her dreams for weeks. That mouth, that greedy-looking mouth, gaping and bloody and cruel. Anne felt her heart leap in her chest. She struggled to catch her breath and instinctively moved backward, away from the water. In her confusion her legs got tangled up and she fell back onto the sand, still staring at whatever was out there.

Her own mouth was hanging open. She felt the wind on her face, felt her skin grow clammy and cold with fear. Then the light went out and the thing vanished. A scream tore through the night. Wheeling around, Anne tried to see who had cried out. Still shaking, she made her way back to the boardwalk and peered beneath it, but all she could make out were the faint outlines of wooden posts and a dark expanse of powdery sand. At the shoreline, the waves broke one after another, sending up plumes of white spray. There was nobody on the beach. No one at all.

She sat by the living room window, watching the sky turn from black to electric blue to a pearly, iridescent white. She couldn't sleep, couldn't think straight.

After she'd gotten home, she'd considered calling the police or at the very least knocking on a couple of her neighbors' doors to see if they'd seen or heard anything. But it was too early to disturb the neighbors. Besides, how would she explain what she saw? There were moments during the early hours of the morning when she began to doubt it herself, when she felt that her eyes were playing nasty tricks on her.

But hadn't there been other sightings these last few weeks? She tried to remember what she'd heard around town. Reports of music, weird singing, colored lights, a black form rising out of the ocean.

Her mind pulled at the possibilities the way she used to stretch saltwater taffy as a kid. It could have been an apparition, her imagination working overtime, fueled by talk of witches and devils. But deep down, Anne knew that wouldn't fly. She'd seen what she'd seen. Period. Next theory: The thing had been real. Only problem was she didn't believe it. There was no Antichrist, no supernatural being with malevolent designs. Evil was strictly the work of humans with scarred and fractured psyches. Still, she could imagine the newspaper headlines—*Sea Monster Sighted in Heights . . . Jersey's Own Blair Witch Project . . . The Devil and the Deep Blue Sea*. Which left choice number three: someone, some tall person wearing a mask, was out in the ocean in the middle of the night playing trick or treat in August. Which didn't exactly sound plausible. Besides, the image had appeared above the waves, not in them.

Anne gazed out the window at the Atlantic. She could barely see the water but the steady shushing of the waves was reassuring, almost hypnotic. What had Tracy written? *The Devil held my hand and guided me through the skies*. Where was Tracy tonight? Why wasn't she home, safely tucked under her skull-and-bone sheets?

Anne took out the spell book and read through it again. The answer was there somewhere. It had to be. She stared at the pages until the words began to blur, until poppets and herbs and spells were all jumbled up in her head, and she fell into a light, uneasy sleep.

Chapter 7

*Peer pressure is at its
peak in the teenage
years. As a parent, it's
important to understand
that your child needs to
fit in with the group
because she
fears rejection.*

At six-thirty, she threw on a sweatshirt and left the
house. The day had dawned cooler than the one
before it. A thin band of clouds smudged the sky,
and the Atlantic was calm and glassy, the color of seaweed.
When she'd finally fallen back to sleep, Anne had dreamed
about Tracy, about looking for Tracy on the beach at night,
stumbling around in the dark, and hearing a girl's voice cry
out, "help me, help me." But she couldn't help. The waves
had reared up, dark plumes of water crashing over her

head, filling her lungs until she could no longer breathe, and she woke with a start in a nest of tangled sheets.

Now she retraced her steps, dropping down beneath the waist-high boardwalk railing and heading toward the water. She studied the ground for signs that anyone had been there recently. But the beach was remarkably free of litter. Turning, she ducked under the boardwalk and walked to the spot where she thought she'd heard music playing. The area was roughly the width of two large porticoes, dotted with thick wooden posts. It was even cooler there, in the shady half-dark. The sand felt soft and powdery beneath her feet. Her eyes swept the area for signs of life. But all she saw were pieces of broken driftwood.

She sat cross-legged and stared out at the beach. The last time she'd been under this boardwalk she was a teenager. She and Larry Baumgartner had just seen *Star Wars* and they'd capped off the evening by coming there. She tried to think back to what she'd been feeling then: fear, excitement, elation, anticipation. To be kissing under the boardwalk, across the street from her house, where her mother sat watching *The Odd Couple* on TV, seemed the height of youthful abandon. She wondered if kids in the Heights still went under the boardwalk to make out. Probably. The years passed, the seasons changed, but the town seemed to stay the same.

She closed her eyes and took a deep breath. No scent of incense lingered from last night, just salt air. She could smell the dune grass and the waves and the worn gray planks of the boardwalk. She loved these smells. She'd lived at the beach her entire life, and it still managed to intoxicate her. Today, it had a calming effect. She felt grounded again, more sure of herself.

Opening her eyes, she scanned the deserted beach.

From this vantage point, she could see the lifeguard stand, the fishing pier, and a good-size stretch of ocean. A flock of gulls circled lazily over the water, then flew off. She could hear Ocean Avenue waking up—doors slamming, children yelling, the roar of cars.

She rose to her feet, brushed the sand from her legs, and climbed back up to the boardwalk. The house to the right of hers was owned by Hannah and Jeffrey Morton, who were away, visiting Hannah's bedridden mother, in Charlottesville, Virginia, and the house was dark and un-inhabited, the curtains drawn, the shutters closed. On the other side of Anne lived Martha Cox.

Miss Cox was what Anne's mother had called a "church biddy." One of those holier-than-thou women who was convinced God had put her on earth to make sure other people obeyed the Good Book to the letter. When Anne's mother was alive and in the throes of Alzheimer's, Martha Cox had led a drive to have her committed to an institution. *It is disgraceful*, Martha had said, *to have that woman parading around town, digging up flower beds like a mongrel dog and raving to herself about Heaven knows what. She should be punished. She should be stopped.* As if Alzheimer's wasn't punishment enough.

For years, Anne had hated living next door to Martha Cox. The old lady seemed to feel that the disease had passed from mother to daughter and was lying dormant in Anne, waiting to spring up without warning. Martha barely nodded if they saw one another entering or exiting their respective houses, and Anne preferred it that way. After a while, they'd lapsed into a mutual stony silence. It wasn't the greatest situation, but Anne was used to it. About the last thing she wanted to do was talk to Martha, but she didn't see any way around it.

She crossed the street and climbed the three steps to Martha's porch. From this vantage point, Anne had a bird's-eye view of her own house, of the worn wicker furniture on the front porch and the geraniums wilting on the lawn. She was surprised to see how shabby her place looked from here—the yellow paint flaking off the exterior, the torn shutter on the upstairs bedroom, the sagging steps. No matter how much money (and there wasn't a lot of it) she sank into the house, it seemed to settle into a state of benign neglect. Maybe the teenage witch idea would change her luck. All she needed was a breakout book, a book that would land on the best-seller list or make the round of the talk shows, and she'd be able to fix the house up, trade in the Mustang, finally do some traveling. Maybe the witch book was the ticket.

She rapped on Mrs. Cox's front door, which was painted forest green and adorned with a brass knocker in the shape of an angel.

"Oh, it's you," Martha said coldly, opening the door.

From inside the house, Anne heard the low murmur of voices.

Martha Cox peered out at her, squint-eyed. At seventy, she had the appearance and demeanor of a malevolent scarecrow. She was so skinny that her pale pink sweater and gray slacks hung loosely on her frame. Her face looked pinched, hollowed out.

"How are you feeling today, dear?" she inquired, taking a step backward as if she feared whatever Anne had was catching.

The question was vintage Martha. Presumably innocent, but tinged with venom and fear. It must have been tough having a neighbor who you were convinced could turn psycho at any moment.

"I'm fine, thank you," Anne said, forcing a note of cheer into her voice. Fairly early in her mother's illness, she'd learned that the best way to counter mean-spirited ignorance was with a show of bravado. "I stopped by to ask if you noticed anything unusual on the beach last night."

Martha Cox crossed her arms and leaned a bony shoulder against the door. Anne could smell something delicious—fresh bread or muffins—emanating from inside the house.

"Of course, I saw," Martha snapped. "I may be old, but I'm not blind. I've been up for hours drafting the petition."

"Petition?"

"Come in. I'll show you."

Martha turned on her heel and Anne followed her into the living room. She'd never been inside the house before. It was nicer than she'd expected, cheerier, more homey. The walls were painted buttercup yellow. The wood floor had been stained and pickled white and featured a stenciled flower border. The furniture was traditional in style, but still managed to look brand-new. Two camelback sofas, an oversize floral ottoman that doubled as a coffee table, floor-to-ceiling cherrywood bookshelves, some with glass doors.

Six people sat on the sofas, another six were seated on folding chairs draped with white cotton slipcovers that tied in the back. Most of the people were from the Heights. Anne recognized a few elderly ladies—Eleanor Granville, Lucille Klemperer, Sally Metzger. The rest were quite a bit younger, men and women who lived in town and were sitting in Martha Cox's living room sipping coffee and eating what looked like homemade banana bread in the early hours of the morning. Strange.

"What's going on?" Anne said.

"We're having a little meeting," Martha Cox announced, "to solve this problem once and for all."

"It's disgraceful," said Lucille Klemperer, rattling her coffee cup angrily. "Next thing you know it won't be safe to walk alone after dark or leave our doors unlocked."

"When we catch the witches," intoned another voice, "they'll be sorry they ever set foot in the Heights."

Anne turned. The speaker had emerged from a room behind her. She stared hard at the man, who was heavyset, in his early to mid-fifties, with a handlebar mustache and graying hair. It was the man she'd seen on the green, across from the tents yesterday morning. But she'd seen him before that. She was sure of it. She just couldn't remember where.

"Noah's right," said Eleanor Granville, whose normally pale face was flushed. "Devil worship is blasphemy. And it has to stop right now."

"Oh, it shall," crowed Martha Cox.

She picked up a piece of powder blue paper that had been lying on the coffee table and brandished it like a sword.

Anne examined the paper, which consisted of one paragraph, written in black ink in a spidery hand:

We, the people of Oceanside Heights, do declare that we will not tolerate aberrant, deviant behavior in our town or on our beach. The beach closes at 5:30 p.m. Those persons found playing music, lighting fires, swimming, disturbing the peace, engaging in drugs and other unlawful behavior shall be fined, punished, and jailed. We live in an up-

standing, God-fearing community. Such persons who mock our Lord Jesus Christ by worshipping the Devil and performing blasphemous, ungodly acts are not welcome here.

It was Holy Roller stuff. She'd heard tons of it growing up. Most folks in the Heights were good-hearted, friendly people who just happened to appreciate old-time, seat-of-the-pants religion. But there was a fringe element in town whose lives were pledged to God, country, and Christianity, who went to church nearly every day and looked askance at anyone who didn't exhibit the same zeal they did.

She surveyed the circle of grim, angry faces before her. There was a collective fury at work here, and it was building to fever pitch.

She handed the document back to Martha, along with the pen.

"You're not going to sign?" Martha said, her eyes flashing.

"I doubt the petition will do much good. Whoever was on the beach last night will just move to another spot or stay indoors. Besides, even though the lifeguards go off duty at five-thirty, there's activity on the beach at night. People walking, talking. It's hardly illegal."

The man named Noah fixed his gaze on her. His eyes were like cold, gray chips of steel. "One girl has already died."

"I know, but that was . . ."

". . . due to witchcraft," Noah finished. "There's a cancer in our midst. If we don't stop them, it will spread."

Anne heard the hatred in his voice and then she remembered who he was. Noah Wright. He'd had a middle management job over at the electronics plant in Freehold.

Last March, he'd been fired, along with 174 other workers caught in a wave of corporate downsizing. But Noah had fought back. He'd organized round-the-clock protests outside the plant and acted as the group's spokesman, appearing almost nightly on News 12's evening broadcast. When a mysterious fire broke out at the plant, halting production for months, Noah Wright had gone on TV to explain why neither he nor any member of his group had had anything to do with it.

"We've notified the sheriff's office and asked for extra patrols," Martha was saying. "And we're planning on organizing a citizen's watch. We'll take turns standing guard. It's a shame you don't care enough about the Heights or this neighborhood to participate."

It occurred to Anne that Martha Cox would have made a great Sunday school teacher or state senator. She had the unswerving conviction that everything out of her mouth was the God's Honest Truth.

"What exactly did you see last night?" Anne asked.

"The same thing you did, I suspect," Martha snapped. "Some idiots dancing around with colored lights, playing funny music, and that monstrosity in the ocean, whatever the heck that was supposed to be."

"Have any of the rest of you seen it?" Anne asked.

The room went eerily quiet. Then Lucille Klemperer spoke up. "I did. Last Tuesday evening. It made my blood run cold."

Noah Wright waved his hand dismissively. "A cheap trick, that's all it is. I'm more concerned that they're worshipping the Devil. Begging him to join them for their lurid pleasure."

"Could you identify any of them?" Anne asked.

Martha let out an exaggerated sigh. "If we could, we

wouldn't be standing here gabbing with the likes of you. We'd be down at the sheriff's office, pressing formal charges. I'll tell you something though. When we do catch them, they'll wish they'd never set eyes on us. My head still aches from the racket they were making."

Anne pondered this a moment. The music hadn't been all that loud. "Do you get migraines?"

Martha gave her an odd look. "I suggest you worry about your own health and the health of this community," she announced.

"Yes," said Eleanor. "It's odd that you won't sign. Could it be that you're hiding something? Protecting someone?"

Anne was about to offer a snappy reply, then stopped. She thought of Tracy Graustark. What would these people do if they suspected Tracy was a witch? How far would they go?

"Maybe she's one of them," Noah said softly.

Thirteen pairs of eyes bored into her, sizing her up, considering whether it were possible.

"Look," Anne said. "The only time I was a witch was when I played Glinda the Good in Camp Somerset's production of *The Wizard of Oz*. I had the opening solo."

Nobody smiled. Anne studied their stern upturned faces. "You're a tough audience," she said, hoping to break the tension.

"You find witchcraft amusing?" Noah asked, in a voice brimming with barely suppressed rage.

"I'd like to get to the bottom of this, too," Anne replied.

"Then sign our petition," he shot back.

"I think I'll pass," she said lightly.

"I should have expected as much," said Martha Cox, with a sneer. "Now, if you'll excuse us, we need to get back to the business at hand."

Anne was glad to go. The circle of avengers was making her feel almost claustrophobic. Closing the front door behind her, she started down the porch steps. Before yesterday, she hadn't given witchcraft a second thought. If she had, she would have called it a bunch of hooey. But there were obviously people who believed very deeply. And belief systems were a powerful thing. She'd grown up around people, good Christian people, who were so devout, so utterly trusting and worshipful of Jesus Christ, that they would have done anything to serve Him.

All of a sudden, she felt very tired. She loved the Heights, but living in a small town taxed her patience at times. Some people wouldn't let the past alone. They fed on history, picking at old scars, old memories, until it might have been only yesterday that her mother was wandering up and down Main Street, raving to herself in a language nobody had understood.

It struck her that if her mother had been alive three hundred years ago, she would surely have been branded a witch. Her executioners, people like Martha Cox and Noah Wright, only wielding more authority, would have tied stones to Evelyn Hardaway's body, marched her into the ocean, then waited to see if she floated or sank.

Anne looked out at the beach and wondered what would have been worse: drowning or bobbing to the surface. Instant agony versus torture and eventual death. She walked home mulling the question over under sweet blue skies that she couldn't enjoy.

Chapter 8

> *We all tend to think our children are the most brilliant, most beautiful, most extraordinary on the planet. But if your needs for your child's success are too great, you may be thwarting his development. This has come to be known as the Superbaby Syndrome.*

Abby Podowski had lived in a small two-story gray cottage facing Wesley Lake, which separated the Heights from Landsdown Park. On each side of the double-leafed door was a small narrow window. On the second story, under the gable, a second door opened onto a narrow balcony. The house had forest green shutters, jigsaw scrollwork on the eaves, and patterned shingles. It was a style of home that the tourists remarked upon, cute and cozy, reminiscent of a dollhouse.

Abby's mother, Suzanne, had converted one room of the house into a store, which was open from noon to four on summer weekends. Suzanne sold unmatched dishes, colored glass seltzer bottles, tablecloths cross-stitched with folksy sayings, kitschy salt and pepper shakers, 1950s cookbooks, lamps with enormous tasseled shades, and assorted other stuff.

The store, called Suzi's Attic, was one step above a yard sale and several rungs below any reputable antique shop. It was not unheard of for Suzanne to sell her neighbors' castoffs. Her prices were low, and once in a while, an object of value turned up.

There was some question about whether Suzanne had the proper permit needed to run the shop, but no one ever complained and one year, *New Jersey* magazine listed Suzi's Attic in an article called "Secret Shore Treasures," which helped business for a short time and turned Suzanne into a mini-celebrity for the entire month the magazine was on the stands.

Anne bypassed the side entrance to the shop, which had a closed sign on it, and knocked on the front door. No one answered, and, hearing the faint strains of music, Anne went around back. She found Suzanne Podowski hunched in a plastic lawn chair in front of an empty clothesline. Suzanne's laundry basket was filled with wet garments, but she looked too tired, too emotionally spent, to begin hanging clothes on the line.

Her entire face was red—her eyes red and swollen, her nose chafed, her skin splotchy. Her long dark hair was greasy, and she wore it pulled back, in a loose ponytail. She'd smeared sky-blue eye shadow over each puffy eyelid, and her mascara had pooled, giving her the look of a sad raccoon. She had on a man's denim shirt that was several sizes too big over loose-fitting white shorts. Her feet were jammed into a dirty pair of Keds, worn like bedroom slippers, so that her heels were visible. Around her neck was a necklace strung with large pearls.

A transistor radio played Sinatra singing "Summer Wind."

"Just leave it on the porch," she said to Anne.

Only her mouth moved. Her body remained slumped in the chair as if she'd been sitting there a long time and had no intention of moving anytime soon.

"Pardon?" Anne said.

Suzanne was in her mid to late forties, and under better circumstances, with the right makeup, she would have made a passable restaurant hostess or senior flight attendant—a no-nonsense, slightly haggard woman with a brusque voice who was used to taking charge. There was a hardness to her demeanor, even in grief. Anne wondered how much of it she'd passed along to her daughter.

"The cake or casserole or plant. Just leave it on the porch, and I'll bring it in later."

"I didn't bring anything," Anne said, a touch apologetically. Perhaps she should have. Muffins or a basket of fruit. Meaningless tokens in a tragedy of this magnitude. But an expression of sympathy and goodwill nonetheless.

"I was the one who found her on the beach. I came by to say how sorry I am."

"Yes," Suzanne said dully. "Thank you."

Anne sat down on a second lawn chair, which sagged in the middle and was coated with dirt.

"I know this probably isn't the best time," she began. "But I was wondering if I could talk to you for a minute. It's about Abby's friend, Tracy."

At the mention of Tracy's name, Suzanne's head jerked up. "That little troublemaker," she said, fairly spitting the words out. "She's the one who got my baby killed."

"What do you mean?"

"I mean Abby would never have thought about killing herself if it wasn't for Tracy Graustark." Suzanne sat up and cast her red-rimmed gaze on Anne. "She was always a bad influence on my Abby: shoplifting, boosting cars, cheating on tests, staying out all night. Abby's not like that. Abby's a good girl."

Suzanne heard herself slip into the present tense and stifled a sob.

Anne's heart went out to her. How could anyone possibly go on with their lives after losing a child? How could it not tear you to pieces?

"I don't understand," she said gently. "Do you think Tracy talked Abby into it?"

Suzanne gripped the aluminum arms of her chair. "She was always putting wild ideas in Abby's head. First it was stealing, then witchcraft."

"I'm not sure if you heard, but Tracy's missing."

A faint smile played around Suzanne's lips. "Is that so? Well, I hope she never shows her miserable face around here again."

"I was wondering if you knew where she might have gone. If she and Abby had anyplace special they liked to go?"

"Abby was a homebody. In bed by eleven most nights. If Tracy Graustark was running around at all hours, Abby wasn't with her."

"I didn't mean to imply . . ."

"Abby was a good girl," Suzanne cut in. "So kind, so generous." Suzanne's fingers stroked the necklace at her throat. "She gave me this just last week. Isn't it exquisite?"

Anne studied the pearls. In the morning light, they looked real.

As if reading Anne's mind, Suzanne said: "They're real all right. I have the receipt from Cartier."

Wow, Anne thought. *The necklace must have cost a bundle. Where would a sixteen-year-old girl get that kind of money?*

Suzanne was going on about how Abby's grades were improving, how much summer school had helped, how Abby planned to go to college and study psychology. The picture didn't fit with the depressed, emotional girl who had crying jags and wasn't eating or sleeping. But then how much did parents ever really know or understand their children?

"She was an angel," Suzanne was saying, choking back tears. "And now she's gone. Gone."

Suzanne fell silent. On the radio, a silken-voiced man was pitching the new Honda Accord. The air was thick with heat. Suzanne had slumped forward in her chair. When Anne got up to leave, Suzanne was still sitting that way, like a misshapen statue carved from stone.

Even in summertime, the high school smelled chalky and musty, as if no one ever bothered to open a window and let the summer breeze in. Anne had gone to school in the yellow brick building, and though it seemed like a hundred years ago, walking down the locker-lined, dimly lit corridors brought it all back to her. She hadn't liked school much, had never been one of the popular kids. For a few years, she'd been taunted and teased mercilessly about her mother, until it got to the point where she started missing days at a time, claiming to be sick, and then actually became sick at the thought of going back.

Whenever she drove by the school and saw kids talking and smoking in tight little clusters or hanging out on the front steps, she wondered if she'd missed out on one of life's pivotal experiences. School had taken up so many years of her life, and she'd spent most of that time counting the minutes until she could be rid of it for good. At her high school graduation, when her class sang "We've Only Just Begun," she felt like crying with relief. It was over. She was finally free.

It had been nice to discover there was life after high school. That ten, twenty years down the line, the football hero or the homecoming queen could be just as messed up and unhappy as everybody else. Still, she'd spent so many years in this building and ones like it—stuffing her brain with useless information and staring out the window—that in retrospect the whole process seemed like a colossal waste of time.

Going to summer school, which fortunately she'd never had to do, would have been the absolute pits. Now, walking down the halls, she saw teachers and students who appeared to share her view. Kids in shorts and T-shirts dragged their books from one class to the next, eyes cast down, burdened not only by knapsacks but by an invisible sense of dread, as if mentally recounting all the things they could be doing if they weren't stuck in Remedial Trig or Sophomore English II. The teachers seemed even more exasperated than she remembered. Deprived of their summer hiatus and the opportunity to kick back and relax after the close of the school year, they barked orders, spitting out instructions and facts like injured birds unable to migrate.

Tracy Graustark was taking two courses in summer school—Biology and English. The biology teacher, a squat, frumpy woman with a lisp whose name was Mrs. Fitzsimmons, told Anne that Tracy had missed half a dozen classes and was on the brink of failing. She had no idea where Tracy could be, and it looked to Anne as though she didn't much care. There were twenty-four kids in her class, she told Anne crossly, and not one of them had the brains God gave an ant. No one cared about biology anymore, much less understood it.

Anne tried to remember what she'd learned about biology in school, but all she could come up with was an unpleasant image of a frog being dissected.

English sounded more interesting. Anne had majored in English Lit at college and if she won the lottery, she knew one of the first things she'd do was get her master's degree in literature for the sheer joy of reading and discussing Dickens and Hawthorne and Faulkner.

As she stood outside the classroom, she heard the final minutes of the teacher's lecture. The topic was Thomas Hardy's *Return of the Native*. Anne remembered the book. The portrait Hardy had drawn of the lonely, willful Eustacia Vye, standing before a bonfire on the mournful heath had struck a chord in her. Eustacia drowned herself in the end. Hardy had meant her death to be symbolic, but Anne thought it was a waste. Eustacia could have toughed it out. She had the guts and the smarts to survive.

When the lecture ended and the kids had filed out of class, Anne entered the room. The teacher's legs were up on his desk and he was leaning back in his chair, reading a blue essay book. He looked to be in his late thirties, with a lanky frame and sandy-colored hair.

"Hi," he said, glancing up. He studied her for a moment, then smiled, as if he liked what he saw. "You're not here to complain about your kid's grade, are you?"

"Hardly," Anne said, laughing.

"I didn't think so. You don't look like a concerned mom." He swung his legs off the desk and extended his hand. "Doug Browning. English teacher extraordinaire."

"Anne Hardaway," she said, taking his hand and shaking it. "Ghostwriter. Literature lover. And troubleshooter."

"Well, you've got my attention," he said, putting the book down. "Tell you what? I've got ten minutes before the next set of disaffected monsters storms in here. Have a seat and tell me what I can do for you."

She sat down in a chair attached to the middle desk in the first row. The desk was so marked up with graffiti she could barely see what color the wood had originally been.

"It's about Tracy Graustark," Anne said, launching into what had become her standard spiel: how Tracy was missing, how she was a friend of Tracy's guardian, how Abby's suicide might fit in, how witchcraft played a role in the girls' lives, how worried she and Delia were.

Doug Browning listened intently while she talked. He wore faded blue jeans, high tops, and a green cotton shirt, with the sleeves rolled up. He looked a little like the Marlboro man—tanned, rugged, like he'd be right at home roping steers in Montana or riding a palomino with a hat slung low over his eyes. They were great eyes, a clear deep blue the color of a freshwater stream.

When she'd finished, he said: "That's incredible. I had

no idea *The Crucible* would lead to stuff like this."

Somehow Anne had expected a stronger reaction from him. He seemed like the sort of teacher who'd be friends with his students, who would take their problems to heart.

"So they read the play in your class?" she asked.

"The first week of school, in June. I like to place great literature in its historical context. For *The Crucible*, I talked about the origins of witchcraft in Europe and America. The government-sponsored witch-hunts. The kinds of torture these women endured. I even threw in a few incantations and spells I happened to come across." He shrugged and turned his palms faceup in a what-can-you-do gesture. "The kids seemed to like it. They're so used to sound bites and MTV, it helps to liven up the subject matter."

"Did Tracy give you any indication she was taking the witchcraft stuff to heart? Do you have any idea where she might be?"

Doug Browning's expression grew thoughtful. His eyes took on a serious cast. "I can't imagine where she'd go or why she'd run off. But girls that age are sensitive. The slightest thing can set them off or be misinterpreted. A bad grade on a test. Breaking up with a boyfriend."

"Was Tracy seeing anyone?"

"I really couldn't say. I try to stay out of the kids' personal lives." He glanced at the clock, then turned his gaze back to Anne. "Listen, I've got some essays to grade before my next class. Are you free later tonight? I've done some research on witches. We could get something to eat, and I'll fill you in. Maybe it'll shed some light on Tracy's disappearance."

Anne thought it over. Tracy had been missing for about

thirty-eight hours. She had to convince Delia to bring in the cops before darkness fell and before Tracy spent another night God knows where. *If Tracy's okay*, a voice inside Anne's head whispered. *If nothing's happened to her.*

Aloud, she said, "Sure. Seven-thirty's good." She took out her notepad and scribbled down her address and phone number.

"Great," he said, tucking the paper into his shirt pocket. "I'll be there."

Anne got to her feet. From the hallway, she heard the sound of kids going back and forth to their classes. Their voices echoed through the long, dim halls, and they suddenly seemed far away, no longer individuals, part of an endless cycle of students who'd trudged through this building, bearing books and pencils and hope. How many of them turned to the unknown for solace, embracing drugs or alcohol or mysterious rituals that held out the promise of power or escape?

"Anything wrong?" Doug Browning asked.

"I was wondering for the umpteenth time why teenagers are so fascinated by witchcraft."

Browning smiled, but the smile was vaguely sad. "There are so many answers to that question. Witchcraft is history's gothic novel. Sure, it's rooted in folklore and superstition. But it's been around, in one form or another for centuries. Did you know the first witch is supposed to have been Lilith, Adam's wife?"

Anne shook her head. Her knowledge of the Bible was a little sketchy. She'd dropped out of Sunday school at a young age and had little patience for church, organized religion, or people who believed they could see and hear Jesus.

"Lilith was accused of injuring babies," Browning continued. "And look what happened to her. She was supplanted in a New York minute by Eve, practically erased from memory. But that's only the beginning. Witches have always been equated with sex, murder, and encounters with the Devil. People have feared, hated, and persecuted them from the beginning of time."

Anne thought back to the drawing she'd seen in Tracy's room.

"What are witch-hammerers?" she asked.

"Witch hunters. Under European law, witchcraft was a statutory offense. Wherever witches were found, they were arrested, tortured, legally convicted, and burned. City after city established 'burning courts' for the sole purpose of dispatching witches. Enter the witch hunters. These guys built a lucrative business from outing suspected witches. Some of them amassed a fortune from the fees they charged."

Browning was silent a moment, and Anne felt a faint tug of uneasiness. "Today, people are a lot more tolerant," he continued. "You could chalk witchcraft up to eccentricity or garden-variety neuroses. Except in the Heights. I expect some people in town are pretty upset to find a bunch of witches in their midst."

"That's putting it mildly."

His gaze slid away, toward the kids roaming the halls. "It's pretty cut-and-dried actually. The Bible says: 'Thou shalt not suffer a witch to live.' "

Chapter 9

> *Scientific researchers*
> *have found high levels*
> *of stress in children as*
> *young as four months*
> *old. Symptoms include*
> *constant fussiness,*
> *erratic eating and*
> *sleeping patterns,*
> *and the inability*
> *to be comforted.*

Baby Face was practically an institution in Oceanside Heights. Founded in the early 1950s, the shop specialized in large, elaborately dressed dolls with creamy porcelain skin, painted glass eyes, and thick, flaxen hair. Rich Podowski had bought the store from the original owners three years ago and hadn't changed much in it, beyond adding a couple of Made-lines and Barbies to the mix. For the most part, Baby Face was still crammed from floor to ceiling with old-fashioned dolls, wearing stiff hand-sewn dresses, intricate doll furniture, and a smattering of plush animals. Music—the type you'd find in an ice-skating rink or a carousel—played softly in the background, and the air always smelled of vanilla potpourri.

As a child, Anne had loved visiting the store and admiring the dolls, picking out which ones she'd like to own. She particularly liked the Madame Alexander dolls, with their serious, almost soulful expressions and their smooth rosy skin. Unlike some other kids in the neighborhood, she'd always obeyed the "Look, but don't touch" signs posted on the glass display cases. The hushed atmosphere had reminded her of church, only better, and she'd adopted a respectful, slightly wary stance the minute she walked through the door, careful to take small steps and keep her hands by her sides for fear of accidentally knocking over one of the porcelain treasures.

Now, she got to the shop a little before noon. Despite three cups of coffee she was feeling exhausted. Behind the counter of Baby Face, Rich Podowski looked like he hadn't gotten much shut-eye either. His chin was cupped in his hand, but his head kept nodding forward. He was a skinny, rawboned man in his mid-forties, with tattoos snaking up and down his arms. His sandy-colored hair hung down past his shoulders and he wore a dirty gray tank top and a pair of faded jeans. About the least likely person Anne would imagine owning a doll shop. Every so often, the shop got written up in the local paper as an old-fashioned relic, a throwback to gentler times, and each time it did, Anne wondered how Baby Face could possibly make any money.

Tourists wandered in during the summer, taking a break from the heat. But they didn't seem to buy much. Kids today were more interested in Playstation computer games and Pokemon cards than in playing with dolls. Serious doll collectors were few and far between on the Shore. In the winter, hardly anyone came into Baby Face except the mailman. Yet Podowski stayed open six days a week and showed little inclination to carry more salable merchandise.

"Hey," he said, glancing up and rubbing his eyes with his knuckles.

"Hi," she answered.

She and Rich Podowski nodded to one another if they passed on the street or at the Mini-Mart, but they weren't on a first-name basis. She'd been in two or three times in the last couple of years to look around, but ultimately she'd ended up going to the mall to buy presents for the handful of children she knew.

"I'm sorry about Abby," she told him. "If there's anything I can do . . ."

A look of discomfort crossed his face, and he nodded brusquely.

"What can I do you for?" he said, with an oily smile that revealed a cracked front tooth.

"I'm looking for a doll for a four-year-old girl. Nothing too fancy."

It was a half-truth. Her goddaughter's birthday was coming up, but she'd been planning on getting Allyson books or a game.

"Take a look around. I got lots of stuff will do."

His eyes fixed on her chest, then darted away, and she was momentarily filled with disgust.

Rich Podowski made her uncomfortable. There was

something sleazy and low-class about him. It wasn't just the tattoos or the habit he had of looking women up and down as if he were trying to undress them. It was the blank, glazed look in his eyes. They reminded Anne of the eyes of a polar bear she'd seen in the old Central Park Zoo in New York City, before they'd torn it down and built a more animal-friendly replacement. The bear had paced back and forth all day long, prompting a spate of psychologists to term its behavior neurotic.

As she maneuvered her way through the narrow aisles of Baby Face, she noticed there was something different about the dolls on the shelves. They looked cheaper and coarser than the ones she'd admired in her youth, with waxy skin and hair that was obviously fake. Years ago, Baby Face stocked only one of each doll. But now, identical models stared down at her with unseeing, glassy eyes. Plump dolls, small dolls, bald dolls, dolls clad in gaudy costumes, dolls whose painted mouths were stretched so wide their smiles looked painful.

She paused at a row of platinum blond dolls wearing white pinafores over powder pink dresses. Years ago, she'd been enamored of a doll with just such a dress that had sat in the window of the shop. It had seemed like such an elegant, delicate creation, and Anne remembered wishing her mother would buy it so she could take it home to her room and have pretend tea parties.

Anne wondered if Allyson would like a doll or if she should just go to Toys "Я" Us and spring for a plastic *Sesame Street* electronic toy. No, the girl was probably sick of Big Bird and company. A doll was more original.

She took down one of the pinafore dolls, noticed a smudge of dirt on its rosy cheek, and set it back on the shelf. She was about to choose another when she saw its dress was slightly torn. Reaching out her hand, she by-passed the front row and grabbed a doll from the back of the shelf. She brought it up to the cash register and set it on the counter.

Rich Podowski stroked the doll's dress, and Anne felt a twinge of disgust she couldn't explain. "That'll be $19.95," he said. "You want it gift-wrapped?"

"Okay."

Rich got out some red paper decorated with tiny green trees that looked left over from Christmas. Up close, she noticed his eyes were bloodshot. A thin layer of stubble coated his cheeks and chin.

Anne said, "It must be hard for you to work at a time like this."

Podowski rubbed at the corner of his mouth. "Yeah," he said. "Well." There was an awkward silence. " 'S a shame," he said finally. "To off yourself when your whole life's ahead of you."

"I didn't know Abby very well. But Abby's friend, Tracy Graustark, is missing. I'm trying to help Delia find her."

He let out a high-pitched giggle. "These kids think they got problems. They should be so lucky."

"Do you remember Abby saying anything about Tracy before she died?"

"Nope. I don't know who Abby hung out with or what all they were up to."

Anne didn't believe him for a minute. Pam and Lauren had told her he'd come around, asking questions.

She took a deep breath and decided to gamble. "I understand Abby had come into some money right before she died."

"That's news to me," Podowski said nervously.

She was sure he was lying. His hands shook as he tried to Scotch tape two ends of the wrapping paper together.

"Really? Your wife showed me the pearls Abby gave her. And one of her friends told me she was spending a fortune at the mall."

"Well, girls will be girls," Podowski stammered.

"Did you know about the witchcraft?"

"Huh?"

Podowski's eyes rested on Anne's face, then danced crazily around the room. His head bobbed up and down. It occurred to her that he was high on something.

"Abby and Tracy fancied themselves witches," Anne continued.

Podowski giggled again. He crumpled the gift wrap and it tore. Scotch tape stuck to the doll's hair.

"Ooooh, Oooh, witchy woman, la da da da da," he sang.

"You know what?" Anne said, carefully removing the doll from his hands. "I can wrap this at home."

She watched as he rang up the sale—head bobbing, fingers twitching—and slid the doll into a plastic bag.

He was still warbling the same tune as she left the shop. *Oooh, oooh. Witchy woman.* For an eerie moment, right before the glass door closed behind her, it sounded like one of the dolls was singing.

When she got home, she realized she was out of wrapping paper. Taking the doll out of the bag, she set it on the window seat. It looked prettier in her living room than it did in the shop, less fake and forlorn. She tried Pam again, got the machine, and hung up.

She was so hot and sweaty that she decided to take another shower. But the minute she got out she started to sweat all over again. She was eating coffee ice cream straight from the container when the phone rang.

"Okay, no more excuses," said the voice on the other end. "I want a detailed outline by the end of the day."

Anne's heart sank. "Phil."

"You remember my name," the publisher said. "That's good. Very good. Now can you remember how many more days you have until the book is due on my desk?"

"Phil, I . . ."

". . . thirty-eight days. God made the world in less time."

Anne tried again. "You wouldn't believe what's been going on down . . ."

". . . you're right. I wouldn't. Just get me the outline by five o'clock. Understood? Or FedEx me back the first half of your advance and I sign up a new writer first thing tomorrow."

"Wait," Anne protested. "You don't understand. I can't make the advice up. And Dr. Arlene's not cooperating. She refuses to . . ."

"I knew you'd see it my way," Phil interrupted. "A detailed outline. By the end of the day."

Before she could respond, he'd hung up.

Damn, she said to Harry, who was staring at her quizzically with his one eye. Damn, damn, damn.

Dr. A. had been out all day. She'd told Anne this morning she wasn't sure what time she'd be back. There were big sales at the Monmouth Mall. The stores were open till nine. The sales tax exemption was too good to pass up. Anne hadn't bothered to argue.

Over the years she herself had mastered the art of procrastination. There were plenty of things she found to occupy her time when she should be writing—playing with the cat, doing hand wash, talking on the phone, straightening up her office, taking a nap, sneaking off to the beach—the list was endless. But when it came to putting things off, she was an amateur compared to Dr. Arlene. It didn't even seem to bother Dr. A. that they weren't working on the book. She didn't make excuses or express any guilt. But then the radio shrink's neck wasn't on the line. Dr. Arlene was irreplaceable. The ghost writer wasn't.

Still, Anne didn't get it. What was the point of this visit exactly? Dr. A. could afford to vacation anywhere in the world. Why had she selected Oceanside Heights for an extended summer sojourn?

And now this. Phil Smedley must be concerned if he was threatening to have her removed from the project. Anne sat down with her checkbook, trying to decide whether she could hold off the electric company longer than the gas company or vice versa. She had exactly thirty-nine dollars and change in her checking account and a couple of hundred more in her savings account. Not a pretty picture.

She put the checkbook aside and turned on the computer. *Chapter One*, she typed. *Beating Breast-feeding Blues*. The outline would have fourteen chapters, she decided. After all, it was just a draft. When the finished product (if there ever was a finished product) was turned in, it didn't have to look anything like this. She typed for an hour, trying to include every topic she thought Dr. A. should address in the book. The outline was heavy on topics, light on advice. When she was finished, she printed the outline out and faxed it to Phil.

There, she thought, pushing the send button. *That ought to buy me a little time.*

She called Trasker and left a message, asking if the autopsy results on Abby were in. Then she went into the living room and began perusing the bookshelves in her living room. She had *The Crucible* somewhere. She'd had it since her freshman year of college when she'd read it for Miss Jablonski's American Literature course. After about a minute she found it—a tattered paperback that she'd bought used more than twenty years ago. She began rereading it and was immediately swept back to seventeenth-century Salem, when the witchcraft frenzy was at its height. She read the first act, captivated by the tale of impressionable teenage girls whose accusations led to their neighbors' torture and death.

Then she went back into her office and logged on to the Internet. A search for "witchcraft" turned up hundreds of matches. There were sites devoted to astral projection, gemstones and crystals, druidry, herbs, oils and incense, spells, animal guides, meditation and chakras, candle magic. She wondered how many people were into this stuff and how many of them were teenagers. There had to be a big market for her witch book. Maybe these web sites could help her promote it.

She called up *witches.com*, which seemed to be among the larger sites, and read the message of the day on the home page: Don't link your life force to anything with glowing red eyes and a black aura. Sure, Anne thought. No problem. She found the message board and sent off the following e-mail: *Looking for practitioner of Wicca to help with a book I'm writing on teen witches. Jersey Shore location preferable.*

It felt a little weird, like composing a personal ad. Had Tracy logged on to these web sites or visited witchy chat rooms? Anne had a sudden sick feeling in her stomach. The newspapers were full of stories of young women who met men through the Internet and were lured unsuspectingly to their deaths.

She thought it over and then sent off a second e-mail: *Looking for a sixteen-year-old witch named Tracy, who disappeared from her home in Oceanside Heights, NJ. Does anyone out there know her whereabouts?*

It was a long shot, she knew. But sometimes long shots paid off.

Chapter 10

Teenagers often don't say what they mean. They react emotionally to every word, action and event they experience. Many of their verbal responses to us are instinctive attempts to protect their feelings or to divert our attention from the immediate issues.

Nagle's served the best ice cream in the Heights—rich, creamy, sweet, melt-in-your-mouth heavenly. Anne found Pam Whitehouse behind the narrow counter, serving raspberry ripple cones and chocolate sprinkle-flecked sundaes to sun-baked tourists. Anne waited her turn in line and ordered a scoop of butterscotch crunch for good measure.

"Can I talk to you for a minute?" she asked, after Pam had thrust the cone, a napkin, and a handful of change into her hand.

"I'm not off until four."

"That's okay. I'll wait."

Anne sat in the shade, savoring the ice cream as it melted away in the heat. Town was bustling. Several store owners had put stuff for sale—T-shirts, watering cans, postcards, baskets of shells—in front of their shops, giving Main Street the look of a summertime bazaar.

At precisely four o'clock, Pam slipped out of Nagle's and started walking briskly in the direction of her house.

"Hi," Anne said, catching up to her. "I wanted to talk to you about that voodoo doll you made of Tracy."

Pam started walking faster, keeping her head down.

Anne decided to get straight to the point. "What do you and Lauren have against Tracy? Why do you want to hurt her?"

"We don't," Lauren mumbled. "Leave me alone."

"Look," Anne said, catching hold of Pam's arm. "Tracy's missing. If you don't talk to me, maybe you'd prefer talking to the police."

At the mention of the word, Pam froze. Her eyes darted up and down the street, as if she were looking for a place to hide. "No one wants Tracy hurt," she stammered.

"Then what was that business with the doll?"

"It was nothing," Pam said nervously.

"The doll was wearing Tracy's shirt and had Tracy's hair. You stuck pins into it and set it on fire. I wouldn't call that nothing."

Pam was panting, although Anne couldn't tell if it was

from fear or exertion. Her cheeks were flushed, her shoulders hunched. "We were just having fun," she said, struggling to catch her breath. "Fooling around, practicing spells. And Tracy lent me that shirt. You can ask her yourself."

"I would if I could find her. Do you know where she is, Pam?"

"No."

Pam looked up and met Anne's gaze, and Anne believed she was finally telling the truth. "There's blood on the trunk in Tracy's room," Anne said. "Whose is it? How did it get there?"

"We had a special ceremony," Pam said, her voice barely a whisper.

"The coven?"

"Yes."

"When was this?"

"The other day. We each pricked our finger and made a wish."

"What did Tracy wish for?"

"I don't know. It was a secret."

Pam hugged her arms to her chest and shivered. On Main Street, people were buying souvenirs and snapping photos, eating pretzels, talking, laughing, oblivious to witchcraft and spells and missing girls.

"Are we done yet?" Pam said. Her face was screwed up. She looked on the verge of tears.

"You said Tracy had betrayed you. You and Lauren. When you were burning the doll. What did you mean by that?"

Am I a traitor, Tracy had written in her Book of Shadows. *Am I a traitor?*

"Leave me alone," Pam mumbled. "Just leave me alone."

She turned and ran, her sandals flapping against the sidewalk. Anne watched her go, thinking that for a girl her size, Pam Whitehouse moved very, very fast.

The teenagers were forty-five minutes late for the focus group and the later it got, the more sure Anne was that Dr. Arlene was going to walk in on the group and wonder what the hell was going on. It would be easy enough to explain away the focus group as research, the equivalent of doing extra-credit work on a school report. But she hadn't told Dr. A. about the meeting because she hadn't wanted her to be there. With the psychologist in charge, Anne was pretty sure she wasn't going to be able to ask about Tracy or witchcraft.

The teenagers—minus Pam, which Anne had expected—finally showed up at a quarter past six, trooping into her living room, plopping down on the furniture, and immediately digging into the Cheez Doodles, nachos, Fritos, pretzels, and assorted other junk foods Anne had laid out.

Lauren and Brian sat on the couch. Leo took the most comfortable seat in the room, an oversize armchair and matching ottoman that commanded a spectacular view of the ocean. Harry eyed the intruders balefully from his perch on the window seat. He considered all of the furniture to be his very own personal scratching posts.

Anne started off with a series of puffball questions—how they felt about school (too many tests, too much paint-by-number learning), how they got along with their parents (okay for the most part), whether college was in their future (yes). She'd armed herself with a legal pad and pen and was taking copious notes, which the kids seemed to get a kick out of.

"There's a section in the book devoted to stress," Anne said. Actually, there was. But it was the parents' stress, not the kids', and Dr. Arlene wasn't averse to recommending the occasional tranquilizer to take the edge off. "When stressful situations come up," Anne asked, "how do you deal with them?"

Lauren confessed that she lost sleep and picked her split ends. Brian said he lifted weights. He'd been the quietest one in the group, staring down at his hands and shifting uncomfortably when Anne asked a question, as if it pained him to talk about anything personal. He reminded Anne of jocks she'd known back in high school: larger than life in big games. But off the playing field and out of uniform, they seemed diminished, as if they didn't quite know what to do with themselves.

"Stress is a no-brainer," Leo said, pushing his black hair out of his eyes. "I just go outside and work on my tennis game. If you spend time dwelling on your problems, it never helps. It's better to forget for a while."

Something in his tone made Anne glance up from her notes. He sounded sad, almost resigned. For a moment, his lively eyes went dead, empty of any emotion except raw, hollow pain. It startled Anne. From what she could see, Leo Farnsworth was golden—he had looks, intelligence, personality, popularity. She wondered what problems he could possibly have that had brought that look to his face.

"What about your friends?" Anne said. "People like Abby Podowski. What could have been so stressful, so bad, to cause her to take her own life?"

"Abby was a drama queen," Lauren volunteered. "Every other minute, there was some kind of crisis going on with her. She was always in love with somebody, and they were always making her cry."

"You mean that teacher she was seeing?" Brian said.

"What teacher?" Anne said sharply.

"Mr. Browning. He's our English teacher at summer school," Lauren said. "He's kind of cute, and I guess he had a thing for Abby. She was all upset about it."

Terrific, Anne thought. *The first available guy to come along in months turns out to be attracted to teenage girls.*

"Abby was a flirt," Lauren continued. "She pretended to be Miss Innocent, but it's not like she didn't encourage him. Staying after school, sitting on the edge of his desk, leading him on the way she did."

Anne threw up her hands. "Wait a minute. What happened between Abby and Browning?"

"Unclear," Brian said. "But she sure was shook up about it. Remember the other day on the beach? She was crying so hard I thought she'd never stop."

Lauren nodded. "I guess he crossed the line," she said. "Because Abby told us she never wanted things to go as far as they did. She ended up reporting him to the principal, and now he's in big trouble."

Now Anne was shocked. The man she'd met with this morning didn't seem capable of forcing himself upon a student.

"But Browning was there today. In class," she said. Not only that, he'd looked relaxed and happy, as if he hadn't a care in the world.

"I think there's going to be an investigation, and it kind of takes a long time," Brian said. "There's a review board. The PTA gets involved. And the district superintendent. Another teacher was accused of the same stuff last year. He got suspended."

"You mean grabby McClansky?" Lauren said, with a laugh. "I had him for algebra. He had the worst breath. It was hard to imagine anyone wanting to kiss him."

"What about Tracy Graustark?" Anne said. "Is she a drama queen, too?"

"Beats me," Leo said. "I don't know Tracy very well."

"Tracy's more together," Lauren interjected. "She probably boosted a car and took a joyride down the shore. She'll be back any day, if she doesn't get arrested first."

Brian pushed the brim of his baseball cap back. "Tracy can take care of herself. She's got more smarts in her pinkie finger than most girls have in their entire bodies."

"Thanks, Bri," Lauren said sarcastically.

"Anytime," he shot back.

"Is this really relevant?" Leo broke in. He turned to Anne. "I thought you wanted to hear about us."

"I do," Anne said. "I was just getting around to your hobbies. Tell me how Devil worship works."

For a moment, nobody spoke. Anne could hear the ticking of the grandfather clock and the waves smashing against the shoreline. It was as if the teenagers had suddenly become strangers on a bus. They'd stopped making eye contact and seemed to shrink deeper into themselves. The esprit de corps, the sense of togetherness and familiarity that had been there minutes ago, had completely vanished.

"What are you talking about?" Leo finally said.

Anne studied his face again. His features were blank, except for his eyes, which registered a wary, almost feral intelligence. Unlike the other two, he showed no sign of nervousness. She felt he was challenging her, daring her to continue.

Lauren said offhandedly, "Pam and I were fooling around with a doll in my parents' tent. And now Miss Hardaway's making a federal case about it."

"I gather that's the party line," Anne said. "But what about the rest? The chanting, the fire, the light show on the beach. The whole nine yards. Especially the Devil part. That was my favorite."

The silence in the room was thick as fog. Lauren examined her nails. Brian stared at the floor. But Leo continued to gaze at Anne with eyes that had turned cold and mocking.

"I think you've been watching too much late-night TV," Leo said. He began to laugh, and one by one, the others joined in, their laughter becoming hoarse, then ragged. She heard the relief in it, felt the tension slip from the room.

"Now chess, there's a good hobby," Brian chortled, wiping tears from his eyes. "Chess or stamp collecting."

"How about bird-watching?" Lauren giggled. She doubled over, shaking with laughter.

Next to her, Brian was practically howling. "Stop, stop," he pleaded, to no one in particular. "I can't take it."

Only Leo was no longer laughing. His eyes danced merrily. A thin, joyless smile played on his lips.

Above the others' raucous peals of laughter, Anne heard the doorbell ring. She stood up and went to answer it, thankful for the chance to escape, feeling like she'd been played for a fool. Douglas Browning stood on her front porch, holding a bunch of wildflowers. Truth be told, she wanted to slam the door in his face.

"Back in the fifteenth century, women who believed they were witches came from the lowest, weakest element of society," Browning was saying. "In general, they had no family or friends and had to depend on the charity and generosity of ungenerous neighbors. They were completely alienated from society and vulnerable to the charges they faced."

He and Anne were sitting on a bench on the boardwalk overlooking the beach, near the fishing pier. It was a clear night. Above them, the sky was strung with strands of glittery stars. The breeze off the ocean smelled briny and sweet.

Two hours earlier, when Douglas Browning walked into her living room, the laughter had immediately ceased. Anne couldn't tell who was more surprised: the teacher or the kids. After about thirty seconds of forced conversation, the teenagers departed. And Anne was left with the puzzle that was Douglas Browning, the man who might have been responsible for Abby's death. All through dinner at the Pelican Café, as she picked at her fried clams and corn on the cob, she tried to determine what made Browning tick.

There was something open and forthright about the way he talked about his life, about what teaching meant to him, how hard it was to reach kids who didn't give a damn about much of anything, how he could relate because he'd been wild as a teenager, uninterested in school, alienated from his family, a waste case heading nowhere, how difficult dating was, how some women he'd met told him he was "too nice," whatever that meant.

Most men were so close-mouthed it was like pulling teeth to get them to reveal anything beyond which baseball team they rooted for; this guy seemed to want to pour out his whole life story. All evening, she'd been waiting for the opportunity to bring up the charges against him. But she kept putting it off. She found she liked Browning. He was good-looking and funny and smart, and she was enjoying his company. So here they were on the boardwalk, not twenty feet away from where she'd heard the singing and seen the flashing, colored lights.

When she told him about it, he listened intently and shook his head, rather sadly it seemed to her. Anne reached into her pocketbook and took out a copy of the symbols she'd written down. "Do you have any idea what this means?" she asked.

Browning looked at the symbols. "Not a clue. Should I?"

"I just thought since you seem to know so much about witchcraft you might be able to help me decode this."

"My best guess is ancient hieroglyphics. But that's probably not much help. Are you sure it has to do with witchcraft?"

"Not really. I guess I have witches on the brain. The last twenty-four hours have been pretty bizarre."

"Sure. But when you think about it, witchcraft isn't so out of place in the twenty-first century. For starters, lots of people embrace witchcraft because they desire power," he said, looking up at the stars. "Power to attain success or love, power over people you want to hurt or who may have hurt you in the past. It's more action oriented than the New Age mumbo jumbo of the nineties. Problem is if you believe in the power, if you really believe, it can get awfully dangerous."

"It's already past that point. One girl is missing. Another one committed suicide."

There. It was out in the open.

"Abby," he said softly.

The word hung in the evening air like a shroud. She watched his face change. It was like flicking off a switch. His body stiffened, and his tone was suddenly glacial.

"She was in one of my classes."

"I heard there was more to it."

"Those kids tell you that?"

Anne nodded. "They said she'd reported you."

Now his eyes were two dark coals, burning fiercely. "You know what an 'improper sexual advance' is?"

Anne inadvertently moved away from him on the bench.

"Do you? Huh?"

"No."

"Anything from patting a kid on the shoulder to statutory rape. Doesn't matter whether it's true or not. Worst case, you lose your pension. You'll never be hired anywhere again. Best case, same as above, only you're sorting mail in the district office because you're fighting this thing and they can't fire you just yet."

"Which scenario are you facing?"

"Neither. Because that neurotic, messed-up little girl took it all back—every last lying word of it."

Chapter 11

A child in the throes of a temper tantrum needs your help to snap out of it. Try to interest him in something that you know he likes, such as a beloved toy or game. If that doesn't work, try ignoring his bad behavior or insisting that he take a time-out in a quiet corner of the house or in his room.

"She took it back? When?"

"On Friday she left a note for the high school principal denying everything she'd said about me."

117

"Did he talk to her personally?"

"There wasn't time. Abby left the note in his mailbox at the end of the day. He'd already gone home, and the first time he read the note was yesterday morning, when Abby turned up on the beach."

How convenient, Anne thought. Right before the girl dies, she suddenly recants her whole story. Leaving Browning in the clear.

She looked over at him. He was gazing out at the ocean, his jaw set, his eyes hard as granite. It was as though he felt dying weren't punishment enough for Abby Podowski. Anne could practically feel his anger, naked yet palpable, like the white curtain of mist that rose from the beach and drifted toward them.

Anne said, "If you don't mind my asking, what exactly did she say about you?"

Browning turned back to Anne. When he spoke, his voice sounded husky, almost raw. "She claimed I forced her to have sex with me. Which is completely the opposite of what really happened. She showed up at my house one night wanting to give me an expensive Rolex watch and practically threw herself at me. I rebuffed her, as gently as possible. I thought she was mixed-up." He let out a sarcastic laugh. "Of course, I felt sorry for her. I even tried to get her to go for counseling. I just had no idea she was emotionally disturbed."

He sounded like he was telling the truth, and she found herself wanting to believe him. She wasn't sure why. Maybe it was because Browning seemed like a decent guy, someone straightforward and aboveboard. Or maybe—and this suspicion crept into her mind reluctantly—she didn't want the first available single man she'd met in months to turn out to be a sex offender.

Browning got up. "Let's walk a while," he said.

They headed north on the boardwalk. On their left stood the rambling Victorian homes along Ocean Avenue. To the right was the dark swath of ocean, which hissed and tumbled as plumes of spray hit the beach. The night air was warm and slightly humid. Fireflies glowed yellow-green for an instant, then disappeared. In the distance, the lights of the abandoned Dreamland Amusement Park towered over the shabby, dilapidated buildings of Landsdown Park.

Browning ambled along slowly, his eyes trained on the beach. His anger seemed to have dissipated as quickly as it had appeared.

"This kind of accusation, it taints you forever," he said quietly, after they had walked half a block in silence.

"What do you mean?"

"Oh, nothing overt. But my colleagues at school, the kids in my classes, they look at me differently now. I can see the doubt in their eyes. Plenty of them think I was responsible for Abby's death. Or else they believe her, in spite of the note."

"It must be very uncomfortable for you."

A sigh escaped Browning's lips. "I thought about requesting a transfer to a school in another district. But this goes on my permanent record. It will follow me wherever I am, like a bad smell. Meantime, there's absolutely nothing I can do. I was interviewed by the police right after Abby killed herself and the principal found her apology in his mailbox. I think the cops believed me. But who really knows?"

Anne thought of Trasker, of how he'd neglected to mention Browning's connection to Abby. But then why should he have? All she'd done was find the body. She had no relationship with the girl. And practically none with Browning. But she felt compelled to find out how and why Abby Podowski had died, to make sense of a terrible, senseless event.

They'd reached the fishing pier at the end of the boardwalk, which jutted into the water like a giant wooden finger. Anne scanned the deserted beach. It was eerily quiet. No sign of the "coven" or the mysterious figure bobbing above the waves. But she could see the exact spot where she'd come upon the corpse.

"Do you think Abby was depressed because you'd rejected her?" Anne said.

"It's possible. Though it doesn't seem like a good enough reason to end your life. Now that you've told me about the witchcraft angle, I have a different take on the whole thing."

"You mind sharing?"

Browning stopped and leaned over the railing of the pier. Standing there, facing the Atlantic, was like being aboard a ship. The surf pounded the rocks beneath the pier, and Anne felt a light coating of spray splash her face. Clouds drifted across the surface of the moon, like dark wisps of smoke.

"Hundreds of years ago," Browning said, "when witches gathered at night, they were 'skyclad,' or naked. Unlike the old myths, they didn't use broomsticks to get around. They concocted special ointments that they smeared on their bodies. It was later found that the ointments were made from plant extracts containing belladonna, which had hallucinogenic properties."

"So they truly believed they were flying."

"Right. Today, you could get the same effect with drugs like Ecstasy."

Anne glanced over at him. "How'd you know about the Ecstasy? It wasn't in the papers."

Browning shrugged. "Some kids at school were talking. Seems like the whole town's heard by now. Don't you think?"

She wasn't so sure about that. The teenagers who'd gathered at her house earlier didn't seem to know Abby's drug of choice. If they did, they weren't talking.

"Enough about death," Browning said abruptly. "That's not why I asked you out."

Asked her out, as in a date? Was that what this was, underneath all the stuff about magic potions and suicide?

"Why did you?" she said, genuinely curious.

"I'd like to get to know you better. When you walked into class this morning, I was intrigued. It's not every day a smart, beautiful woman enters my life and starts asking me about witchcraft."

"Thanks for the compliment," Anne said, with a smile.

"I mean it. Really. Are you seeing anyone right now? I've been trying to figure that out, but you don't give much away."

An image of Trasker flashed through Anne's mind. Trasker leaning toward her in the car, brushing her hair off her face.

"No. Actually, I'm not."

"Great. Then maybe we could get together again. Are you free Tuesday night? Would you like to come over?"

"Okay." The word was out of her mouth before she had a chance to stop and think. Was it okay? Had this guy been telling her the truth about Abby?

Doug Browning leaned forward and brushed his lips against her cheek, then straightened up. He smelled faintly of pinecones and tobacco.

"I love the beach at night," he said quietly. "It's so mysterious and still."

Anne gazed past the sand, at the black expanse of water. Far out toward the horizon, lights from a few scattered boats shone like earthbound stars. Actually, the quiet was starting to unnerve her. She felt edgy and uncertain, as though she couldn't quite get her bearings. Everything familiar about the Heights, about this stretch of beach and boardwalk she'd known for so long was changing, clouded by a haze of ancient superstitions. To settle herself, she breathed in the clean, salt air, ran her hand over the smooth wooden railing of the pier. She watched the fog creeping over the sand and heard herself tell Douglas Browning that she loved the beach at night, too.

Delia Graustark officially reported Tracy missing at 8 A.M. the next morning. It had been more than sixty hours since she'd last seen her grandniece, and Anne had finally convinced her that too much time had already elapsed. After she'd made her report, she immediately phoned Anne. Her voice sounded so small and sad that Anne didn't recognize it at first.

"You did the right thing," Anne said, trying to sound reassuring. "I'm sure the cops will be able to find her."

"But you'll keep looking, too. Won't you?"

"Of course. I've already talked to Tracy's teachers and some of her friends. I'm afraid I haven't found out very much, but I'm not going to give up."

"I had to tell the police that I lied to them at first, that Tracy hadn't been visiting relatives."

"I know."

There was silence on the other end of the phone. "You don't think . . ." Delia began. Her voice cracked and she started over. "Nothing bad could have happened to her, right?"

"I'm sure Tracy's fine." Actually, she wasn't sure at all. But there didn't seem much point in upsetting Delia further with all the horrific, violent things that could have befallen a sixteen-year-old girl who'd vanished. "She'll be home safe in no time," Anne told Delia before hanging up the phone. "Try not to worry."

Dr. Arlene looked up from her omelet and raised one perfectly tweezed eyebrow. Anne tried to ignore her. Which wasn't easy. Dr. Arlene had completely taken over Anne's house. The psychologist's clothes were hanging in Anne's closet. Her floppy disks clogged Anne's computer. Low-fat salad dressings, weird-looking fruit and designer yogurts crowded the refrigerator shelves. The entire living room had been turned into Dr. A.'s office by the sea, overflowing with files, books, notepads, tapes of her radio show, and other assorted detritus she'd brought from New York. Harry wasn't crazy about the situation either. He was a creature of habit. He didn't appreciate having his favorite snoozing spots turned into clutter magnets.

"What was that all about?" Dr. Arlene asked. "Don't tell me you're tracking down a runaway."

"I'm just trying to help out," Anne said, stirring her coffee. "Listen, we really should get some work done this morning. How about we get started on the temper tantrum chapter?"

"Can't do it today. I have another engagement."

Anne stared at her in disbelief. She'd showed Dr. Arlene the outline she'd faxed to Phil. It hadn't seemed to make an impression one way or another. If she didn't know better, she'd think the good doctor was carrying on a clandestine affair. But Dr. A. was between marriages. And there were certainly enough eligible guys on the streets of New York. You didn't need to come to Jersey.

Anne gave it one last stab. "If you don't feel like having me interview you, you could talk into a tape recorder. Carry it with you all day and speak into it when you have a free moment. Then I'll transcribe the tape and . . ."

"Unfortunately, I won't have any free time today. My schedule is completely booked."

"Doing what?" Anne said angrily. She couldn't help it. This was ridiculous. Soon, she'd have to start charging rent.

Dr. Arlene looked over at her. But instead of reacting, she coolly changed the subject. "That missing girl you're trying to help: Is there a shelter around here where she might have gone? An agency she would have turned to?"

Anne felt exasperated. "This isn't New York. And Tracy's not exactly homeless."

Keep cool, she told herself. *You have nothing to gain by antagonizing her.*

"Look," Anne said, in a calmer voice, "you probably know something about this. When teenage girls run off, do they tend to stay close to home or head for a large city or what?"

Dr. Arlene pushed her breakfast plate away and popped a pink piece of gum between her lips. She was trying to stop smoking and needed to either be chewing, drinking, or sucking on something every waking moment.

"Most teenagers don't have much of a game plan when they leave," she said slowly. "They have this romantic notion of life on the run, that it's glamorous or exciting or fun. Completely unrealistic, of course. It would also depend on why she was running away. Abusive parents?

Drugs? Boyfriend troubles? Your garden-variety mixed-up kid feeling alone and misunderstood?"

"Tracy's parents are dead and she had a so-so relationship with her guardian. I'm not sure about drugs or boys. I didn't know her all that well."

Dr. A. shrugged. "Not much to go on then."

Anne had a sudden brainstorm. "Do you think you could mention something about it on your show? Give Tracy's description, an 800 number people could call?"

Dr. Arlene stared hard at Anne. "It's a *national* radio broadcast," she said slowly, enunciating each word as if she were teaching phonics to a dim-witted third grader.

"I know. I just thought . . ."

"No public service announcements," Dr. Arlene cut in. "I'm sorry."

No, you're not, Anne thought, as she went upstairs to get dressed. Not the least little bit.

Chapter 12

Take your child's concerns about popularity seriously. When offering advice, do so in a casual, nonjudgmental manner. Above all, guard against dismissing or ridiculing your child's friendships or lack of them.

Three blocks from the beach was a beauty salon called The House of Blondes. It was one of those old-fashioned places where women of a certain age still came in twice a week for the privilege of sitting under beehive-shaped hair dyers and having their tresses teased, blown dry, and sprayed into helmets. A sign in the window said, *Haircuts: $14.* Below that was a second sign welcoming *Monsieur Andre, hairstylist to the stars*.

Shortly after 10 A.M., Anne walked in and asked for a pedicure. Jolene Baker, who owned the salon, indicated a wall rack containing dozens of shades of polish. Jolene was pushing fifty, but tried to hide it. She wore her skirts too short and her shirts cut too low. Her skin was so tan it looked leathery, and her hair was the color of tapioca pudding. She'd been pretty once—you could see it in her bone structure, in the way she sashayed across a room— but instead of allowing her beauty to fade she had tried to prop it up with layers of makeup.

"You here for a cut and comb today, hon?" Jolene called out.

Jolene thought Anne should wear her hair short, which was the latest fashion. But Anne didn't agree. You had to maintain short hair. You had to style it and blow it out and use mousse and gel to keep it looking good. Unlike long hair, which you could pull back in a ponytail and basically forget about. Anne got her hair cut every six months or so. She had wash 'n' wear hair: shampoo, comb and go. No dryers, diffusers, or curling irons, except on rare special occasions.

As always, the salon buzzed with conversation. Pink-smocked ladies chattered back and forth to one another like crows in a cornfield. In the background, an oldies radio station played Elvis crooning "Are You Lonesome Tonight?" The air smelled of hair spray and cigarettes and burnt coffee.

"What do you think of this devil business?" Anne asked Jolene.

"I think it's a hoot. If I didn't know better, I'd swear the mayor dreamed the whole thing up to get more people down here in the summertime. Might do my business some good, and I'm all for that."

"Isn't summer your busiest time?"

"Honey, when's the last time you saw someone from New York or Philly getting a comb-out in here? The tourists don't set foot in my place. It's strictly ladies from the Heights."

Anne picked out a reddish-orange color called Cinnabar, and Jolene led her past a row of vinyl chairs where a thin, mustached man who Anne assumed was Monsieur Andre was busily rolling pink curlers into Martha Cox's thinning gray hair. There were two more chairs in the back, facing the front door. A middle-aged woman occupied one of them, reading the Bible and smoking. In the other sat a bored-looking blond teenage girl. Melissa Baker, Jolene's daughter.

Melissa waved hello. Then she got up and filled a plastic tub with water and pink soapy liquid. The water in the tub was hot, and Anne gratefully dunked her feet into it. Running fifteen miles a week wreaked havoc on her tootsies. Every once in a while she treated herself to a pedicure. It was one of the few things in life that didn't cost all that much and still felt terrific.

"How've you been?" she said to Melissa.

"Okay, I guess. I'm only working here another couple of weeks. When school starts, I'm getting a job waitressing at the Pelican Café."

Melissa was wearing a UCLA tank top over a pair of pink shorts, and her long blond hair was swept up in barrettes. It was gorgeous hair. Blond as corn silk, thick, cascading down her back. Melissa had probably never had a split end in her life. Or a Saturday night without a date. Or countless diary entries bemoaning the fact that she didn't have a boyfriend, that she might not be asked to the prom, that she had given up trying to understand what guys wanted and how to give it to them. She had the easy, confident air of a girl who's always known she was pretty and took her looks for granted.

Anne gave Melissa a once-over. If Melissa were ever a witch, she'd be the cute, perky kind that Melissa Joan Hart played on the TV show *Sabrina*—a witch who twitched her nose and got the guy in her algebra class to ask out her best friend or who switched the casting of the school play so she got the lead and then felt guilty enough to switch things back.

Melissa bent over Anne's toes, and she and Anne made small talk for a while. In the middle of the salon, Monsieur Andre finished styling Martha Cox's hair, removing the pink towel from around her neck with a grand flourish. Two other women gathered around Martha's chair to admire the result: Martha's gray locks blown and styled into a feathery do that reminded Anne of the way the young Dorothy Hammill had looked in the 1970s.

Anne turned to Melissa and lowered her voice. "You know Tracy Graustark, right?"

"Uh huh."

"Did you know she's missing?"

Melissa looked up, her face a blank. "I heard she ran away from home."

"Do you have any idea where she might be?"

Melissa shook her head. "Nope. We weren't that close."

"Even though you're both in the coven."

Melissa made a sharp shushing sound and glanced nervously around the room. "How do you know about that?"

"From Tracy's great-aunt."

"My mom will freak if she finds out," Melissa said, eyeing Jolene, who was mixing dye for a permanent. "It's really no big deal. We wear black. We chant a little. It's a kick. Besides, I only joined because Leo was into it. Have you met Leo? He is such a sweetie."

"Is Leo part of the coven?"

Melissa dabbed pink lotion on the soles of Anne's feet. "He's a boy, silly. Boys can't be witches."

"Did he go to the meetings?"

"Nope. He's just interested is all. He thinks it's funny." Melissa rubbed the lotion in. "It is pretty comical, when you think about it. Spells. Incantations. Secret powers. Do you watch *Charmed*? It's a pretty good show. And I love Shannon Dougherty's hair."

Anne was beginning to understand Melissa's involvement. Melissa wasn't serious about witchcraft. She was merely slumming.

Anne thought back to the burning doll, dressed in what she was pretty sure were Tracy's clothes, with Tracy's streaked hair.

"Has Tracy been in here lately?" Anne asked.

"She was in last week for a trim."

"What about Pam and Lauren?"

"Lauren comes once a week for a manicure. And Pam helps my mom out on Tuesdays and Fridays."

So it would have been easy to get samples of Tracy's hair, Anne thought. *And teenage girls borrowed each other's clothes all the time*.

Aloud, she said, "Did you know Abby Podowski very well?"

"Not really," Melissa said evasively, massaging the soles of Anne's feet.

"I heard she was into drugs."

Melissa shrugged. "Who knows? Abby was the type to do anything for a little attention. She was really insecure. I even heard she threw herself at this teacher at school," Melissa said, keeping her voice low. "God, she was always giving it away. But then who wouldn't be screwed up with that wacko stepfather of hers. He's psycho, don't you think?"

Just as Anne was about to answer, the front door of the salon swung open and Brian Miller walked in. His eyes searched the room. When he saw Melissa, he grinned and made a beeline for her. "Hey, can I talk to you a sec?"

Melissa made a face and waved the nail polish at him playfully. "Can't you see I'm working?"

Ignoring the question, Brian directed his smile at Anne. "That was fun last night. If you need any more help, we'd be glad to come back."

Melissa glanced up, her expression curious. "You two know each other?"

Anne filled her in on the focus group session and who had attended.

"That sounds so cool," Melissa said. "Can I be in it next time?"

"Sure. How about later today if you're free, say around sixish?"

"I'll let everyone else know," Brian said. "Meantime, do you mind if I steal Mel away for like, two minutes?"

"Go ahead. I'm not in a hurry."

Melissa got up, and Anne saw her check her face in the mirror hanging on the wall behind the pedicure chairs. She wiped her hands on a towel and followed Brian into a small back room that was used for bikini waxes and massages.

Anne looked around the salon. Monsieur Andre was taking a coffee break, and the ladies had gathered around Jolene, who was wrapping sheets of dye-smeared silver foil on Eleanor Granville's head. Over the radio came the plaintive sweet strains of Sam Cook singing "Stand By Me."

"To obey is better than to sacrifice," a voice intoned.

Anne glanced up. Martha Cox was standing over her. Anne suppressed the sudden urge to giggle. Martha's feathery hairdo and wispy schoolgirl bangs looked patently ridiculous.

"What did you say?" Anne asked.

"To obey is better than to sacrifice," Martha pronounced slowly. "And to hearken than the fat of rams. For rebellion is as the sin of witchcraft."

Anne stared at Martha Cox. She wondered whether the old lady had spent too much time under a hot blow dryer.

"I'm not following you."

"The Book of Samuel. Suffice it to say, problem solved. Without your assistance. I've taken care of it myself."

"What problem are we talking about?"

Martha rolled her eyes. For a moment, she looked like something that had been left out to spoil on Halloween. "The witchcraft problem. Is your memory faulty, dear?"

Anne sat up straighter in her chair. "No, Martha. I'm just not used to people talking in riddles."

Martha leaned in so close that Anne could smell the cherry cough drops on her breath. "Then let me spell it out for you," Martha whispered. "There will be no more witches cavorting in the Heights. Not after tomorrow night."

"Why's that?"

Martha drew an imaginary line over her pale, thin lips. "Don't ask, don't tell," she said, with a giggle.

"Is this about your petition?"

Martha laughed so uproariously she was practically cackling. "I've decided to adopt a harder line. Fight fire with fire, if you know what I mean."

"I'm afraid I don't."

Anne was sick of Martha Cox's riddles. What was the old lady planning this time? She saw Melissa and Brian emerge from the back room. Brian had his arm around Melissa's shoulder.

"Mrs. Cox," Melissa called out, slipping out from under Brian's grasp. "I love your hair."

"Why, thank you, dear," Martha said, patting her feathery head lovingly. "Monsieur Andre is a genius, don't you think? Nobody does hair like the French."

With a wave of her hand, Martha Cox floated away on a cloud of hair spray and self-satisfaction.

"Andre's from Hoboken," Melissa said softly, when Martha was out of earshot. "But his accent is killer."

Brian laughed. "Don't ever try to put anything past Mel," he said. "It'll never work." He shot Melissa an adoring look. "Think about what I said, okay? Let's talk more later."

"Sure," Melissa said.

But Anne could tell that her heart wasn't in it.

"See you around six," Brian said to Anne. He waved at both of them and loped toward the door.

Melissa had picked up the bottle of Cinnabar and started painting Anne's big toe. She brushed it on once, twice, then smeared polish on the toe itself. Shaking her head impatiently, she grabbed for the nail polish remover.

"Everything okay?" Anne asked.

Melissa prided herself on never making mistakes while applying polish. Her mother called her The House of Blondes' own Rembrandt.

"Oh, it's no biggie. Bri and I used to go out. We broke up a couple of months ago, and he can't accept that it's over. I keep telling him we can still be friends. But he wants more."

Anne could see that Melissa was used to the adoration. It came with the territory when you were young, leggy, and drop-dead gorgeous.

"Brian's a nice guy," Melissa continued. "And he's not full of himself the way some of the football jocks are. He doesn't brag that he's already been recruited by four or five colleges. Even after that big game against Rumson, when he ran three hundred yards, it wasn't like he thought he was God's gift to the world."

"Then what's the problem?"

"Brian has a bad temper. I guess maybe that's why he's so good at football. The aggression and all." Anne looked at her quizzically. "Oh, don't get me wrong," she continued. "It's not like he ever laid a hand on me or anything. But it can be exhausting to be around someone who's got such a short fuse."

"Was there anything else?"

Melissa let out a mock sigh. "Bri's got a chip on his shoulder the size of Rhode Island. Not that it's his fault," she added quickly. "His parents don't care what he does. They're not paying for college. They don't come to his games. They just want him to go into the family business. Plumbing supplies." She made a face. "Not exactly the NFL, is it? But no matter how they ignore all that Bri's accomplished on the field, he worships them. I think that's why he started playing football in the first place. To get their attention."

"About the breakup," Anne said. "It's none of my business, but was it because of Leo?"

Melissa's face lit up. "Isn't he amazing? Did you know he speaks, like, five languages? And he can body-surf. And he's got the coolest car. It's a blue Corvette Stingray, from the sixties. He retooled it himself."

"What else do you know about him?"

"He goes to some fancy private school outside of LA. His parents have, like, tons of money and a pool and all these servants. But he isn't stuck up in the least." Melissa had regained her expert technique and was applying polish evenly to Anne's toes. "He's like, incredibly smart. He could get into any college he wants. But he's probably going to Yale because they have this great chemistry department and one day, he's going to win a Nobel Prize for some really cool experiment or invention or something."

"Sounds like the two of you are pretty good friends."

Melissa's cheeks turned a becoming shade of pink. "It's nothing serious or anything. We've hung out a few times. Down at the beach."

"The beach," Anne repeated.

"Leo knows all about magic and astronomy. He can find the Milky Way in, like, a second. He even named a star after me."

Melissa was rattling on about planetary moons and asteroids and comets. But Anne wasn't listening. She was doing the math in her head: A working knowledge of chemistry and magic plus a magnetic personality equaled one charming Devil.

"So what do you think?" Melissa was saying, fanning Anne's feet with a towel.

"I'm sorry. I spaced out there for a minute. What do I think about what?"

Melissa grinned. "About how far away is Yale?"

Chapter 13

Some children are daredevils from the day they're born—fast crawlers, early walkers, exploring every inch of their world. During the preschool years, keep a careful eye out so they don't fall off the top rung of the jungle gym or choke on a small intriguing object.

Anne found Leo Farnsworth entirely by accident. After the pedicure, she'd gone home, slipped a bathing suit on under her clothes, stuck a book and a towel in her tote bag, and crossed the street to the beach. She was getting nowhere in the search for Tracy.

She was making absolutely no headway with Dr. Arlene. She felt tired, stuck. Maybe what she needed was a quick swim to clear away the cobwebs.

She was considering where to spread her towel when she happened to spot Leo at the far end of the fishing pier, a pole idly dangling from his hands, his face partially covered by a Los Angeles Dodgers cap, his eyes hidden by a pair of oversize mirrored sunglasses.

"How's it going?" she said, walking up to him. "You catch anything?"

"Only a mild case of sunburn. The fish aren't biting. Or I'm using the wrong lure. Either way, it's been a bust."

He cast the pole farther out and surveyed the ocean glumly. All up and down the pier, fishermen were nursing poles, attaching bait, scanning the water for a sign. No one seemed to be having much luck.

"I've been looking for you," Anne said.

"Well, here I am. What's up?"

"I'm interested in learning about magic. And I understand you're quite the magician."

She couldn't see Leo's eyes, but the corners of his mouth turned up in a half-smile.

"Who told you that?"

"Melissa Baker."

"Aaaaaah, the lovely Melissa. You know, girls who look like her are a dime a dozen back in LA, but in Jersey, she stands out like an orchid in a field of daisies."

"Seems like all the girls in town are crazy about you."

"Or maybe they're just plain crazy." Leo leaned his pole against the railing and lit a cigarette. It was the hottest time of the day, and though there was a pleasant breeze off the Atlantic, a thin sheen of sweat coated his face. "I'm a curiosity, I guess. West Coast kid. Not one of the townies who everybody's known since kindergarten. Plus, I've got that bad-boy rep working for me. You'd be surprised how far that can take a guy."

"Does the bad-boy stuff extend to witchcraft? Maybe playing Devil for a few of your admirers?"

Leo wheeled around to face her, and Anne saw that the skin near his left eye was swollen and eggplant-colored.

He said, "You're not going to let this go, are you?"

"Not until I find Tracy Graustark. No."

Leo took a puff of his cigarette and gazed at the ocean. Farther out, a half-dozen boats perched on the water, like large ungainly birds. They were so far away that they appeared not to be moving at all. The wind was blowing hard from the west. It ruffled the feathers of the ring-billed gulls, who swooped low over the waves, in search of lunch.

"*Are* you playing Devil?" Anne asked.

"I don't know what you're talking about," he said sullenly. "And what does it matter anyhow?"

Anne studied him, trying to determine if he was telling the truth. "I think witchcraft has something to do with Tracy's disappearance."

Leo tossed his cigarette off the pier and tugged on his fishing pole. "Tracy struck me as a girl who can take care of herself."

"I thought you said you didn't know her that well."

"Did I?" Leo mused. "Must have been a first impression then. Tracy always seemed like a tough cookie."

"So was Abby Powdowski apparently. Were you involved with her?"

Leo tugged gently on the pole again and began reeling the line in. "If you're asking me whether we slept together, the answer is no. She was a little too out there for me, if you know what I mean."

"I'm afraid I don't."

"She took stupid risks. Shoplifting, driving drunk, sleeping around. Abby was the sort of girl who'd cross a highway blindfolded if you dared her to. Believe it or not, I'm more the careful type."

Anne pointed to his face, which seemed to negate his point. "How'd you hurt yourself?"

"You mean the shiner? It's nothing," Leo said carelessly. "I got up last night to go to the john. It was pitch-black, and I walked smack into the bathroom door. Pretty dumb of me, right?"

Anne watched the tension on his pole increase. He had something on the line and he was reeling the fish in carefully, keeping his back straight, his elbows bent, straining to exert just the right amount of pressure.

"Does it hurt?"

Leo tightened his grip on the pole and jerked it upward. Anne saw the line go slack.

"Damn, lost him." He wedged his pole in between the rails of the pier and folded his arms across his chest. "This is not my lucky day," he said. "But, hey, if you're serious about the magic, I can teach you a thing or two. Nothing hokey or grandstanding. I don't pull flowers out of my sleeve or saw beautiful women in half. What I practice is subtler, more unusual."

"I would love to see a demonstration."

Leo flashed the full wattage of his smile on her. "I think you believe you already have."

The ocean was so cold it made her skin ache. Anne dived under a wave and swam with her eyes open, the water rushing and tumbling over her body, the wave so powerful she was momentarily blinded. She used to swim

every morning, doing self-imposed laps across the surface of the Atlantic for nearly an hour—the crawl, followed by the back stroke, then the crawl again. When
she'd finished, she always felt spent, but exhilarated. She
didn't know why she'd stopped, why she'd begun to re-
place the laps with quick, twenty-minute jogs. As she
swam back toward shore, she promised herself that she
was going to start swimming again before summer gave
way to fall.

Half the beach was still cordoned off by police tape.
But the tourists didn't seem to mind. They flocked to the
other half, gawking at the empty field of sand where
Abby's body had lain. They'd come equipped for a long
hot day in the sun, toting sunscreen and umbrellas, cool-
ers laden with sandwiches, cookies, soda, and potato
chips, plastic toys for the kiddies, sand chairs, radios, cell
phones and any other convenience they could manage to
carry. Anne had spread her towel as close to the water's
edge as possible. The waves helped drown out radios and
the sound of other people. Still, snippets of conversation
drifted over:

"So I told her to back off and mind her own business. If
I want to carbo load, it's no skin off her banana."

"When you talk to God, it's prayer. When God talks to
you, it's schizophrenia."

"Stop putting peanut butter in your nose!"

"I'm better off without him. He just doesn't know it yet."

Anne closed her eyes. She liked the beach better off-
season, when the tourists had gone home and this particular stretch of sand became her very own private front yard.
She wished she was on vacation, lying on an unfamiliar
beach where straw huts dotted the sand and white-jacketed
waiters served drinks with impossibly silly names. Or on

the Riviera, where the ground was rocky and sherbet-colored villas sprang from the cliffs above the sea.

"Mind if I join you?" said a familiar voice, interrupting her reverie.

She opened her eyes. Mark Trasker stood over her, wearing navy blue bathing trunks.

She felt several things all at once—surprised, pleased, self-conscious, nervous.

"I'd be glad to have some company," she told him.

"Great. I'll go get my stuff."

She watched him plow through the sand, zigzagging past bronzed sun worshippers and toddlers dripping ice cream. She was grateful she'd worn her one-piece suit, instead of her bikini. She felt slightly less exposed in the one-piece, although it was odd enough to be with Trasker in any state of undress.

Actually, she'd never pictured him as the beach type. And she'd never seen him in anything but expensively tailored suits. He had a nice build: athletic and muscular, but not so toned and buff that he looked like a gym rat.

"Aren't you working today?" she asked, when he'd come back and spread a large blanket next to her towel.

"I logged so much OT this week that the chief gave me some extra time off. I've got to be back on the job by two, so there wasn't time to take the boat out." He reached into a cooler and took out a sandwich wrapped in tin foil. "Want one? I brought tons of food."

"Sure."

He unwrapped the sandwich and gave it to her. Egg salad on rye, flecked with celery and paprika. She took a bite. Delicious. Digging her feet into the sand, she looked out at the water. It was the most incredible shade of turquoise, more like the Caribbean than the Atlantic

Ocean. Scraps of pearly clouds drifted across the distant horizon. But overhead the sky was eggshell blue. She breathed in the briny air and practically sighed with contentment. She had the exhilarating feeling that she was playing hooky, which she supposed was absolutely true.

Trasker dug into the cooler and brought out another sandwich, two Diet Cokes and a giant bag of tortilla chips. She noticed he looked tired. There were faint circles under his eyes, and he seemed to be moving at a slower pace than usual.

"You busy tonight?" he asked, handing her a Coke. "I've been working late all week, and I could use the break. I was thinking we could head down to Wildwood, go for a ride on the Great White."

"Sounds like fun, but I can't."

The Great White was one of the biggest, baddest roller coasters on the Jersey Shore. Anne always had to force herself to go on it, but once she did, she loved the giddy, wild excitement-laced fear the ride produced.

"You still trying to pin down the radio shrink?" Trasker asked.

"Actually, I have a date," she said, carefully watching his reaction.

"A date," Trasker repeated, sounding puzzled.

"You remember dating," Anne laughed. "When you get dressed up and go for dinner and a movie and make small talk and try to decide whether you like each other, whether the chemistry's right, whether you'd ever go out with this person again or you'd rather be home watching reruns of *ER* on the tube."

"Right," Trasker grinned, biting into his sandwich. "It's all coming back to me. Who's the guy?"

She felt vaguely disappointed. She'd been hoping for

even the smallest display of jealousy or any sign at all that he cared she'd be out with another man.

"He's a teacher over at the high school."

"A teacher, huh? Sounds intellectual. What's his name?"

Anne hesitated a second, then said, "Doug Browning."

Trasker's eyes scanned her face. "As in the Doug Browning who was accused of sexual misconduct with a minor. You do know about that, don't you?"

"I heard he's been cleared," she said defensively.

"It helps if the victim dies, don't you think? There's nobody left to press charges."

"Look, Mark, he told me all about the letter Abby wrote recanting her story. She obviously made the whole thing up."

Trasker shook his head, as if surprised by her naïveté. "For starters, we don't know under what conditions she wrote the note."

"Are you telling me Browning is a suspect in her death?"

"There's been no ruling of homicide, but our investigation is still pending."

He sounded very formal and official, as if they had never discussed Abby's death before.

"Are the autopsy results in?" she asked.

"Yes. I was going to call you later today."

"Was it a drug overdose? The Ecstasy pills?"

Trasker shook his head. "It's a bit bizarre, actually."

She looked at him expectantly.

"Abby went into respiratory arrest, caused by a poisonous herb called jimsonweed."

Anne thought back to Tracy's Book of Shadows. Jimsonweed was one of the herbs Tracy had written down. But she'd never shown the book to Trasker, never handed it over to the police. Aloud, she said, "I think jimsonweed is popular with witches."

"I can see why. It produces delirium with hallucinations. Practically every part of the plant is poisonous— the seeds, the roots, the leaves. You can jump on a broomstick, travel around the world, and never leave the ground. We questioned Abby's friends again. They claim to know nothing about it."

The tide was starting to come in. Anne watched the water sweep toward them, staining the sand a shade darker. "Where did she get it from? How was it ingested? When did she take it?"

"We don't know yet."

Something in his voice made her glance up. "What?" she said. "What else haven't you told me?"

When he spoke he sounded official again. "We've received two reports from unrelated persons claiming they saw Tracy Graustark leaving the beach at 1:30 A.M. on Friday night, which the medical examiner says is approximately when Abby died."

Anne couldn't quite believe what she was hearing. "And . . . ?"

"And there's a possibility that Abby Podowski was deliberately poisoned. And that the person who poisoned her is the missing Tracy, who fled because she murdered her friend."

"What about the Ecstasy? And the suicide note? I thought you said an expert claimed it was genuine."

"It sounds from all accounts like Abby was depressed. Maybe she wrote the note, then lost her nerve and couldn't go through with it. Maybe she thought about taking the Ecstasy. Or maybe Tracy has absolutely nothing to do with this, and Abby ingested the jimsonweed deliberately, all on her own."

"Has the lab analyzed the blood in Tracy's room yet?"

"Looks like the Whitehouse girl might have been telling the truth. A few different blood types turned up on the trunk. It could have been caused by a finger-pricking ritual."

"How about Tracy? Any word?"

Trasker finished his sandwich and took a long swallow of soda. "*Nada*. The more time passes, the harder the girl is to trace. Her friends still claim they don't know where she could be. We've notified the FBI and the National Center for Missing and Exploited Children. We've checked motels and inns within a sixty-mile radius of the Heights. We've accessed phone records to see who called the house in the past few months, turned the place upside down. We've even been able to get copies of Tracy's e-mail. You know what that all adds up to? Absolutely nothing."

He threw a handful of chips to a seagull, who devoured them greedily.

"I've got to get going," he said. "My shift starts soon."

Anne sensed that something was wrong between them. She wondered if he was mad at her for not telling him about Tracy sooner. She refused to believe Tracy had poisoned Abby. Tracy was a handful for Delia, but Tracy wasn't a murderer. If only she had talked Delia into reporting Tracy missing as soon as she heard the girl was gone. If anything happened to Tracy . . .

Trasker started to gather up his stuff, then abruptly stopped. He gazed down at Anne with eyes that had taken on a serious cast. "I want you to watch your step with Browning. I interviewed him myself the day Abby died. I don't trust the man. Not for a second."

Chapter 14

*Tip for the Terrible
Twos: Avoid any
questions that can
be answered by "No,"
such as "Do you want
to have your bath now?"*

When Anne got home from the beach, she found
sixty-seven new e-mail messages on her computer, all pertaining to witchcraft. The writers had
names like Raven Moondancer, Lady Enchantress, Silver
Wolf, and Sky Belle. Not one knew anything about a
missing girl named Tracy. Instead, they wanted to know
Anne's astrological sign, what her book was going to be
about, whether she was thinking of forming a coven, if
she'd had her cards read, her colors analyzed, her aura
cleansed. Four men (she hadn't realized men could practice Wicca) expressed an interest in getting to know her

better and three women offered to teach her candle magick. The only one who lived in Jersey was somebody named Allegra Goodbody (otherwise known as alleywitch), who included her phone number. Anne dialed it and left a brief message.

She was starting to feel hopeful about the teen witch project. Maybe she could finagle an article in *Seventeen* and *YM* magazines. Meantime, there was the parenting book, which weighed upon her like a millstone hanging from her neck. Dr. Arlene still wasn't back (no surprise there). And Phil had left a hysterical message on her machine, shouting that the outline was thin, that he wanted the first five chapters on his desk by Monday or there'd be hell to pay. Anne wondered if Dr. A. had received similar missives on her machine in the city. Somehow, she tended to doubt it.

She sat down at the computer, logged on to wicca.com again, and posted the following message: *Does anyone know where I could get hold of some jimsonweed?*

Then she reluctantly gathered up her meager notes and tried to work. Harry jumped onto her lap, eager to play, and she gently eased him off. Where to begin? Toilet training? Managing aggression? Discipline? What to do when your four-year-old claims there's a scaly green monster beneath the bed?

"Later, kiddo," she said to the cat. "Gotta tackle this stuff first."

Harry gazed at her reproachfully and slunk out of the office. A moment later, she heard him rummaging around the living room, batting pages of the newspaper around, chasing his Ping-Pong ball, probably clawing the furniture for good measure.

She turned back to her notes and nearly threw her hands

up in despair. They were a mess, a jumble of unconnected snippets, advice for dealing with four-year-olds and fourteen-year-olds mixed together. Wading through the morass, Anne wondered why people chose to have children in the first place. Sure, she daydreamed about finding the right guy and getting married. But those dreams never seemed to include drooling, screaming babies who would one day grow into sullen, barely coherent teenagers.

Did that make her mean-spirited, unnatural, less of a good person? She didn't dislike kids necessarily. She just didn't want one of her own. Maybe she wasn't cut out to be a mother. She was frazzled and overworked enough without having to deal with all the demands kids placed on you. On a day like today, when she hadn't slept well, when her job was frustrating, when she felt like she was spinning her wheels and getting no place fast, it seemed like too much trouble simply to look after the cat.

There was no way they could make the deadline. They'd be lucky if they had a finished draft six months from now. Still, Anne figured she had to start somewhere. If she could get Dr. Arlene to focus, it would help. In the meantime, the best she could do was try and put the material in chronological order. That meant beginning with babies. She sifted through her notes. Where to start? Dr. A. had touched on so many topics: guilt over not breast-feeding, the pros and cons of pacifiers, how to tell if your baby is colicky or merely cranky, baby-walker risks, learning through touch. There was enough here for ten books on babies alone. She had to get Dr. A. to stop rambling and start thinking like a harried parent who wanted advice spoon-fed quickly and easily.

Anne created a new file and typed in several subheads: When to Call the Doctor, Dos and Don'ts, Ages and

Stages. Then she tried to plug the information she had collected into the appropriate slots. It was like working a puzzle, connecting the various pieces so they formed a recognizable picture.

A salt-laced breeze wafted through the open window as she worked. She heard screen doors slamming, the roar of a lawn mower, the lilting medley of the Good Humor truck. And then a different sound. A muffled crash from the back of the house. She stopped typing. Okay, Harry. What have you done this time?

She pressed the save key and got up. Hopefully, it wouldn't be as bad as last week, when the cat had accidentally knocked over a delicate Spode creamer that her mother had adored. Anne had to remind herself to put things away. Not that there was much valuable stuff in the house. But Harry was like a heat-seeking missile. If there was panty hose to chew or a half-eaten plate of food to pick at or a new throw pillow to scratch, he'd find it.

She headed to the kitchen, alert for signs of destruction. On the floor, by the sink, lay the remains of a geranium in a broken clay pot. Dirt had spilled onto the linoleum floor. The cat had climbed onto the counter and was staring balefully at the mess.

"Oh, Harry," Anne exclaimed. "What have you done this time?"

A sharp knock sounded on the back door. Anne went to open it and took a step back in surprise. Rich Podowski was standing there smiling at her, and he was just about the last person she expected to see.

He looked rumpled, as though he'd slept in his clothes and hadn't showered. But his eyes were clear and the vacant, spaced-out expression he'd worn in the doll shop was gone.

"I got to talk to you," Rich said. "Can I come in?"

She opened the door wider and he stepped inside.

"How you doing?" he said.

"Fine."

She took out a broom and dustpan and began sweeping the dirt and the fragments of the broken pot off the floor. She didn't know whether to be annoyed or scared that Rich Podowski was standing in her kitchen as if he owned the joint.

"How'd your little friend like the doll?" he said.

"I haven't given it to her yet. Her birthday's not for a couple of weeks."

"Oh." He reached out to stroke Harry and the cat leaped off the counter and stalked out of the room. "The doll's not really why I'm here. I came by to apologize for yesterday. You were asking about Abby and witchcraft, and I kind of blew you off."

Anne studied him. He looked and sounded sincere, contrite even.

"I wasn't feeling so good yesterday," he continued. "Had a twenty-four-hour bug. Fevers, chills, the whole shebang. Guess I shouldn't have come to work."

"You seem better now."

"Yeah," he said. "Still, it got me to thinking. About the witchcraft. It's kooky is all. To pretend you're a witch. It's beyond weird."

Anne threw the mess from the broken pot into the trash can. "Did you ever see Abby doing weird things?"

Rich cocked his head and tapped his finger against his cracked front tooth. "She would walk around the house mumbling to herself. Scheming and plotting. She used to give me the evil eye. Made my blood run cold."

"I understand she was especially unhappy the week before she died. One of her friends found her crying on the beach."

"Oh, Abby was usually moaning about one thing or another. She was spoiled. Always wanting more." He stopped short, as if realizing he sounded too harsh. A pained expression appeared on his face. "At heart, she was a good kid though," he amended. "At heart, she meant well."

His contrite tone reminded Anne of a man she once knew—a friend of her father's—who winced every time someone leaned against the hood of his Lincoln Town Car. Anne couldn't read Podowski. What was he doing here? What did he want?

"It was those friends of hers," he said. "They hooked her into this witchcraft garbage." He leaned across the table. "You know how kids are at that age. They like to play follow the leader."

"And who would that be?"

"The Graustark girl maybe. Or Lauren Jensen. You been talking to them, right? They tell you anything?"

"Like what?" she asked sharply.

Anne was growing more wary by the minute. Podowski was after something.

"Oh, I don't know. Abby was always mouthing off, causing trouble. She made stuff up about that teacher of hers. Not that it took me by surprise. She could twist things into knots, when it suited her."

"What do you mean?"

"Just that Abby stretched the truth sometimes."

Anne had a sudden urge to shake Rich Podowski. She felt like he was playing games, tiptoeing around whatever he'd come to say.

"Did Abby use drugs?" Anne asked.

Rich shook his head vehemently. "Not that I ever seen. Worst her and her friends did, far as I know, was smoke cigarettes filled with some bad-smelling herb."

"I heard she was flashing around lots of cash right before she died. Do you know where she got hold of so much money?"

Rich shrugged. His eyes narrowed. "I don't want to say nothing bad about my stepdaughter."

Right, Anne thought. *That's why you've spent the last couple of minutes bad-mouthing her.*

Aloud, she said, "Are you implying that Abby got the money illegally?"

Rich's body tensed up. He jammed his hands in his pockets and ducked his head. "She liked men, if you get my drift," he said slowly. "Wouldn't surprised me if every once in a while, one of them paid her."

Anne tried to imagine Abby Podowski as a teenage prostitute. It wasn't hard to do. There was, after all, a certain hardness about the girl, a sense of having seen the worst of what life had to offer. But Anne didn't completely buy what Rich Podowski was selling either. Abby seemed more like the type who fell hard for men, who got schoolgirl crushes on the wrong sorts of guys. So why was her stepfather trying to paint her as a whore?

Anne said, "Do you know who any of these men are?"

"Nope. Abby didn't tell me her secrets. We weren't close."

"Then what makes you think . . . ?"

"Forget I said anything," Podowski interrupted, moving toward the door. "Like I told you, I just came by to apologize for yesterday."

"Look," Anne said, trying hard not to show how exasperated she'd become. "Tracy's still missing. Do you know anyplace the two of them hung out? Anyone else they were friendly with?"

Powdowski thought it over. "You try over in Landsdown?"

"Why Landsdown?"

"Maybe Tracy was hooking, too."

At ten past six, the front doorbell rang and the five teenagers clomped into the living room, their faces bright with anticipation. All except Pam, whose eyes remained downcast. To Anne's surprise, Dr. Arlene was home—had been home for nearly an hour—and pronounced the focus group idea an inspired stroke of genius.

Anne couldn't figure Dr. A. out. For two weeks, the radio shrink hadn't expressed an iota of interest in anything to do with adolescents. Now, she couldn't seem to hear enough from them. She wanted their views on dating, drugs, peer pressure, sex, the whole enchilada.

Anne listened carefully, observing the psychologist's technique, which boiled down to trying to connect with each member of the group. Dr. A.'s manner was sympathetic and nonjudgmental. She took notes on a yellow legal pad while the teenagers talked, but even while she was writing, she offered encouraging remarks and made it clear that she took their problems seriously.

It was a side of Dr. Arlene that Anne had never seen before. The caring, compassionate side. The kids seemed to feel it, too, opening up in ways they hadn't done during the first focus group session, when Anne had been running the show.

Brian said he was afraid he wasn't good enough to play college ball, despite what his statistics on the football field showed. Lauren confessed that she hated her mother. Melissa talked about how her looks made some people think she was stuck-up. Pam, who ignored Anne but seemed enamored of Dr. Arlene, revealed that her earliest memory was of feeling fat. Only Leo remained aloof, studying the radio shrink with his usual bemused expression.

"I'm curious about something," he said to Dr. Arlene, when there was a break in the conversation. "How are you able to tune into kids' lives so well? You must be what? In your early forties."

Anne smiled inwardly. Dr. Arlene was pushing sixty, though she looked about ten years younger because of the work she'd had done on her face. But then Leo would know that. California was the plastic surgery capital of America.

"Well, Leo, I have two teenage sons of my own. I try to listen when they talk to me. It's the key to being a good parent."

Anne wondered why Dr. A. couldn't apply this philosophy to her own sons. Maybe they wouldn't be so angry if she did.

"What about your daughter?" Leo asked suddenly.

Dr. Arlene was taken aback. She looked stunned. "Who?"

"Your daughter. I only know about it because my mom writes for the *LA Times*. I mentioned I was coming here tonight, and she told me how you'd given your little girl up for adoption when she was born. She'd be about our age now, wouldn't she?"

Anne saw Dr. Arlene's jaw go slack. Fear flickered in her eyes. Anne realized it was the first time she'd seen Dr. Arlene lose control.

A hush had fallen over the room. The others leaned forward expectantly.

Dr. Arlene grabbed her legal pad and started scribbling furiously. When she'd finished, she had regained some of her composure. "I think your mother must be mistaken," she said firmly. "Because of my show and who I am, I'm often the subject of unfounded rumors. I hope your mother knows that if the *Times* ever printed something like that, I could sue for slander."

Leo flashed a wicked grin. "I'll be sure and tell her."

"You've been awfully quiet," Dr. Arlene said, in the silken, reassuring tone she used on the radio. "Isn't there something you'd like to discuss? I'm sure I could help you if you let me in."

Leo stretched his long legs and clasped his hands behind his head. "Thanks. But I've had my fill of shrinks for a while. I'm sure you mean well. It's just that I don't think group therapy, or analysis, for that matter, is the answer. We all have to sort stuff out for ourselves. There's no such thing as a quick fix."

"I agree completely, Leo. Therapy is hard work. It can take years to eradicate the pain of an unhappy childhood." She turned to the rest of the teenagers. "I'm thinking of starting a new feature on my show," she said. "It's called teen hot line. Kids who are in trouble can call in and get referred to local agencies in their area. Depending on the problem, we might direct them to say, a homeless shelter or an alcohol abuse program."

Anne looked at Dr. A. in surprise. This sounded like the ultimate public service announcement. Was it prompted by Tracy's disappearance?

"Do you guys know of any places like that around

here?" Dr. Arlene asked. "I was thinking of starting with my next broadcast."

From the teenagers' blank faces, it was clear that they didn't know.

"Okay," said Dr. A. "Let me put it a different way. If you were in trouble, where would you go?"

No one spoke for a moment. Anne felt a surge of gratitude to Dr. A. for trying to help Tracy. The radio shrink had her good points. Look at the hundreds of people she helped every day. Look at the way she tuned in to these kids.

"I'd talk to my friends," Pam piped up.

"Yeah," Lauren said. "That's what I'd do, too."

The boys nodded their assent.

Dr. Arlene smiled, but it looked like a reflex. Her heart wasn't in it. She put down the legal pad and rose to her feet. "I feel this has been a most productive session. If any of you would like to come back and chat privately, feel free."

The teens filed out quickly, not talking, reminding Anne of the way people sometimes looked leaving church, their expressions cleansed and soulful. She and Dr. Arlene stayed on the porch, watching the group disappear down the block. Daylight was fading. The sky had a soft, ivory cast, as though it had been bleached clean of color.

"Thanks for trying to help find Tracy," Anne said.

Dr. A. looked puzzled for a second. "Oh, right," she said, nodding vaguely. "The missing girl."

Then again, maybe Tracy had nothing to do with it. Maybe public service announcements would help boost ratings further.

"What was that business about your daughter?" Anne asked.

Dr. A. rolled her eyes. "It's tough being a celebrity," she complained. "You're fair game for every rumormonger with a laptop. Did you know there are negative web sites about me and my show?"

"No, I didn't." Anne made a mental note to look them up.

Dr. Arlene knelt and picked up something white that was fluttering on the bottom porch step.

"It seems one of our adolescents has a message for your eyes only," said Dr. A., handing over a folded piece of notebook paper with Anne's name on the front.

Anne unfolded the paper. It contained three scrawled lines: *Meet me at Ravenswood, 10 o'clock. Come alone. Don't tell Aunt Delia or the cops.*

Anne felt her heart racing. Tracy. Tracy was alive.

"Is that from young Leo? A youthful crush perhaps?" Dr. Arlene teased. "I noticed he was staring at you for a good part of the evening."

"Really? I didn't think so."

Dr. Arlene smiled condescendingly. "Don't let these kids fool you. They look as if they're ready to take on the world, but inside they're a quivering mass of insecurities."

"I'll bear that in mind," Anne said, with more than a hint of sarcasm.

She glanced over at the radio shrink, wondering if she'd gone too far, but Dr. Arlene was gazing out at the ocean. There was a tranquil, almost beatific expression on her face.

It figured. What Dr. A. lacked in irony she made up for in self-absorption.

Chapter 15

If your child is afraid of the dark, create a nighttime kit containing a high-powered flashlight, her favorite books and cassette tapes, and family photos. Discuss how she might use the kit before she falls asleep or should she wake up. Every time she uses the kit to calm herself down, it's real progress.

 Built at the turn of the century, the Ravenswood Inn was a sprawling white Victorian house, two blocks from the ocean, with black shutters and a

wide, sweeping front porch. At one time, it had been one
of the premier places to stay in the Heights, an architectural gem that attracted wealthy businessmen and their
families from New York and Philadelphia.

But in the mid-1970s, the state had begun housing former mental patients from county psychiatric hospitals at
the historic inn. The number of patients, most of them
elderly, grew, until there were no more paying guests and
Ravenswood began a precipitous decline. The inn had
closed down for good the previous summer and now it
had the abandoned, dilapidated air of a house that had
never been cared for or lived in.

Shingles had come loose from the roof. The wood on
the front steps had rotted, and the porch itself seemed to
sag. The paint on the facade was so weather-beaten and
faded that the house looked gray, even in sunlight. Shutters had broken off and were never replaced. Railings
were missing pieces of wood and had the gap-toothed appearance of sad jack-o'-lanterns.

A *For Sale* sign was planted in the weed-infested front
yard, but so far, there hadn't been a single offer. The cost
of restoring the inn was so great there was some talk that
the owner was considering cutting his losses, tearing the
place down, and selling the vacant lot outright.

The front door had been boarded over and nailed shut,
but someone had pried open one of the side doors, which
swung creakily on its hinges. Anne stepped through it
carefully and was immediately enveloped by a dank
musty odor, worse than any mildewed attic or basement
she'd ever been in. Ravenswood smelled dank and sour,
and, for a moment, Anne felt the urge to flee.

She'd had to cancel her date with Doug Browning, and
she'd much rather have been spending time with the

teacher than brushing cobwebs away from her face.

She'd brought a flashlight, and she shined it on the scarred wood floors, taking care to avoid the holes that appeared without warning, like small black craters. The only other illumination came from the streetlamps on Main Street and the moon that shone weakly through the dirty, shattered windows.

As she made her way through the first floor she could see traces of the inn's former grandeur: patches of peeling rose wallpaper, a tufted horsehair settee coated in dust, pieces of Oriental carpeting worn thin by time and neglect. Her flashlight cast weird shadows on the walls, making ordinary objects—chairs, paintings, an old piano—appear to sprout ghostly tendrils and spikes.

"Hello," Anne called out. "Anybody here?"

Her voice echoed back, sounding thin and strained. She glanced down at her watch. It was exactly ten o'clock. Ahead lay a curved staircase leading to the second floor. She ascended it slowly, one hand on the mahogany banister, mindful of loose steps that gave way without warning. Everything sounded too loud: her footsteps, the stairs groaning beneath her, even her own breathing.

When she reached the top she found herself in a narrow hallway, with rooms branching off each side. Most of the doors were open and Anne peered inside each one. Some rooms were completely empty. Others contained dark mahogany beds and dressers that had once represented the height of furniture fashion but now were so old and scarred they looked like you couldn't give them away at the rattiest flea market.

A hot breeze blew in through the broken windows, riffling the worn, moth-eaten curtains. Anne felt something touch her shoe and stifled a scream. She looked down in time to see a large gray rat with a long tail disappear into a hole in the baseboard. Ugh! The place was probably infested with rodents. She shined her flashlight in wide sweeping arcs, trying to spot any other creatures lurking in the shadows. None were visible, but a soft, rustling noise emanated from the next-to-last room on the left side of the hall.

Approaching cautiously, she reached the doorway, pointing her flashlight at the interior as if it were a gun.

Tracy Graustark was curled up in a corner of the room, clutching a khaki-colored knapsack. She looked dirty and tired and small. Her hair, normally shiny and blow-dried, was pulled back into a loose, wispy ponytail. She wore no makeup, which made her seem younger. Her eyes were bloodshot, her face streaked with dust and soot. But she was here and she was alive, and Anne felt a surge of happiness at how pleased Delia was going to be to finally have her great-niece back home.

Tracy stared up at her. "What are you doing here?" she said finally, her voice a creaky whisper, as if she hadn't used it in days.

"I got your note," Anne said gently. "Don't worry. I haven't told anyone where you are."

Anne entered the room and knelt on the floor about three feet away from Tracy. Her eye fell on Tracy's wolf tattoo. The skin around the tattoo looked red and raw. "Where have you been? Are you okay?"

A confused expression appeared on Tracy's face. But an instant later it was gone, replaced by fatigue and the gritty will to tough out exhaustion that Anne had seen on athletes who had pushed themselves beyond what they were able to endure.

"I need money," Tracy whispered.

"What for?"

"To get away."

It struck Anne for the first time that Tracy had no intention of going home. That's why she hadn't gone there first or contacted Delia directly. Tracy needed money to make her escape, and Anne hadn't been part of the plan.

"Who did you want to meet you here tonight?" Anne said.

Tracy waved the question away. "Never mind. You're here now. You can help me."

Anne studied the girl. Tracy's shorts were filthy. Her T-shirt was smeared with stains, her sneakers looked like they'd been dipped in mud.

"What's going on, Tracy? Where've you been?"

Tracy shook her head impatiently. "Never mind that. I need five hundred dollars. In cash. Will you help me?"

Through the broken window, Anne could hear faint sounds of life on Main Street: the distant hum of voices; the roar of cars; laughter and footsteps and barking dogs.

"Your Aunt Delia's been frantic with worry," Anne said. "If you just go home and talk to her, I'm sure she'll understand. No matter what's happened. It's going to . . ."

"No," Tracy interrupted, her voice shrill, laced with panic. "I have to get away from the Heights. Now. Tonight."

She leaped to her feet so suddenly that Anne inadvertently moved back, blocking more of the doorway.

"Is this about Abby?" Anne said. "About the way Abby died?"

Slowly, Tracy nodded. Her eyes were glazed and unfocused. She looked as if she was in some kind of trance.

"The police know about the jimsonweed. And they know you were with Abby right before she died. What happened?"

Tracy gazed past Anne at a spot on the wall. Her mouth had dropped open, and she was taking short, shallow breaths.

"If you tell me," Anne said softly, "I can help."

Tracy started to speak, then abruptly stopped. A sullen expression crossed her face. Wrapping her arms tightly around her chest, she rocked back and forth.

"You won't believe me," she said defiantly.

"Try me."

Tracy's lips trembled. "Nobody ever believes me. Not Aunt Delia. Or my friends. If my mom and dad were here . . ."

"They'd want you to come home. They'd want you safe."

Tracy's laugh was brittle. "I don't have a real home." She backed away from Anne, toward the window. "Can you get me some money? Please." Her tone was plaintive, the voice of a tired, frightened child. "I'll write to Aunt Delia and tell her where I am when I get settled."

"About Abby. Did she kill herself? Or was it just set up to look that way?"

"I don't want to talk about it," Tracy interrupted.

Anne saw that the girl wasn't going to say anything more.

"Okay," she told Tracy. "I have to get to an ATM machine. It'll take about ten, fifteen minutes. But you have to promise me you'll let Delia know where you are after you get settled."

Tracy sank down onto the floor and picked up the ragged knapsack. "I will. Honest."

"Do you need anything else? Can I bring you some food?"

"Just the money."

Anne backed out of the room, reluctant to let Tracy out of her sight. "Wait here. I'll be back as soon as I can."

Retracing her steps, she went back down the stairs, almost stumbling in her hurry. The flashlight made wide sweeping arcs as she ran, its beam careening off the walls. She rushed past the lobby and exited through the side door. At the corner was a phone booth. She dialed Trasker's number, her eyes trained on the inn.

"It's Anne," she said, when he picked up. "I found Tracy Graustark. She's at the Ravenswood Inn on Main Street, in the Heights. Can you get over here right away?"

"I'll be right there."

After Anne hung up, she ran across the street and waited in the doorway of the launderette. Curved Victorian streetlights lined Main Street. But the entrance to the launderette was set back far enough that it allowed her to keep an eye on Ravenswood. She gazed up at the second floor, trying to figure out which room Tracy was hiding in. It was next to impossible. Ravenswood was pitch-black, a skeletal hulk of a building that looked like it had been abandoned for years.

Where had Tracy been all this time? Hiding in the Heights? In the inn itself? It had only been three days. But Tracy Graustark seemed like a shadow of her former self. All her bravado had faded away. Anne could almost smell Tracy's fear.

Anne kept her eyes trained on the inn. Who had Tracy been expecting to meet? Somebody who'd been at the focus group? Why had that person passed Tracy's note on to Anne?

After about ten minutes, Trasker pulled up in front of Ravenswood. He got out on the driver's side of the Camry and another man whom Anne had never seen before emerged from the passenger side. She was glad there were no uniformed policemen, no patrol car to scare Tracy with its flashing red lights and sirens.

"Anne, this is Bill Duffy. He usually works out of Toms River. But he's with the squad this week."

Anne and Duffy exchanged brief greetings, then the three of them entered the inn. Anne led the way, shining her flashlight up the dark, battered stairs. She was thinking of Delia, of how Delia was going to have to work with Tracy, to really talk to the girl. Delia loved Tracy. Anne was sure of it. But Delia didn't trust her grand-niece. Anne saw that now. Delia neither trusted nor believed in Tracy. And Tracy knew it.

As they approached the room where Tracy had been hiding, Anne slowed her steps. She had a sudden vision of Tracy cowering in fear, knowing she was cornered, trapped.

"Let me go in first," Anne whispered to Trasker. "She's scared half out of her mind. I don't want her to freak out."

Trasker nodded and motioned Duffy to stay out of sight.

As Anne stepped into the room, she kept the light trained low. "I'm back," she said, peering around at the bed, the dresser, the boarded-up window scarring the wall like a blind black eye.

There was no one to hear. The room was empty. Tracy was gone.

It took close to an hour to comb Ravenswood from attic to basement. The search uncovered a couple of rats, a multitude of spiderwebs, and the back door of the inn, which was ajar and banged forlornly against the side of the house each time the wind picked up.

"I should never have left her alone," Anne said. "I should have stayed with her all night if I had to."

Duffy had returned to the sheriff's office to file a report, and Anne and Trasker were sitting at a window booth in the Ocean Diner on Route 35, downing coffee and cheeseburgers smothered with onions. It was a few minutes after midnight, and the diner was practically empty, save for two truckers hunched over the counter. The air conditioner was broken and a couple of fans pushed hot air around the room.

"At least Tracy's okay," Trasker said. "Listen, we'll find her. As far as we know, she doesn't have a car. The State Police are covering the local train and bus stations. She can't have gotten very far."

"What about her friends?"

"The Staties are going door to door right now, talking to friends, neighbors, anybody who might have seen her tonight. When we're done here, I'm going to join them."

"Oh, God," Anne said. "I really messed up."

He reached across the table and took her hand in his own. "You did fine, Hardaway. Don't let anyone tell you different."

His hand was warm and comforting, and Anne realized with a pleasant shock that it was the first time she had ever held it. As if he were having the exact same thought, Trasker suddenly dropped her hand and reached for the ketchup, which he poured liberally over his remaining fries. He smiled at her, almost bashfully.

"It's going to be a long night," he said.

"What can I do to help?"

"Your friend Delia probably won't be getting much sleep. We've put a trace on her phone, in case Tracy calls. But from what you've told me, I don't think it's likely.

Maybe you could talk to Delia, see if there's anything we might have missed."

Anne swallowed the rest of her coffee. She could feel the caffeine coursing through her system, the instant rush of adrenaline that made it seem as though she could stay up all night. "I know Delia hasn't exactly been cooperating with the police."

"She distrusts us. And she's scared of us. Not the best combination when you're hoping to elicit information."

"I've been trying to figure that out actually. Delia's relationship with Tracy is . . . well, it's complicated. But all along, I've felt Delia's been holding something back."

Anne stared out the window. The red neon sign in the parking lot was reflected in the plate glass, spilling red rings of light onto the asphalt pavement. She thought of the circle traced around Abby's body. Why would Abby have bothered to draw it? Or was the circle created by someone else?

"Abby's suicide note," Anne said. "Could I take a look at it?"

Trasker looked at her in surprise. "What for?"

"There's something I want to check out."

"I can't get you the actual note. But I guess I could make a copy."

"Thanks."

She knew it was against the rules, that Trasker could get in trouble. But she also knew he'd do it, even without an explanation. Because he trusted her. Because in some inexplicable way, they connected. Because they were friends. What was it that prevented them from becoming more than friends?

"Mark . . ." she began. She rarely used his first name. It tasted strange on her tongue. "About the other night."

She wanted to ask him how he felt about her, about their relationship. She wanted to tell him how often she thought about him, how she'd imagined what kissing him would be like, that he'd taste like honey and tangerines, that his skin would be smooth and sweet to the touch, that they'd wake up one morning and find that something had shifted and what they were searching for in other people had been right here all along. But she couldn't find the words.

"The other night?" Trasker repeated. His face betrayed no emotion. It was closed, blank, a cipher she couldn't read.

Who was she kidding? Where she and Trasker were concerned there was no "us," no bright romantic future. The whole thing was hopeless. "I wanted to thank you again for dinner," she said lamely, not trusting herself to look at him. "It was really fun."

"Yeah. We should do stuff like that more often. Get dressed up, go to restaurants where the beer doesn't come in a bottle."

"I know."

There seemed to be nothing more to say on the matter, so they sat in silence for a while, not eating or making eye contact. Somewhere in the night a car horn blared. The wind rustled lazily through the trees. It was hot in the diner. Anne pushed the food around on her plate. She wondered where Tracy Graustark had gone and whether Tracy was hungry.

Delia was in her kitchen, furiously clipping recipes from a 1982 issue of *Family Circle* when Anne walked in.

"Any news?" Delia said quickly, her eyes hopeful yet wary of what she might hear.

"Not yet."

Delia seemed to have aged ten years in three days. The lines on her face had formed deep, pouchy creases. Her cheeks sagged. Her faded blue housecoat hung loosely on her thin frame. Her hair, which was usually combed and fluffed into a soft, white cloud, looked stringy, exposing pale pink patches of scalp. Delia was seventy-six. It was the first time Anne had thought of her as old.

"She looked okay," Delia said, "didn't she? You said on the phone she looked okay."

"She looked fine."

"Tell me everything again."

So Anne did.

After she'd finished, Delia put down her scissors and stared at them as if they were a strange unknown object. "I tried," she said. "I honestly did." Tears formed at the corners of her eyes but did not spill down her face. "When Tracy's parents died, there was no one else to take her in. No one."

With a wave of her hand, Delia scooped the recipes she'd been clipping into a cardboard file folder. "I don't know what I was expecting," she said, biting her lower lip. "No, that's not true. I did think about what it'd be like, us living together. I thought we'd bake cookies together and go shopping and she'd tell me about crushes she had on boys in her class and I'd make her a dress for the junior prom. Green taffeta with a sweetheart neckline." Delia let out a small, weary sigh. "Just shows you how foolish I can be. Tracy's not interested in proms, and if she was, she'd wear black, a short, tight black dress that plunged low in front. Nothing homemade."

Delia got up and shuffled over to the stove. She poured water from a kettle into two mugs and dunked a tea bag into each.

"You must think I'm terrible," she said, putting the mugs on the table. "Tracy's missing for days, and I'm going on about evening wear."

Anne reached over and patted her friend's arm. "There's nothing terrible about it. You're upset."

Delia shook her head impatiently. "Not at first I wasn't. I should have been. I can't sleep for thinking about it."

Delia picked up her mug. Her hand was shaking. Tea sloshed onto the table, splashing the pile of magazines.

"In the beginning," Delia said, "I told myself Tracy was just acting out, trying to get my attention. The poor girl had lost her parents. She was practically alone, except for me. And what do I know about raising children? Nothing. That's what. Never married. No kids. I like quiet and order. I'm set in my ways."

"You're doing the best you can."

The words were meant to comfort Delia, but as soon as they were out of Anne's mouth, they sounded wrong, false. Delia was a wonderful friend—supportive, loyal, encouraging, the most competent person she knew. But up until a few years ago, Delia had had no experience as a parent. Yes, she provided the girl with shelter, food, and clothing. It was, she'd once said to Anne, her duty to do so. Beyond that, she'd kept her feelings about her grandniece to herself.

Anne wondered if Delia loved Tracy, even a little. What must it feel like to grow up in a house where you were tolerated, cared for, but basically ignored?

"There's something else," Delia said quietly. "I didn't tell you before because I knew it looked bad. But now . . ."

"What is it?"

Delia swallowed hard. "Tracy and Abby had a big fight the morning Abby died. I was here, in the kitchen, but they were yelling so loud I heard parts of it."

Anne felt a curious sensation of dread. It was like watching a car you knew was seconds away from crashing.

"What was the fight about?" she asked.

"Tracy was telling Abby not to do something. It had to do with the coven, I think. I've never known Tracy to get so upset. She said to Abby, 'If you do this, you'll die.' Those were her exact words."

Anne looked at her friend. Delia's face was ashen. "Do *you* think Tracy had something to do with Abby's death?"

Two tears slid down Delia's face. "I don't know anything anymore, Annie. If only she hadn't run off. You see, it got to where I started to expect her to disappear. What could I do? Lock her in her room? I cut off her allowance. I threatened. I pleaded." Delia wiped at her face with a cloth napkin. "Is it running away if you keep coming back?"

Anne didn't know. It was strange how you could be close to someone for years and suddenly see a completely different side of her, like stumbling upon a locked door in the house you grew up in.

"I hate thinking Tracy capable of hurting anyone," Delia said quietly, picking at the frayed edge of the tablecloth. "But I don't know who she is anymore."

Anne thought back to what Tracy had said at Ravenswood. *Nobody ever believes me.* It was hard to trust a liar. Harder still to be taken seriously once you'd violated people's trust.

Anne looked over at Delia, who was holding her head in her hands and rocking back and forth. "Where is she?"

Delia whispered. "Where on earth could she be?"

The phone rang sharply. Once, twice. Delia picked it up on the third ring. She cupped the receiver to her ear. Anne saw her stiffen, then visibly relax.

"Tracy?" Anne mouthed.

Delia shook her head no.

Anne listened as Delia answered questions: yes, no, I don't know.

She felt helpless and tired and angry at herself. She'd let Tracy Graustark slip away into the night. If anything happened to Tracy, she was responsible.

Delia hung up the phone. "It was the police," she said wearily. "Someone thought they saw Tracy in Bradley Beach. But it wasn't her."

Delia's face was bewildered, her eyes flecked with pain. "How can I make it up to Tracy? How can I fix it between us?"

Anne didn't know what to say. She hoped that the time for fixing things hadn't come and gone. That it wasn't already too late.

Chapter 16

No parent can predict the future. But we can dream about the life we want our kids to have. Make a list of the qualities you most want to see in your child. Then decide how you can best help them be each of these things.

Visitors to Cape May were usually struck by how picturesque the seashore village looked. Hundreds of Victorian "painted ladies," with their bric-a-brac, gazebos, cupolas, and dados, had been meticulously restored to their previous splendor. Awash in a historically correct color palette, from sunflower yellow to azure blue, the houses were larger, grander, and

more imposing than those in Oceanside Heights. Anne
was never quite sure if this was good or bad. It meant Cape
May attracted more tourists than the Heights. Room rates
were twice as high and many of the bed-and-breakfasts
were open year round. There were more antique shops,
more Victorian teas, bird-watching expeditions, and
tours—guided trolley tours, mansions by gaslight tours,
horse-and-carriage tours—plus lavish costume dramas,
music festivals, and whale watching, to boot.

As Anne drove through Cape May the next morning,
passing Georgian Revival "cottages" that looked like
mini mansions and Italianate-style inns with graceful col-
umn porches, she couldn't help but compare it to her
hometown, which seemed, in the face of such land-
marked splendor, like the proverbial country mouse.
When it came to marketing, Cape May left the Heights in
the dust. Her town's annual sand sculpture contest and
fish and chips dinner hosted by the Ladies' Auxiliary
didn't quite measure up.

Allegra Goodbody lived on Perry Street, in a three-
story Second Empire cottage with a mansard roof and
dormer windows. It was painted a cheerful shade of
cherry red and had a multicolored slate roof. An American flag hung from a white pilaster decorated with fanciful scrollwork and curlicues. A wrought-iron fence
surrounded the house, which was situated on a corner lot
not far from the beach. The steps creaked as Anne walked
up to the broad sweeping verandah, which wrapped
around three sides of the house.

If she ignored the salt-tinged breeze blowing off the
Atlantic, Anne could practically imagine she was in the
antebellum South. The verandah seemed intended for
ladies with alabaster complexions and long voluminous

skirts. The house itself was stately enough for the pages of *House and Garden* magazine. Yet it had a homey quality, too. Wind chimes tinkled pleasantly. A plump calico cat was stretched out on a striped canvas beach chair.

Allegra herself turned out to be a short, solidly built woman in her mid-fifties, with thick, curly gray hair that nearly reached her waist. She was dressed all in white— white slacks, white sandals, embroidered white peasant blouse. Nothing about her suggested she was a witch, not her kindly, welcoming face or her soothing, soft-spoken manner or her lilting voice.

Anne had been expecting someone with harder edges, someone who wore her eccentricity like a badge of honor. But at first glance anyway, Allegra could have passed for an apple-cheeked grandmother.

"Come right in, Miss Hardaway," she said, ushering Anne into a sun-dappled parlor furnished with expensive mahogany antiques and a large baby grand piano.

The air in the room was laced with a woodsy-smelling incense. Two mugs of steaming tea rested on an ornate coffee table with ball-and-claw feet.

"I've taken the liberty of brewing my favorite blend," said Allegra. "Rose hips and fennel, with a dash of mint. I do hope you like it."

Anne brought the mug to her lips. The tea was slightly tangy, with a hint of sweetness. "It's delicious."

"Good," said Allegra, settling back against a long, low divan piled with needlepoint pillows. "Now, then. Tell me more about this book idea of yours."

Anne began talking about the teenage witch proposal. It would be geared to girls between the ages of twelve and eighteen and would include wiccan rituals, fashion tips, room design, and, of course, spells. Anne would probably need to conduct a series of interviews, some in person, some over the phone. If Allegra agreed to help, she'd be mentioned in the acknowledgments page and her web site would be listed in the Resources section at the back of the book.

"Sounds like fun," said Allegra. "I'm sure there's interest in the subject. More than half the visitors to my web site are teenage girls."

"Really? Where I live, in the Heights, some girls have formed a coven," said Anne, launching into the *Reader's Digest* version of what she'd learned so far about Tracy and company.

When she'd finished, she asked if Allegra had any idea where a runaway teen witch might seek refuge.

Allegra removed a cigarette from a silver box on the coffee table, lit it, and inhaled. "There aren't any organized hideaways, if that's what you're getting at. I suppose in the olden days the young lady could have found a cave or a leafy glen in which to hide. But there simply isn't a modern equivalent."

"Is there any way Tracy could have hooked up with other young witches in Jersey? An address list on the Internet? A café or shop that's popular?"

"Not that I know of," said Allegra. She blew a perfect smoke ring, which drifted to the ceiling before evaporating. "Tracy may have corresponded with other girls, but it was probably on a one-to-one basis."

"Where might she have gotten hold of an herb called jimsonweed?"

Allegra frowned. "I have no idea. But from what you've told me, it sounds like Tracy was involved with black magic. Wiccans like myself practice white magic."

"What's the difference?"

Allegra stood up. "Come with me."

Anne followed her to the back of the house. The incense smell was stronger there. Allegra pushed open a door that had been closed and led Anne inside a small, dark, wood-paneled room lined with books from floor to ceiling that looked as if it had once served as a study. The first thing Anne noticed was the fireplace mantel, which had been turned into an altar. On it were two white candles, a cone-shaped incense burner, a bell, a gilt-edged dagger, a silver chalice, a tarot deck, a five-pointed star enclosed in a circle, and a carved figure of what looked like a goddess dressed in a long, flowing robe.

An astrology chart hung on one wall. Opposite it was a framed charcoal drawing of the palm of a hand, with a road map of lines running through it. In the center of the room, five folding chairs were arranged in a circle. The rest of the room was empty.

Heavy burgundy drapes shrouded the windows, dimming the sunlight. The half-light, the incense, the sense of being in a sacred space, gave the room a mystical air.

"Is this more along the lines of what you were hoping to find?" Allegra asked.

Anne smiled. "Sort of."

Allegra sat down in one of the chairs. Anne took the chair next to her.

"You know," Allegra said, "witches have always gotten a bad rap. Look at the Wicked Witch of the West. Or *Hansel and Gretel.* What do you see? An old crone with a big, hooked nose and a nasty disposition. But Wicca is a religion of love and joy. It's about healing, about spiritual growth. When we gather at our *esbats*—our meetings—to chant and dance, we are celebrating life. You should come to the next *esbat*, by the way. It's a week from Thursday. I think you'll get lots of good material for your book."

"What else happens at an *esbat*?"

"Certain rituals are performed by a priest or priestess whom we have elected to lead us. We celebrate nature, we sing, we recite verse, we give thanks. It is simple and complex at the same time and hard for a *cowan* like yourself to understand."

"A *cowan*?"

"A nonwitch." Allegra stubbed her cigarette out in a silver ashtray and immediately lit another. "You see, for us, Wicca is a religion. It is like a star that guides us home on a dark, windless night, the keeper of all that is good and holy in the world."

Anne pointed to the dagger on the mantel. "What is that used for?"

"For marking the circle at the start of an *esbat*."

Seeing Anne's puzzled look, Allegra explained that Wiccans used circles to mark a sacred space, to keep unwanted people out and magical energy in.

"What about the moon?" Anne asked. "Is there a certain phase of the moon that works best for the practice of witchcraft?"

Allegra thought a moment. "Most *cowans* associate witchcraft with the full moon, which isn't entirely correct. The full moon works well for fertility rituals and spells that increase psychic ability. The waxing moon is best for spells that bring about love, good luck, and wealth. The waning moon would be the best time to practice destructive magic—hexes, jinxes, curses."

Anne removed the strange hieroglyphics from her handbag and showed them to Allegra. "These are an ancient language known as runes," Allegra said. "But there are dozens of different types of runes, and I don't recognize these particular ones. I have a lot of books on the subject. I could look through them and see if I come up with anything." Allegra went over to one of the shelves and started plucking out several books. "In the meantime, you can borrow these."

"Thanks."

"It sounds as if the young lady you're concerned about is flirting with danger. In the wrong hands, spells and conjuring can have a boomerang effect."

"What do you mean?" Anne said quickly.

"Novices who cast spells, especially dark ones, are often subjected to retribution from a source more powerful than themselves."

"You're talking about the Devil?"

"We do not accept the concept of absolute evil nor do we worship any entity known as Satan or the Devil. Satan sprang out of Christianity and Wicca has been around since long before the birth of Christ. But the craft is powerful. There are certain forces in nature that one should not interfere with."

Anne felt the force of Allegra's belief just then, and for a split second she experienced a flicker of envy. She'd never been able to become passionate about her religion, had never, truth be told, entered the Church by the Sea convinced she was in the presence of God. What must it be like to believe with all your heart? Maybe you became a calmer, more centered person. Maybe, like Allegra, you had a clear sense of your own purpose on this earth.

Allegra said, "You're afraid some harm has come to Tracy, are you not?"

Anne nodded. She glanced around the room again, taking in the tarot cards, the astrology chart, the giant hand. An image popped into her head: the Wicked Witch of the

West gazing into a crystal ball and spying Dorothy and her friends en route to Oz. If only she could use cards or tea leaves or astrology to figure out where Tracy might be. But she didn't have a clue. She stared at the hand on the wall. The lines crisscrossing its surface reminded her of a maze.

"Are you interested in palmistry?" Allegra asked.

"I really don't know much about it."

"Let me see your left hand for a moment."

Anne extended her hand with the palm facing up, and Allegra took it in her own. Anne had never given much thought to the lines in her hand. Now, looking at them, they appeared to resemble faint, delicate cuts in clay. Allegra was studying Anne's hand intently.

"What do you see?" Anne said, a tad apprehensively.

She'd always been wary of fortune-telling, but she didn't disbelieve it either. Two summers ago, a fortune-teller in Landsdown Park had produced the Death card in Anne's tarot reading and sure enough, before the week was over Anne was knee deep in murder.

"You have a long life ahead of you," Allegra said. "But the road may not always be smooth."

Anne's heart sank. "What do you mean?"

Allegra touched Anne's palm. "This is your heart line," she said, running her fingertips over a horizontal line in the top part of Anne's hand. "See the way it looks like a chain and the way it curves as these other smaller lines intersect it?"

Anne looked at her heart line, which ran nearly the length of her hand and which she'd never noticed before.

"A chained heart line can mean frustration," Allegra said. "There will probably be many ups and downs before you find your true soul mate." Allegra's gaze met Anne's. "How's your love life?"

"At the moment, not very scintillating. I've been in kind of a dating slump."

Allegra let go of Anne's hand. "Well, that will change. But it may take a while to find Mr. Right."

Tell me something I don't know, Anne thought.

Aloud, she said, "About the book, can I count on your help?"

"Absolutely. It sounds like a terrific idea." A ray of sunlight peeked through the drapes, casting a warm, yellow glow on the altar. "Who knows? Once you've done some research, you may decide to become one of us."

Anne tried to picture herself as a witch. The part about nature sounded okay. The dancing and chanting she could live without. She had a sudden flashback to when she was a child watching *The Wizard of Oz* for the very first time. The Wicked Witch of the West had scared her. That acid green face, the cackling voice, the evil winged monkeys who did the old hag's bidding. But then Glinda the Good was no great shakes either. Glinda was a crashing bore.

Dr. Arlene wasn't there when Anne got back. But she'd left a note: *Gone fishing. We'll catch up later*. Anne felt more relieved than irritated. She was in no mood to dispense advice to hapless parents. Although she was beginning to believe they could use it.

The gap between parents and children seemed to have widened into a deep, unforgiving chasm. She thought about Delia and Tracy, about how unconnected they were to one another, beyond the vagaries of biology.

She got out the phone book and looked up tattoo parlors. There was only one on the boardwalk in Belmar. The phone was answered by a man named Sal. Anne described Tracy and asked if she'd been by in the last couple of days.

"We got dozens of girls who look like that in here every day," Sal said.

"She has a tattoo of a wolf right above her left ankle."

"Yeah, I remember. I put it on myself. She was with a couple of other girls. They all wanted animals. Must be a new fad. Most girls go for roses."

"I was wondering if she'd been back to have it taken off."

"Taken off?" Sal sounded shocked. "She just had it put on."

"I know. But she's run away from home. I think she wants to start over. New image, new everything, and I thought she might want to have it removed. Could you do me a favor? Could you call me if she comes back or call Detective Mark Trasker in the Neptune Township Sheriff's Office? He's looking into her disappearance."

"I guess so."

Anne gave him the numbers. "Thanks."

After she hung up, she stared at the phone for a moment, remembering the raw skin around Tracy's tattoo. Then she went through the Monmouth County phone book and called every tattoo parlor listed. The answer was the same at each one: No, a sixteen-year-old girl hadn't been by to have a wolf tattoo on her ankle removed. Yes, they'd call if she showed up.

Anne realized she was grasping at straws, but she didn't know what else to do. She changed into shorts and a T-shirt, laced up her running sneakers, grabbed her Walkman, and left the house. She hadn't been for a jog since the morning she'd found Abby's body, and she realized the minute her feet hit the pavement how much she'd missed the exercise.

It was the wrong time of day to run. One o'clock. When the sun was strongest and the heat seemed to rise off the boardwalk in waves. Still, she forced herself to maintain her usual pace—nine minutes per mile.

Halfway through, she could feel the beginnings of a shin splint forming in her right leg. Sweat stung her eyes. Her breath came in short, ragged gasps. She turned the volume higher on the Walkman and forced herself to keep moving.

Passing the stretch of beach where Abby's body had lain, she averted her eyes from the dune grass. This was why she hadn't run before now. She hadn't wanted to re-live the experience.

Why the beach, she asked herself. It would have been easier and more private for Abby to have ended her life at home. Why pick such a public place, where she'd be so exposed, so vulnerable. Anne realized that's how she'd come to view Abby, as a victim. Despite the tough-girl veneer, despite Rich Podowski's teen-prostitute scenario, despite the power that witchcraft supposedly conferred, Abby was a victim. But of what? Or of whom?

Could Tracy have poisoned Abby? Or was someone else responsible for Abby's death?

It didn't matter whether Anne continued to run by this spot or not. Abby was imprinted on her brain. She couldn't stop thinking about all the whys.

After she got home, it took half an hour to stop sweating. She fixed herself a cream cheese and jelly sandwich and a glass of milk, then washed the lunch down with a bowl of rice pudding. Comfort food. At this rate, she'd gain at least ten pounds before Labor Day came and she could safely put her bathing suit away.

She checked her e-mail, but no one had gotten back to

her about the jimsonweed. It was probably a waste of time. In all likelihood, the people affiliated with wicca.com practiced white magic. They'd have no need of jimsonweed or the other poisonous herbs listed in Tracy's Book of Shadows.

She felt like taking a nap, but knew if she closed her eyes she'd sleep for hours and wake feeling heavy and listless. She sank down on the sofa, and the cat immediately jumped up onto her lap. Where could Tracy be? The fact that Tracy had picked Ravenswood as a meeting place indicated that she probably hadn't left the area. Which in turn suggested someone was helping her, sheltering her. Was it one of Tracy's friends? Could Tracy be staying at a friend's house without attracting their parents' attention?

If only she hadn't left Tracy alone. If only she'd called the police before she went to Ravenswood so they could be stationed outside, watching. If only she'd been able to talk Tracy into going home. If only she'd positioned herself better, so she could see the back door of the inn as well as the front. If only Tracy were still okay.

She stroked the soft fur between Harry's ears and gazed out the window. It was so crowded on the beach that you could barely see the color of the sand. The doll sat squarely on the window seat. With the sun streaming through the panes of glass, its skin seemed less waxen and pallid. Its glass eyes appeared to glitter. Anne's mind drifted to Rich Podowski, sitting day after day in his shop, surrounded by hundreds of plastic and porcelain dolls. There was something unsettling about that man. She could picture him working as a mechanic or a plumber. But he could not have been less at home among all those smiling, frilly little girls.

Anne let out a sigh and reached for the cordless phone. Sensing that cuddle time was over, the cat jumped off Anne's lap and crossed noiselessly to the other side of the room. She watched him climb up onto the window seat, his favorite sunbathing spot. She dialed Delia's number and let the phone ring a dozen times before hanging up. Maybe Delia was over at the sheriff's office. Or maybe she wasn't answering the phone. Anne pictured Delia at the kitchen table, not having slept or bathed or eaten since last night. Listening to the phone ring again and again.

Harry purred contentedly. He blinked his good eye and started to stretch, luxuriating in the afternoon sun. Far out in the ocean, Anne saw two boats approach each other in slow motion, like lovers preparing to kiss. As the cat extended his body the length of the window seat, his front paws knocked against the doll, which lurched forward and tumbled to the floor. Anne heard a cracking sound as the doll's flimsily constructed right leg broke off.

She stared in wonder at the place where the doll had fallen. A pile of fine white powder had seeped out of the doll's leg and lay in a heap on the wood plank floor. She got up and walked over. The crystalline powder had been packed tightly into the leg. Picking up the doll gingerly, she broke off the other leg. More powder. It had no odor. She stared down at the stuff that had leaked out. It looked like a small pile of fresh snow.

Chapter 17

It can sometimes be tempting to lose control and yell at your child. When you are seized by such an impulse, walk away, count to fifty and revisit the situation with a clear head and a fresh perspective.

"Heroin," Trasker announced. "Podowski claims he has no idea how it got in the doll. But he's under arrest, on a drug-dealing charge. We checked the shop. There are thirty-nine other dolls in a back room packed with the same stuff. The one you bought must have slipped by him somehow. It should have been in the back with the others."

Anne twirled the phone cord between her fingers. "Imports?"

"From Taiwan, via Turkey. It's a lucrative business for Rich. We figure he brings the dolls into the country and delivers to a network of dealers in Landsdown, who sell bags on the street for two, three hundred bucks a pop. Of course, he's denying everything. Says he was set up."

Anne had taken the phone onto the porch and was ensconced in the wicker swing, her bare feet tucked under her knees. It was four-thirty in the afternoon. Couples strolled by the water's edge, their fingers laced together. Toddlers snoozed on blankets. A group of teenage boys were engaged in a spirited game of volleyball.

The sun wouldn't set for another couple of hours, and the accumulated heat and humidity of the day seemed to leak out into the air, enveloping the town in a curtain of heavy, moist air.

Anne pressed the receiver closer to her ear. She could hear the background buzz of the sheriff's office—phones ringing, the hum of voices, papers rustling.

"Is that where Abby got the Ecstasy?" she asked. "From her stepfather?"

"Could be. We think Podowski was dealing marijuana and speed, among other goodies. We found quite a stash in his bureau drawer."

"What about his wife?"

"Hear no evil, speak no evil, if you know what I mean. She swears she never even takes Tylenol."

"Do you believe her?"

"I think it's hard to live with a drug-dependent man and be blind to what's going on. By the way, did you learn anything else from Delia?"

She hesitated a moment, and then repeated what Delia had overheard about the argument between Abby and Tracy.

"Interesting. This puts a whole new spin on things." He paused, and when he spoke again a note of concern had crept into his voice. "You doing okay, Hardaway?"

She considered the question. "I'm annoyed at myself for letting Tracy get away."

"We'll find her again. Remember what it was like to be her age? I was a mass of insecurities. Tried to hide it by playing tough guy. You had to in my neighborhood or you'd get your face bashed in. What do the French say? *Plus ça change*. Kids today act just as tough. From what I've seen on the job, they think they're invincible. Even the suicides like Abby, they never really believe they're going to die."

"Speaking of which, did you get hold of a copy of the suicide note for me?"

"You never told me why you wanted it."

"The witchcraft angle. Maybe something in that note will lead us to Tracy." She told him about her meeting with Allegra Goodbody. "I'd like to show Allegra the note. I know it's grasping at straws, but I figured it couldn't hurt."

"Okay. I'll fax it over as soon as I can."

"Thanks. By the way, you've looked for Tracy in Landsdown, right?"

"We've scoured Landsdown. Practically pasted her picture on every lamppost. Why?"

Anne thought of Rich Podowski saying that Tracy and Abby were hookers. "Landsdown is as good a place as any to get lost in. It's where I'd go if I were trying to hide."

"I don't know, Hardaway. A white-bread girl like Tracy among the druggies and prostitutes? She'd stand out like a sore thumb."

"I guess you're right."

After they hung up, Anne shifted her gaze across the street to where the volleyball game was in full swing. Leo and Brian were playing on opposite sides of the court. Leo was a showman—diving for the ball, making spectacular leaps, punching the ball over the net. But Brian was the better player. He had the natural grace and smooth moves of a born athlete.

Anne got up and crossed the street to the beach. The afternoon stretched out ahead of her, a clean, empty space that she could use however she chose.

Dr. Arlene had called an hour earlier from the Freehold Mall, raving about how great it was that the state of New Jersey had no sales tax on clothes. It sounded like she'd hit every big department store before setting off for Spring Lake, a quaint town with a shady park, a swan-bedecked lake, and elegantly appointed shops selling everything from antique beaded evening dresses to rare books. She would be back late, she told Anne. After dinner and a movie. Don't wait up.

No word from Dr. A. on when they'd begin work on the book. The days were passing quickly. The deadline loomed nearer. And they still had months of work ahead. Anne pictured Dr. Arlene hunkering in for the winter: lighting a Yule log in the fireplace, curling up on the sofa with a paperback best-seller and a cup of hot chocolate, asking where she could go ice-skating or cross-country skiing. The very thought of it made Anne shudder.

Positioning herself on the sidelines, she watched the volleyball game unfold. A bunch of teenage girls were grouped near the court, acting as a cheering squad. Anne saw Lauren slouched on a plastic lawn chair, a hand-rolled cigarette dangling from her lips. She wasn't wearing makeup, and she looked young and tired. Pam and Melissa sat next to her, also smoking.

Anne surveyed the girls. When you were a teenager, life was like an endless soap opera: who said what to whom, who was dating whom, who had slept with whom. It had been years since she'd played volleyball on the beach, years since she was a pimply-faced adolescent who blushed when she talked to boys and dreaded anyone finding out how crazy her mother had become. Thank God it was all behind her.

She wondered how many of the boys on the volleyball court knew Tracy. In their baggy shorts and backward baseball caps, they seemed interchangeable—lanky, loose-limbed, pumped to win. She watched Leo try to spike the ball. He jumped in the air, timed his return badly, and slammed his fist against the ball, sending it skittering out of bounds.

"Game over," one of the boys called out. "Unless you guys want a rematch."

No one did, and several of the boys began to drift away. Anne caught Leo's eye and he smiled at her. Lauren got up and started toward him, but Melissa was quicker. She whispered something in his ear and laughed. Without answering, he draped an arm around her shoulder and leaned into her.

Just then, a man strode toward the volleyball court. He was tall and heavyset and wore a Hawaiian print shirt over white Bermuda shorts. His stomach spilled over the bottom of his shirt.

"Leonard," the man shouted. Anne saw Leo turn and wince. "Get your sorry self over here before I haul you back myself."

"Hi, Dad," Leo said, with a deprecatory shrug. "What's up?"

Leo's father had planted his legs in the sand and was glaring at the boy. "You know what time it is?" he yelled. "Of course, you don't. You never bother to wear a watch."

"It's time to remind me what a lazy, selfish kid I am," Leo said wearily.

Leo's father's face turned a deep shade of crimson. "You've got a smart mouth, mister. You better watch it if you know what's good for you."

Leo muttered something under his breath. A half-dozen kids were watching the interaction and pretending they weren't.

Leo's father came two steps closer, and Leo winced again. His body seemed to close in on itself, as if he were trying to make himself disappear.

"You were supposed to meet me at the marina an hour ago," Leo's father said.

"I know," Leo said. His expression was pained, embarrassed.

Melissa stepped forward and flashed Leo's father a 150-watt smile. "Hi," she said. "I'm Melissa Baker. I don't think we've met."

Leo's father nodded curtly.

"I'm the reason Leo was late," Melissa said. "I talked him into playing volleyball. I'm sorry."

"Melissa," Leo said, with a grimace. "Don't . . ."

"You have girls sticking up for you now?" Leo's father said scornfully. "Listen up. You better be at that marina in ten minutes, mister. I mean it. We got to retool that engine today. You hear? Ten minutes. Or you'll be sorrier than the day you were born."

Turning on his heel, Leo's father plowed back through the sand to the boardwalk.

No one said anything. Brian kicked at the sand. Lauren lit up another cigarette. Melissa watched Leo's father leave, then reached out and took Leo's hand. Lauren stared at the two of them, looking as though someone had slapped her.

"You don't have to take that from him," Brian said to Leo.

"What's he supposed to do?" Lauren countered. "Run off, like Tracy did?"

"He could fight back, stand up for himself," Brian said angrily. "I wouldn't take that garbage from anybody."

Pam got up and walked over to Anne. Her jaw was set, her gaze stony. She stared at Anne accusingly.

"I thought you could help," she said. "Guess I was wrong."

The anger in the girl's voice surprised Anne. "What are you talking about?"

"I'm talking about last night."

It took Anne a few seconds to catch on. "Tracy left that note for you, didn't she? Tracy wanted *you* to meet her at Ravenswood."

The others were staring at them.

Pam waved her hand dismissively. "I thought you'd know how to handle the situation. You with your focus groups and advice books."

"Have you seen Tracy?"

"Yeah, I have."

"Where is she, Pam? What was she so scared of?"

Pam bit down on her lip. She looked as if she was about to start crying again. She started to walk away, then turned around. Her voice trembled when she spoke: "I guess now you'll never know."

Anne ran after Pam, her feet sinking into the hot sand. "Pam, wait up. I need to talk to you."

It was clear the feeling wasn't mutual. As Anne caught up to her, Pam wheeled in the opposite direction and walked quickly toward the ocean.

"Look," Anne said. "I want to help. But I'm flying blind here. I can't help Tracy until you level with me."

The beach had thinned out a little. Many of the tourists had packed up and left to shower and change for dinner. Overhead, the sun was a high white wafer in the sky. Dune grass waved languidly in the breeze.

Anne reached out and touched Pam's arm. The girl pulled away.

"Leave me alone," Pam said.

Anne felt as though she were dealing with a petulant child. But she softened as she caught a glimpse of Pam's tear-streaked face. They had reached the shoreline, and Pam waded into the ocean. Kicking off her sandals, Anne followed, the water so cold it numbed her ankles.

"I don't understand," Anne said, "how you can want to help Tracy when you were sticking pins into a voodoo doll replica of her."

Pam began to cry harder. Water licked at the hem of her shorts.

"Tracy's my friend," she sobbed. "I never meant anything bad to happen to her."

"What about the doll?"

"It was Lauren's idea. She was mad because Tracy wanted to drop out."

Anne could see Lauren and the others standing on the beach, watching them.

"Drop out of what?" she asked.

"Of the coven."

"Why?"

Goose bumps had broken out on Pam's arms. "Tracy said it was dangerous. She said if we weren't careful, someone would get hurt."

"When was this?"

"The night Abby killed herself."

"You all met on the beach that night, at the *esbat*, right? The five of you?"

Pam nodded, wide-eyed.

"What about Leo and Brian? Were they there too?"

"No."

"What happened that night, Pam?"

Pam cast a fearful glance at the beach, where the teenagers had gathered. From here, they looked like distant stick figures.

"We cast a circle and summoned the Devil."

Anne's legs had adjusted to the ocean somewhat, but the water was still painfully cold. "Then what?" she asked.

"We chanted and danced and finally, he appeared."

"The Devil?"

"Yes." Pam's eyes were dreamy. "I saw myself in a past life, at a masquerade ball. In a ballroom with crystal chandeliers. I was dressed as a peasant girl in rags, and I was dancing and dancing." Pam's eyes shone. "A bell started to ring and all of a sudden the rags fell away. I was wearing the most beautiful dress. Black velvet with long, sheer black sleeves. Everyone else in the room just melted away." Pam hugged her arms to her chest. "And then he took my face in his hands, and he kissed me."

Pam's expression was so joyful it made Anne's heart begin to ache. She wished Pam's Cinderella fantasy would come true, wished that all the overweight, unpopular teenage girls could be transformed into whoever they most wanted to be. But it took more than magic or witchcraft for that to happen.

Anne had a sudden vision of her own younger self staring out her bedroom window, her face pressed to the glass, as the boy she loved kissed a dark-haired girl beneath the soft glow of lights on the boardwalk. She'd wanted to trade places with that other girl, to become her, to experience that kiss. Standing in the icy ocean, so many years later, she still remembered her fierce desperate desire to change.

"Leo kissed you?" Anne asked.

Pam's face flushed. "In my dream. Not in real life. I was . . . we were all a little out of it."

"Because of the jimsonweed?"

Pam's face closed up. Why won't any of them admit it, Anne thought. It's not like they were taking illegal drugs that would land them in jail.

"Was Tracy out of it, too?"

"I guess. I don't know."

"What about Abby?"

Pam nodded.

"Tracy and Abby had a fight, didn't they?"

Pam's eyes widened. "How did you know?"

Ignoring the question, Anne said: "Tracy wanted Abby to drop out of the coven, right? And Abby wouldn't listen."

Pam's face darkened. "Abby was acting real crazy. She said colors were exploding inside her head. She said there were insects crawling into her eyes."

"Were all of you on Ecstasy, too? Is that why you won't talk about it?"

Pam's jaw was set. "Forget I said anything. Just forget it."

"Okay. Okay." Anne's body was starting to ache from the cold. She could see Lauren making her way down to the ocean, with Melissa trailing behind. Pam saw, too, and blanched. "What happened after that?" Anne asked.

"One of the witch-hammerers came. We had to run."

"A man or a woman?"

"Man."

"Do you know him? What did he look like?"

"He had a mustache, I think. And gray hair."

Lauren had reached the water and was wading determinedly toward them. Anne sensed she was running out of time.

She said, "Tracy contacted you. So I know she must trust you. Is she here in the Heights? Do you know where she's hiding?"

"No," Pam cried out. "I have to go."

She dived under and started swimming away, her strokes sure and strong, her thick legs slicing the water like knives. Anne shivered, though the wind blowing off the ocean was barely more than a whisper. Witchcraft. It all led back to witchcraft. She was sure of it. If she could only find the link.

Douglas Browning lived in a gray weather-beaten cottage at the southernmost end of Bradley Beach. It was a nondescript house with faded blue shutters and a porch that sagged into a low, wide frown. On the front lawn a small Sunfish perched on blocks, its sails furled, its mast listing to the starboard side.

The house was badly in need of repair. The paint had flaked off the clapboard exterior, giving the cottage a pockmarked appearance. The bricks on the lower half needed repointing and a portion of the roof had become discolored, as if stained by heavy rain.

Browning had invited Anne over for an early supper. She found him in the back, working in his garden. It was so lovely it took Anne by surprise. Long-stemmed roses in creamy shades of pink and coral. Stately delphiniums. Tiny purple-blue pansies growing in shady nooks. Lush, blowsy peonies. Old-fashioned hollyhock and lily of the valley. A small fountain where huge orange goldfish frolicked. Topiaries shaped like swans, elephants, and dancing bears. All flourishing within the confines of a neatly manicured lawn. The fragrance alone was intoxicating.

"Hey, there," Browning said, glancing up from where he was kneeling, patting the soil around an elegantly mottled foxglove with deep maroon and white flower spikes. "You found the place."

"You give good directions." She looked around, taking in the cast-iron furniture, the boxwood lined path, the leafy topiary. "This place is gorgeous."

"Thanks. It's Victorian. I did some research and found out what flowers would have been popular in the mid-nineteenth century. Of course, if I was gardening back then I'd be wearing a vest and trousers and a proper hat."

Instead he had on khaki shorts and a T-shirt that said: *Those Who Can, Do. Those Who Can Do Better, Teach.*

"I heard about Tracy disappearing again," he said kindly. "I'm really sorry. Her aunt must be beside herself."

Anne nodded. When she'd stopped by earlier, Delia's face had been splotchy and swollen from crying. The sedatives weren't working, and Delia's doctor had suggested hospitalization, but Delia wouldn't budge. Anne thought about her own sense of guilt, the what-if scenarios she kept spinning in her mind. If you multiplied them by a hundred, it wouldn't come close to what Delia was feeling.

"It's hard," she said aloud.

"Hard for you too, I imagine."

"Yes."

Suddenly, she didn't want to talk about Tracy. She wanted to put Tracy out of her mind, if only for a short while. She sank into a rustic-looking cast-iron bench adorned with winged griffins. "It's so peaceful out here." Being in the garden was like escaping to another world, a world without pain or hurt or dying. The flowers, the steady droning of the bees, soothed her.

"I love it out here," he said. "It's like finding religion."

He took off his heavy gloves and sat opposite her in a high-backed wire chair that looked as though someone had spun it out of lace. "Would you like some wine?" he asked, motioning to what looked like an expensive bottle of Cabernet on the table.

"That'd be great."

She inhaled deeply, drinking in the heady floral scent. She had the odd feeling she was in a Merchant-Ivory film and an English butler would be appearing momentarily with a tray of hot hors d'oeuvres. She'd pegged Browning as a renegade, a maverick teacher who made up his own rules as he went along. The image didn't jibe with the formal, meticulously laid out garden he obviously lavished so much attention on.

He poured her a glass of wine and smiled broadly as he handed it to her. "You look beautiful tonight."

She could feel herself blushing. "Thank you, kind sir."

It was the garden. The garden cried out for formal language, formal clothes. The pale green sundress she'd picked out to wear—chosen with care, after she'd tried on and discarded half a dozen other outfits—didn't entirely suit the profusion of extravagant blooms. She should have worn a long sweeping skirt, if she owned such a skirt, which she didn't.

But she'd been expecting barbecued burgers and potato salad. Not the miniature mushroom crepes that he served with the wine.

"So," he said, leaning back in his chair. "Tell me about Anne D. Hardaway."

She grinned. "How'd you know about the D?"

"I looked you up in the phone book."

He looked her up in the phone book. Wow. She did that from time to time with old boyfriends. To see if they'd moved, if they were still around.

"What's the D stand for?" he asked.

"Danielle."

"I like it," he said. "It suits you. Wait a sec." He lifted his glass. "We forgot to toast."

They clinked glasses.

"To the rest of the summer," he said.

Anne took a sip of her wine. It tasted heavenly.

"So. Anne Danielle Hardaway," he said, "start talking. I want to know everything about you. Your childhood. Your work. Where you went to school. Who your favorite author is. What you like to do on rainy days. Tell me."

And she did, over salmon steak and delicate flaky potatoes, a salad made with fresh greens and Jersey tomatoes, a second glass of wine.

Browning appeared to drink in the facts of her life like a bee sipping nectar from one of the many long-stemmed roses. He vowed to read her last book, the autobiography she'd ghost written for a Hollywood actress with an oversize ego. Anne knew he'd buy the book and read it, cover to cover. He wanted to know how she selected which material to include and which to edit out. And he seemed fascinated by the witchcraft book, which he felt sure would be a best-seller.

They talked about art, politics, baseball, education. He had firm opinions on each of these subjects, but he also seemed to respect her views, even when they differed from his own.

The sun was starting to set in the west, and the sky was shot through with pink-and-orange streaks. A butterfly with velvety spots on its wings danced in the air above the rosebushes. Two robins landed on the edge of the fountain, stared with interest at the fat goldfish, then flew away. In the fading light, the garden was as soft and muted as an Impressionist painting. Anne realized that Browning had planned the color scheme so that one hue seemed to melt effortlessly into the next. A wooden fence surrounded the property and the shade trees were large enough to block out the view of neighboring yards. It was like the rest of the world had ceased to exist.

The perfumed scent of the garden had grown even stronger. It made Anne feel a little dizzy. Clouds of bugs swarmed to the light around the back porch. Each time one hit the electric bug zapper and died there was a flash of light, followed by a tiny sizzling sound.

She was telling him about her meeting with Allegra

Goodbody, about Allegra's house, and what Allegra had said about Wicca.

"It sounds a lot different from black magic," Browning said. "Take what she was telling you about circles. I read that witches trace a circle on the ground to summon the Devil."

"The Devil," Anne repeated.

"Witches worship Satan as God. And in exchange, the Devil promises to empower them with magical, supernatural powers."

Anne thought of the creature she'd seen rising out of the ocean, with its gaunt, hollow cheekbones and gaping mouth.

"So witches need the Devil."

"And he needs them. They live to serve him. He, in turn, feeds off their obedience and fear."

"Fear," Anne said sharply.

Browning's teeth gleamed as he smiled. "The Devil is a complicated fellow. You never know when he'll decide to bite the hand that feeds him."

She took the fax she'd received from Trasker out of her pocketbook and gave it to him. Abby's suicide note wasn't addressed to anyone. It was written on a torn page of lined paper. Anne had read it a dozen times in the last couple of hours, had faxed it over to Allegra, and practically knew the whole thing by heart. "Is there anything in here that has to do with witchcraft?" she said. "Any phrase or word that has a double meaning?"

Browning glanced at the fax. "What is this?"

"Abby's suicide note."

His face seemed to shut down. Then he raised a quizzical eyebrow. "I didn't know the cops handed out stuff like this to civilians."

"I have a friend on the force."

"Oh."

He looked at the note, holding it at arm's length as if he were slightly repelled by it, and squinted to see the writing in the fading light. She watched his face change as he read, his expression shifting from the cold, detached manner he wore when anything associated with Abby came up to one of puzzlement.

"*This* is the note the police found by Abby's body?"

"Yes. In her pocket. What's wrong?"

When he spoke, his voice sounded peculiar, as if he'd swallowed helium. "It's not a suicide note."

Anne leaned forward in her chair. "How do you know?"

"Because it's part of an exam the kids had to do for class. Write an essay in the voice of a character we've read about."

"I don't understand."

Browning dropped the note on the table. The edges of the paper fluttered softly in the breeze. It was almost night. The sky had turned a smoky purple.

"We were studying *The Crucible*," he said. "Everybody chose a different character. Abby picked Elizabeth Proctor. Do you remember the play? Elizabeth's husband, John, had had an affair with their servant girl. He stood accused of consorting with the Devil and was sentenced to be hanged. Elizabeth put a brave face on things, but it was terribly hard on her. Abby felt that underneath, the character was depressed."

Anne sat very still, sifting through the possibilities. "Are you sure this is the essay Abby turned in?"

Browning nodded grimly. "I gave her a B on it."

Chapter 18

Adopted children should be told that they are adopted as early as five years old and definitely before they reach adolescence.

There was no sound in the garden, except for the droning of the bees and the sizzle of the electronic zapper. An upstairs light was on in the house, and the bushes and flowers cast spiky shadows on the lawn.

Anne's mind was racing. There had been something off about Abby's death from the beginning. Something calculated and sinister. Something . . . contrived. Yes, that was it. Each element—the circle in the sand, the amber necklace, the pills Abby clutched in her fist—carefully orchestrated, staged for effect. Still . . . still . . .

"You knew Abby," Anne said slowly. "Is it possible she was talking about herself and not Elizabeth Proctor in that paper and rather than compose a new note, she decided to use the assignment as her good-bye to the world?"

Browning laced his hands together and studied them, as if the answer lay there. "I never should have said anything."

He dropped his hands in his lap and sat perfectly still. When he spoke, his voice sounded like a spray of gravel beneath the wheels of a car. "If you tell the police, they'll think I was involved. It will start the whole thing up again."

"Any one of her friends could have gotten hold of that paper."

He turned toward Anne. "Tenth graders don't show each other their homework assignments." He took a breath and exhaled audibly. "Trust me, they don't."

"If you had anything to do with Abby's death, you would have kept quiet about this."

As soon as the words were out of her mouth, Anne realized that she wanted them to be true. She wanted Douglas Browning to be her "interesting man."

"I hope the police agree with you," he said quietly.

"I know they will."

Actually, she wasn't entirely sure Trasker would see this in the most favorable light.

"I heard Abby died of jimsonweed poisoning," Browning said. "Not exactly a plant that I cultivate."

"Are you familiar with it? Did you come across jimsonweed when you were researching witchcraft for your class?"

"No. I wouldn't recognize it if I tripped over it."

Browning got up and went over to one of the rose-bushes. His back was turned to her, but she could hear the *snip-snip* of his gardening shears. In a minute, he was back. "Here," he said, holding the flowers out to her shyly like a boy presenting his prom date with a corsage. "I'd like you to have something from the garden. As a remembrance of tonight."

Browning finished the wine in his glass. "This evening has taken a rather unusual turn," he said. "I want to get back on track."

She lifted the roses to her face, breathing in their sweet, strong scent. They smelled better than fine perfume. He was looking at her as though he wanted something, and then he was kissing her amid a crush of roses. She closed her eyes and kissed him back. When she opened them, the moon over his shoulder was milky white, a large white teardrop pasted onto the sky.

She drove in a cloud of roses, with the flowers resting lightly on the backseat. Above the ocean, stars glittered like cheap rhinestones. It was a hot, sultry night, and she'd rolled the windows down, hoping the breeze would clear her head. She didn't want to go straight home, so she headed north, toward Landsdown, with the radio cranked up high, blasting Aretha singing "R-E-S-P-E-C-T." She liked to drive fast at night, whizzing by houses and streets, the low beams of her headlights only revealing what was just up ahead.

She could have stayed in the garden longer, could have taken Browning up on his offer of coffee, warm pecan pie. The other offer she saw in his eyes—come inside, come upstairs, stay the night. But she'd mumbled something about Dr. Arlene, the book that was stalled in neutral, and then she'd left, in a state of confusion.

She wanted to shut down her thoughts, to drive until she outraced them as she sped through the empty streets of Landsdown. Even the bars seemed quiet tonight, their neon signs missing letters, winking blearily at the night. The town seemed more menacing after dark. The abandoned storefronts and shantylike houses had a skeletal, almost sinister quality. The car's headlights swept over graffiti-smeared buildings, smashed in windows, weedy vacant lots strewn with garbage and broken glass. She turned left, then right, then left again, driving down deserted side streets and dirty, narrow alleyways. She scanned the pavement, peered at shadowy doorways, and realized she was searching for Tracy again, going down streets she hadn't covered the other day.

Her thoughts swung back to Browning. If he'd planted the note in Abby's pocket to make her death look like a suicide, he would never have implicated himself by admitting he knew that the note wasn't real. Of course, he had nothing to do with Abby's death. Browning had been Abby's teacher, nothing more. To prove herself right, she tried to imagine him kissing Abby the same way she herself had just been kissed. Passionately. Slowly. With genuine feeling. The image reared up at her like a slap in the face, and she swallowed hard to get rid of it. Be careful, Trasker had said. *Careful. Careful.* And she drove right through a stop sign, not seeing it until afterward, as if to prove how careless she had become.

She swung the car around and headed back to the Heights. A light rain had begun, and the air was thick with mist. She drove slower, concentrating on the road, turning the volume on the radio down and rolling up her windows.

When she pulled up to her house, all the lights were

on, and the front door was open, flapping in the wind. She stared at the scene in amazement, a hard knot of dread forming in her stomach and traveling up to her throat where it lodged like a stone. What was going on?

She got out of the car and ran up the front walk. It was raining harder now. A crooked streak of lightning hit the sky and disappeared. When she reached the porch she froze, her eyes riveted to the door. Something was nailed to it, and that something was bleeding. She felt a weakness in her knees, but she forced her legs to keep going until she was almost to the door—her own familiar front door that she'd opened and closed thousands of times in her life—and she saw what the thing was.

A small fleshy red heart pierced with twigs had been nailed to the center of the door. A thin trickle of blood dripped from the heart and snaked its way down to the wood plank floor. She stared as if transfixed, her mind reeling. Behind her, waves crashed against the beach. She heard footsteps and whirled around.

Dr. Arlene stood on the walk, her mouth gaping open.

"Oh my God," she shrieked, pointing to the door. "What is that thing?"

"I think it's a heart."

Being in the presence of someone more panicked than she was made Anne feel a certain degree calmer. She peered inside the house, then turned back to Dr. A., who was soaked through and shivering.

"Did you just get back?" Anne asked.

"I got home about an hour ago and decided to go for a walk along the beach. I came back when it started to rain."

Dr. Arlene was shaking. She clearly wanted to go inside and dry off, but she couldn't seem to bring herself to walk past the heart.

"The lights?" Anne said.

"I turned them on. They were on when I left."

"Did you lock the front door?"

Dr. A. looked startled. "No." Her bangs were plastered against her forehead and she looked as wet and miserable as a stray dog who'd been tied to a tree in a thunderstorm. She took a tentative step forward, her eyes still glued to the door. "It's not like you live in New York City, where people are going to break in."

Anne walked up to the door and examined it more closely. The blood was still fresh. Whoever nailed the heart up had been there recently.

"I thought it was safe here," wailed Dr. Arlene.

"So did I."

The house itself was undisturbed. As far as Anne could tell nothing had been taken, nothing was out of place. She found Harry asleep in his basket upstairs, which proved what she'd always suspected to be true: Cats could not be relied upon to guard the home front. Not when they'd eaten an entire dish of Purina Cat Chow and were curled up with a blanket and a squeaky toy mouse.

Trasker had taken one look at the heart and said it was too small to be human. It came from a chicken, he'd speculated. Or a rabbit. They'd know more in a few hours, when the lab could run an analysis. Anne thought of the chanting on the beach. Was this another bizarre witch ritual? Why pick her door?

She'd told Trasker about the paper Abby had written for English class. Doug Browning was innocent, she told herself. He had nothing to hide, so what did it matter? Although she noticed how Trasker's face had clouded over when she told him. For a moment, she'd thought Trasker was going to warn her about Doug again, but he'd just scribbled something down in the notebook he always carried in his breast pocket and patted her arm sympathetically, as if she'd suffered an unmentionable loss.

"Rich Podowski's out on bail," Trasker had said as he was leaving. "After what you found in that doll of his, he's not your biggest fan."

"This doesn't seem like his style," she'd replied.

"Why not?"

"Too creative."

Dr. Arlene lay on the couch, a damp Tension Tamer herbal tea bag over each eyelid. She'd taken a shower and washed her hair and spent a good half hour pacing the living room, discussing whether stress could affect one's cholesterol level and the amount of serotonin in the brain.

"I was having such a phenomenal day before this happened," she complained to Anne. "I vegged out all morning on the beach. And there was a great sale at Nine West in the mall. They actually had three pairs of shoes in my size. Do you know how hard it is to find a size ten in a C width?"

Anne didn't.

"I had dinner at this wonderful Jamaican place in Bradley Beach. The Blue Marlin. Fantastic jerk chicken. Have you ever been? God, I can't believe this is happening. I feel so violated."

Anne watched Tension Tamer tea dribble onto her chintz sofa cushion.

"Dr. A.," she began. "Arlene. Why exactly are you here?"

"For the project, of course."

"Since you arrived, we haven't worked on the book at all."

"I'm soaking up ideas. Getting inspired," Dr. A. said, stretching her legs and sinking deeper into the sofa.

Anne considered her options. At this rate, the book wouldn't be finished until next spring. And the radio shrink showed no signs of vacating the premises.

Anne sighed and plunged ahead. "Every day you say you're going shopping, but you never seem to buy anything. Or you claim to be on the beach, but your skin is still pale. I don't even think you brought your bathing suit."

Dr. Arlene raised her head, and the tea bags slid onto her cheeks. She plucked them off her face and deposited them on a plate of toasted raisin bread. Then she looked over at Anne as if seeing her for the first time. She reached for her coffee, put the mug back, and patted her hair. She didn't seem to know what to do with her hands and finally settled on picking at her nail polish, which was already starting to chip.

"Can't a girl go shopping without making a purchase?" she asked somewhat coyly.

"Sure. Only you're always talking about what you bought. Those size ten shoes, for instance. Where would they be?"

"In the trunk of my car," Dr. Arlene said evenly.

But Anne could tell by the uncertainty in her eyes, a quick flicker of movement, that she was lying.

They stared at one another for a long moment. Anne thought about what would happen if she had to give back her advance—the unpaid bills, the roof that needed to be replaced before winter set in, the fact that she hadn't been able to afford a vacation in over three years.

Luckily, Dr. Arlene blinked first.

"Oh, all right," she snapped. "I haven't been maxing out my Visa card."

Anne looked at her expectantly.

"My kids were driving me crazy. Acting out. Coming in at four in the morning. Getting in all kinds of trouble. I decided to let my housekeeper deal with it and I needed an escape route. And you fit the bill."

"What else?"

Dr. Arlene reached for her coffee and took a long swallow. It had been sitting on the table for over an hour, and Anne knew it was stone cold.

"Why does there have to be something else?" Dr. Arlene demanded.

"Because there are dozens of other more glamorous places you could have chosen. You said so yourself. The Hamptons. Bali. Monaco. The Jersey shore isn't exactly the French Riviera."

"It's not so bad," Dr. Arlene said grudgingly. "Good boardwalk fries."

"But why the shore? Why me?"

Dr. Arlene picked at her polish so vigorously she tore a nail and let out a little yelp. "You always interrogate your houseguests like this?"

"I do when they're trying to put one over on me," Anne shot back.

Dr. Arlene threw up her hands. "Oh, all right. I was going to tell you eventually." She hesitated, then blurted out: "I'm looking for my daughter."

Anne was surprised but tried not to show it.

"The baby you gave away at birth?"

"Yes.

"Then Leo was right."

"Yes, he was right. His mother's name is Kelly Farnsworth. She works at the *LA Times*. She's been floating this rumor about me for months. She just can't get the paperwork to prove it yet. And I don't need the bad publicity."

"You think your daughter's *here*, in the Heights?"

"She may be in the area," Dr. Arlene said, her voice jangling slightly like an out-of-tune guitar. When she talked about her daughter, her face took on an anxious cast. Anne couldn't tell if she was concerned about herself or the girl. "Sixteen years ago, when I gave birth to a baby girl, I was living in Illinois and I'd just begun my career in radio, as a Gal Friday on a talk-radio station. My second husband and I were fighting all the time. I had a one-year-old at home, and my husband was constantly on the road. On one of his trips to the coast, I foolishly had a brief fling with a married man. My own marriage was on the rocks. I could barely take care of my son. So adoption seemed the only way out.

"The problem was I didn't do it legally. I wanted to leave my husband and move to New York. I needed cash. Lots of cash. More than the agencies were willing to pay. I found a lawyer. He took care of everything. All the arrangements and the details. He worked out a deal in the low six figures. Cash. It was the best thing for the baby, believe me."

Anne could tell Dr. Arlene had convinced herself of this a long time ago. "Why are you trying to find her now?"

"She found *me*. I got a letter a few weeks ago from a girl named Olivia Smith, claiming to be my daughter. She'd found out I was her birth mother. Said she wanted to meet me."

"And?"

"She never showed. I thought she'd changed her mind

until I got a phone call right before I came down here. It was Olivia. She said she'd run away from home. Her adopted parents were horrible, she said. Abusive drunks who'd never cared about her. But this time she wanted money."

Anne heard the anger in Dr. Arlene's voice, anger tinged with fear. "Or?"

"Or she'd go to the press. Tell them who she was, her whole sad story. Can you imagine the field day they'd have? Prominent radio psychologist sells baby, screws up daughter's life. News at eleven. How could anyone ever take my advice seriously again? Why would anyone buy my book?"

Why indeed, Anne thought. *The blow to Dr. A.'s ego, her lost parenting guru status, would sting as much as poor sales in the bookstores.*

"How do you know your daughter's here?" she asked. "Did Olivia give you her address?"

Dr. Arlene waved the question away. "All I have to go on is the postmark on the letter Olivia sent. It was mailed from here."

"Did you try looking her up in the phone book?"

Dr. A. rolled her eyes. "I called every Smith in New Jersey, and I didn't turn up one single Olivia."

"The girl might have made the name up. In any case, how do you know she's telling the truth?"

"When I gave her to that lawyer—a horrid man, I heard he was arrested for stock fraud a couple of years ago and that he died in prison of a heart attack—anyway, when I gave her to him I enclosed a silver locket shaped like a heart, on a silver chain. It had belonged to my grandmother, who passed it on to me, and I wanted Olivia to have something of mine. Call me sentimental."

Anne could think of lots of things to call Dr. Arlene. Sentimental wasn't one of them.

"Anyway," Dr. A. continued, "Olivia described the locket in her letter."

"What *have* you been doing every day?" Anne asked.

Dr. A. stood up and walked over to the window. Rain drummed against the pane, fat drops that slid down the surface of the glass. It was raining so hard you could no longer see or hear the ocean. The beach was vast and black, punctuated by the blurry lights of the curved Victorian streetlamps.

Dr. Arlene reached over with her finger and traced a heart against the glass. Without warning, she leaned her head wearily against the windowpane. Anne suddenly felt sorry for her. It can't have been easy—no matter how you justified it—selling a part of yourself, not knowing whether the baby would be safe or loved.

Dr. A. said, "I've been nosing around a lot. Looking through records at town hall. Checking with social services. If Olivia's parents are alcoholics, they might be involved in AA, or they might have gone to a local detox program at some point." She ran her fingertips lightly over the surface of the heart, erasing the image. "Sometimes I walk the streets or I walk around the mall, looking for a girl who looks like me."

"Why not hire a detective?"

"The fewer people who know about this the better. Besides, the Heights is a small town, and I'm practically a household name."

Anne finally got the picture. Forget the charm of the shore and the rotten kids back home and the small-town hospitality. "You're hoping Olivia will find *you*," she said.

Dr. Arlene nodded and looked out at the driving rain. "I'm prepared to pay Olivia to keep quiet. All she needs to do is show up."

Anne thought of the bloody heart nailed to the door, and shuddered. "Maybe she already has."

Chapter 19

*If your kids ask you
if you ever took
recreational drugs and
the answer is yes, be
honest about it.
Otherwise, if they find
out the truth, they may
never be able to respect
you again and you lose
your moral authority.*

After Dr. A. had gone upstairs, Anne took out her phone book, looked up a number, and dialed.

"This is Tina. May I help you?" said the voice on the other end, a professional, businesslike voice.

Tina Lassell worked nights. She always sounded businesslike at her job, no matter what the hour.

"Hi, Tina. It's Anne Hardaway."

"Annie, how are you?" Now Tina's voice was exuberant, bubbling over. "Did you hear the news?"

"What's that?"

"We finally got funding. The museum's a go! We're renting the top floor of a button factory in Camden. We've got lots of stuff—clothes, weapons, guns, even the retractable ice pick used by the alien bounty hunter."

Anne smiled. "Congratulations."

Tina Lassell was a systems analyst for Bell Atlantic. She was also president of the New Jersey chapter of the X-Files Fan Club. Anne had met her a few years ago when she was writing *A Viewer's Guide to Unauthorized Secrets of the X-Files.*

It had been a fun assignment, getting paid to write about plots involving conspiracy theories, double agents, and genetic anomalies. There had even been a witch story line or two, she remembered. Now the X-Files Museum was finally getting off the ground. Maybe it would do for Camden what Victoriana had done for the Heights.

"I'll send you an invitation to the grand opening," Tina was saying.

"Thanks. In the meantime, could you do me a favor?"

"For you? Anything?"

"Great. I need the home phone number and the street address of a girl named Olivia Smith. It's a long shot, so don't worry if you come up empty. All I know about Olivia is she lives in Jersey, she's sixteen, and the number might be unlisted. I was hoping she has her own phone."

Tina chuckled. "What girl doesn't nowadays? Geez, seems like they all have cells and pagers. Remember those princess phones from the seventies?"

"Are you kidding?" Anne said. "I had a pink one by my bed."

"I had a white one. Yakety yak all night long. It was practically my lifeline back in high school. Anyways, I'll look Olivia up now. It'll only take a few minutes."

"Thanks a million."

"No problem. About the museum, do you think there's any chance we could convince David Duchovny to fly here for the opening? It'd be great if we could auction off his Glock 19."

In the early part of the seventeenth century, teenagers were put to death for renouncing God and participating in witch dances and ceremonies held in forests, hidden caves, ruined castles, and other desolate places. The young people were believed to have committed the following acts of maleficent magic: passing through locked doors and solid walls, changing themselves into cats or other animals, controlling people's thoughts and emotions, flying through the air, and drinking the blood of infants they had strangled.

It was a little before 10 P.M. Anne had spread Allegra's witchcraft books out on the floor of her office and was trying to soak up as much information as she could. It was all here: covens and rituals, music and chants, herbalism, auras, initiation ceremonies, necromancy, Devil worship, amulets, talismans.

Outside, the rain poured down, lashing against the side of the house; the wind seemed to make the floorboards quake and shudder. Inside Anne's office, the lights flickered but stayed on. She pulled her sweater closer and kept reading. It was 1692, in Salem, Massachusetts. Witches were led in chains to the hangman, choked until black in the face.

The chief accusation against them was that they'd made a covenant with the Devil, and the deeper Anne got into the history of the times, the more she began to understand how it could have happened. In 1692, the year of the witch-hunts, the winter was cruel and bitterly cold. Taxes were too high, smallpox had broken out, the French army was a threat to the New Englanders, and Indians raided the villages, killing many of the townspeople. There was a need for a scapegoat, someone to bear the blame. It was part of a larger movement to restore moral order in a time of great crisis, coupled with the genuine belief that witches were powerful women who could cause real harm. Behind the accusations lay an element of superstition, even terror. To the Puritan clergymen, the Devil was every bit as real as God.

Then why, Anne asked herself, couldn't the Devil help witches to escape? After swearing allegiance to him, Anne read, he marked or branded their bodies with his talons, producing a scar, the *stigma diabolicum*, or Devil's mark. The presence of such a scar was often sufficient to confirm a prisoner's guilt and enable the authorities to use torture, which the books described in painstaking detail. Sleep deprivation, thumbscrews, pulling out fingernails and toenails, burning, hanging, drowning. In the face of such violent pain, most witches revealed more coconspirators in the vast Satanic plot.

And here Anne discovered the greatest irony of all: Once the witches were imprisoned, Satan robbed them of their powers. No more passing through locked doors and solid walls. No more magical powers, no means of escape whatsoever. The imprisoned witches were at the mercy of their captors, who showed none. The Devil, having abandoned his disciples, ultimately helped to destroy them.

Anne picked up a battered gray book, whose binding was coming loose, titled *Magick Made Easy: A Study of Witchcraft from 1600 to Present Times*. A special gathering of witches, she read, was called the witch's Sabbath. Sometimes sacrifices to the Devil were made at these meetings, involving small woodland animals.

Her mind returned to the heart nailed to her door. Had it been part of a sacrificial act? On an impulse, she got up and thumbed through the dictionary on her bookshelf, looking for the word *sacrifice*. There were several definitions: an act of offering something precious to a deity, the killing of a victim on an altar, the destruction or surrender of something for the sake of something else. She paused at the last one: something given up or lost.

Like a baby sold on the black market. A baby that helped launch Dr. Arlene's career. She closed her eyes and listened to the rain drumming against the roof. She was stretching things too far, she knew, grasping for answers where none existed. Trying to connect the dots into a clear, coherent picture. Images tumbled through her head: the burning rag doll, a circle in the sand, white powder tumbling out of a small plastic leg, the devil rising tall and monstrous from the sea. Her eyes snapped open, and she slammed the book shut.

She sprawled in the big armchair by the window, her legs looped over one of the fat rolled arms, and continued leafing through *Magick Made Easy*. There was a whole chapter devoted to herbs. Traditionally, she read, witches always cut their herbs with a small, sickle-shaped knife called a boleen.

She pictured a half-dozen old hags, dressed in black, gathered around a steaming cauldron in the woods, mixing Lizard Tongues, and Swine Snouts and Donkey's Eyes. Get real, she told herself, with a laugh. That was then, this is now. She thought of the herbs in Tracy's Book of Shadows. She couldn't see Tracy whipping up

Lizard Stew. But then what did she really know about Tracy Graustark? Not nearly enough.

She went into the living room, took out her dog-eared copy of *The Crucible*, and read it through to the end. When she'd finished something nagged at her, something that didn't fit. She called Trasker at home and at work and left the same brief message on both machines.

When she put down the phone she heard the whirring of the fax machine and glanced up at her watch. Ten-thirty. Who would be faxing her so late?

Upstairs, the floorboards groaned. The door to the guest room swung open with a creak and Anne heard Dr. Arlene pad down the hall. The sound of water gurgled in the tub. Dr. A. was fond of taking late-night bubble baths. H_2O therapy, she called them.

Anne went over to the fax machine and picked up the one-page fax she'd been sent. It was from Allegra Goodbody.

> *Have decoded your runes. There are more variations of runes than any other alphabet. Germanic. Scandinavian. Anglo-Saxon. Theban. The runes you showed me are from an obscure Germanic language that dates back to the 12th century. These are the letters they correspond to. Hope it's helpful.*

Anne stared hard at the name the runes spelled out, trying to make sense of things.

PAM. They spelled out PAM.

It was a little before midnight, and the rain had slowed to a light drizzle. The air was damp, bloated with humidity. Though the downpour had cooled things off for a few hours, the hot muggy weather had returned with a vengeance. Anne was wearing a sweatshirt and jeans, and she hadn't gone more than a block from her house before she started to perspire. She couldn't sleep, couldn't get the runic symbols out of her mind.

Spaced out along the boardwalk, about thirty feet apart, people stood holding flashlights, which were trained on the beach. The lights swept back and forth, revealing the empty beach, the lifeguard stands, the odd gull startled by the brightness into taking flight.

Witch finders.

Anne crossed Ocean Avenue, skirting the puddles left by the rain, and walked up to Noah Wright. He was dressed entirely in black, with a cap and T-shirt that said *Citizens Watch*.

"What's going on?" she asked him.

"Night patrol. We're taking shifts until dawn."

"See anything interesting out there?"

Noah stared at her, but didn't so much as crack a smile. "Not yet. If they know what's good for them, they won't be back."

Anne met his gaze and held it. "This is different from the other night, isn't it? When you chased those kids off the beach?"

He looked startled. For a moment, his confidence seemed to wane. But then he pulled himself together and took the offensive. "This is an organized effort by a group of concerned citizens," he said softly, leaning in to her. "Since you've refused to join us, I have to conclude that you're in league with them, that you worship the Devil yourself."

Anne instinctively took a step back, recoiling from

what she heard in his voice. The steady, focused sound of fanaticism. She could see it in his eyes, which gleamed with the force of his mission here on earth. To wipe out witchcraft. To make the world safe for God-fearing Christians. She wondered if he had a wife, a family, if he knew how close he was to slipping over the edge.

Aloud, she said, "You know exactly who those kids are, don't you? You've known the entire time."

His smile chilled her heart. He swept his flashlight over the sand in a slow careful arc. She noticed for the first time how large his hands were, large and powerful.

"Do you know where Tracy Graustark is?" she said, almost dreading his reply.

Without warning, he snapped his flashlight off. He leaned in so close she could feel his dry, sour breath on her face. "If I did," he said, still smiling, "you'd be the last person I'd tell."

Anne headed away from the beach, walking quickly. Her encounter with Noah Wright had unnerved her. If he knew who the witches were, why bother with the charade of the night patrols? Why not confront the girls directly? Turn them into the police for trespassing on the beach or some other trumped-up charge. She felt like he was playing some kind of cat-and-mouse waiting game. Biding his time, lurking in the shadows. But why? What was he after?

She headed south on Pennsylvania Avenue and walked a few blocks until she came to Inskip Avenue. The houses in this part of the Heights were somewhat smaller and less interesting: one-story bungalows with low, overhanging gables and narrow front porches, one step off the ground. They'd been built in the late-nineteenth century by the Camp Meeting Association and seemed like sturdier, taller cousins of the tents surrounding the Church by the Sea.

The Whitehouses lived in one such bungalow, painted white with forest green shutters. It was situated so close to the houses on either side of it that you could reach out the window and hold hands with your neighbors.

The house was dark. Anne stood on the pavement and considered what would happen if she rang the bell and asked to speak with Pam. Mrs. Whitehouse, a loudmouthed overweight woman with peroxide blond hair and a habit of spraying saliva when she talked, would come to the door and demand to know why she'd been roused out of a sound sleep at this ungodly hour. She probably wouldn't bother waking Pam. And if the girl had, by any chance, already been disturbed by the commotion and ventured forward, Mrs. Whitehouse would in all likelihood send her straight back to her room. Tomorrow it would be all over the Heights how Anne Hardaway really was just like her crazy mother—ringing bells at all hours, spouting nonsense about runes—a regular public nuisance. What was the point? Better to talk to Pam tomorrow.

Anne wandered aimlessly down the street, unsure where to go next. The Heights was asleep, her neighbors tucked into their beds behind lace curtains and window boxes brimming with impatiens and petunias. There wasn't one store open in town at this hour. She supposed she could go home, get her car, drive to the diner. But it seemed like too much trouble, so she kept walking.

Dark wispy clouds skated across the face of the moon. The Victorian houses, with their turrets and widow's walks, their gingerbread fretwork and wraparound porches, appeared oddly two-dimensional, like big, turn-of-the-century dollhouses.

Anne passed by Liberty Park, a block-long square dotted with benches and shrubbery. Fireflies glowed green, then disappeared into the night. Off to the right, she caught a glimpse of the tents, which looked peaceful and still, like rows of sleepy white moths. She was moving slower now, weighed down by the heat, and she found herself drifting toward the marina, on the westernmost edge of the Heights.

About half the people in town owned boats. Anne herself occasionally went fishing with Trasker or with her friend Helen who owned a motorboat called *The Shore Thing*. As she approached the docks, she heard a splashing, and she stopped and peered into the darkness. The marina wasn't lit at night. The only illumination came from the lamps outside the houses up the street.

Anne could make out the silhouettes of sailboats, motorboats, and the occasional larger pleasure craft bobbing gently in the moonlight. The water was an inky shade of black. The air smelled damp and fishy. Anne heard a strangled-sounding cry. The splashing grew louder.

Without warning, red lights flooded the sky, like flashbulbs exploding. A leering monstrous face hovered over the bay. Those hollow fiery eyes, the twisted horns, the jaw gaping open as if to devour everything in sight. For one terrible moment, the face of the Devil towered over the Heights and then, just as quickly, it vanished.

Anne stood rooted in place, a faint ringing in her ears. Red spots danced before her eyes. A scream tore the air. She forced herself toward it, stumbling in the darkness. She heard footsteps off to her left. Someone there. Someone running. A muffled sobbing up ahead.

She hurried over to the docks, following the sound of the cries. The weather-beaten wood shook beneath her feet. She could feel the worn planks sway. The water on either side had a thick black sheen. The cries stronger now, the boats dark and ghostly in their slips.

She heard a second loud splash, saw someone swimming out into the murky bay.

"Oh, God," a girl cried out.

"What's going on?" a second girl shrilled.

Anne turned toward the voices, which were directly ahead, on one of the boat slips. She walked faster now, her arms out in front of her, as if feeling her way in the dark. The splashing had stopped, the water was still, a vast, black pool reflecting the moonlight. Anne found herself holding her breath. Then something broke the surface of the bay and started swimming toward them. Or were there two swimmers in the water? Anne couldn't tell.

She reached the girls at last. Lauren and Melissa, their faces ghostly pale, taut with fear.

"Did you see?" said Melissa, grabbing tight to Anne's arm.

Lauren was crying.

"I . . ."

Before Anne could speak, the swimmer had reached the dock.

"Help me," he gasped.

Anne lunged forward, with Melissa close behind. The swimmer was trying to push a bulky sack onto the dock. Anne grabbed hold of the sack and pulled. It was heavy and looked a little like a mummy. Even with Melissa helping, they couldn't get the thing out of the water until Leo—for Anne saw he was the swimmer—heaved himself out of the bay and helped them.

He was soaking wet and fully dressed, down to his shoes. He fumbled to untie the sack, which was about five feet long and fastened in several places with thick leather straps.

Kittens, Anne thought. Someone had tried to drown a litter of kittens in the bay.

She knelt next to Leo and plucked frantically at the straps. It seemed to take a very long time, and after a while the crying stopped. Anne felt sweat sting her eyes. Her fingers were starting to ache as she grasped the last strap and yanked it free. The cloth finally gave way. Not kittens. No.

Anne peered at the body on the dock. The girl was soaked to the skin. Her face was white as the moonlight spilling onto the bay. Her hair clung to her scalp, forming damp tendrils.

Anne touched two fingers to Pam Whitehouse's throat, searching for a pulse. Pam's skin was clammy and cold. No pulse. Leo bent over her, laboriously administering CPR.

"Get help," Anne shouted to Lauren.

But Lauren appeared immobile, gaping down at the body with a dazed look on her face.

Anne turned to Melissa. "Call 911," Anne urged her. "Do it. *Now*."

Melissa ran toward the marina.

Anne looked at Pam, who lay motionless, oblivious to Leo's mouth on her lips, his hands thumping her chest, and Anne knew in her bones that Pam was dead.

An ambulance came to take Pam away, although by that time—ten minutes later—there was no point in it, really. The EMTs had already pronounced her dead. Anne heard them do it.

"Call it," one said.

"Twelve-nineteen," the other one said.

Then they strapped Pam onto a gurney and drove away. About two dozen people were milling around the docks, people who lived close by and had heard the siren or had seen the apparition over the bay. Anne noticed several of the witch finders, including Noah Wright, huddled on one of the boat slips, whispering conspiratorially.

It was still so very hot and humid out, though the air was pregnant with moisture, as if it were going to rain again. Two police officers were talking with Leo and Melissa. Lauren had drifted over to the very end of the dock, where she sank down, her legs dangling in the water, staring at the bay with dull vacant eyes. She wore a long black dress and her feet were bare. An amber pendant was fastened around her neck. She looked wan and dizzy.

Anne knelt beside her, and they sat that way for several minutes, with the dock swaying beneath them, the water lapping gently, the masts of the sailboats swaying back and forth as if pushed by invisible fingers.

"It was a test," Lauren said finally, breaking the silence.

Her voice was thick and fuzzy sounding. She blinked her eyes, as if she was having trouble focusing. Drugs, Anne thought, remembering what Browning had said about witches in the olden days who took hallucinogenics.

"A test of what?" she asked Lauren.

"Faith."

Anne slapped at a mosquito that was biting her ankle. The rocking motion of the dock was starting to make her queasy. "I don't understand," she said.

It was true. She didn't. How could seemingly intelligent, sensible girls believe in the Devil?

"The witch's cradle," Lauren said, laughing giddily. "The ultimate journey."

Anne said, "Tell me."

Slowly, in fits and starts, Lauren did. The witch's cradle was a device invented centuries ago to help separate mind and body. First, the witch was wrapped in a mummylike shroud of cloth and leather and her arms were fastened down as if she had on a straightjacket. Then the witch was briefly submerged in a pond, a lake, or a vat of water for complete sensory isolation. During this time, her consciousness was projected beyond her physical body, and she could travel through time and space at will.

"Is that what Pam just did?" asked Anne, trying to keep her voice flat, devoid of emotion.

Lauren nodded. "She was chosen to perform the test. I just didn't . . . I never thought . . ."

"How was Pam chosen?"

"We wrote down our names in a secret language and scattered them to the wind. Whichever name surfaced first would be the first one to wear the cradle." Lauren's head drooped as if she were on the verge of nodding off. "Then we summoned him. But the witch finders came. We had to run."

Anne could feel herself growing tense. "This happened the night Abby died?"

"Yes. We couldn't finish the ceremony." Lauren was speaking louder, gesticulating wildly with her hands. "Don't you see? He was there. Hiding in the shadows. Watching. Like always. You found Pam's name. You saw it yourself. He picked her." Her speech was starting to slur. Her voice was cottony.

"Who picked her, Lauren? Who was watching?"

"Who do you think?"

Anne hesitated. "Leo? Was he the one who asked Pam to put that thing on?"

Lauren gazed at Anne as though she were looking at a child too young to comprehend what could not be fully understood. "You don't believe, do you? Even though you saw with your own eyes."

There was something eager, almost beseeching, in her tone.

"Lauren," Anne said gently. "What I saw wasn't real. It was a trick, an illusion."

Lauren smiled again, this time with pity.

"There is no Devil," Anne said.

"You're wrong. I've seen him. I've talked to him."

And now two of your friends are dead, Anne thought to herself.

Lauren moistened her lips with her tongue and for a moment, Anne thought she would speak. But she merely tilted her head and stared fixedly at the moon, as if mesmerized.

Then Lauren got up unsteadily and weaved her way over to where a police officer was standing, notebook in hand, to take her statement.

Chapter 20

Whether your child knows it or not, the mother-daughter bond will shape her growth and influence her choices for the rest of her life.

For the second day in a row, Anne was driving down the shore. It was early in the morning, and the traffic hadn't yet started to build. She stayed on the Garden State Parkway for most of the way. Then she got on Route 72 east, passed through the town of Manahawkin and drove over a series of bridges that led to Long Beach Island, a skinny, eighteen-mile-long barrier island that sat four miles off southern Ocean County. Driving down Long Beach Boulevard, the asphalt ribbon that extended the length of the island, she passed surf

shops, shell shops, bait-and-tackle shops, and a smattering of seafood restaurants.

As she drove, she puzzled over Pam's bizarre death.

"It's the damndest thing I've ever encountered,"
Trasker had said, when he'd called that morning. "You
know what the whole mess reminds me of? A hazing
stunt. Like when you're trying to pledge a fraternity or
sorority, and they make you do all kinds of crazy stuff before they'll let you in."

"I suppose that's what this is, in a sense," Anne had
mused. "A sorority of witches."

"God, what could that poor girl have been thinking?"

"Maybe that the Devil would save her," Anne had
replied. "I don't think she intended to die."

Trasker had told her he'd learned that the coven was
supposed to meet on the docks at midnight, at which time
Pam was going to don the witch's cradle. According to
Melissa and Lauren, they'd arrived separately, a few min-
utes late, and had seen someone floundering in the bay.
Leo, as it turned out. Leo trying to save Pam.

They'd found all of this apparatus in the boathouse,
Trasker had said. A small projector, flares, cels from an
old comic book showing a horned creature, and Leo
had admitted—not right away, but a few hours later—at
the station house, when cold, tired and wet, he broke
down and confessed he'd been playing Devil since
June.

He had told Trasker he'd just finished conjuring up his
latest apparition when he'd heard splashing and a few
faint, frantic-sounding cries. He'd run over to the docks,
saw something in the water, figured someone had fallen
in, and had swum out to rescue them.

"Apparently, Leo's father has been knocking him around for years," Trasker had said. "This might have been Leo's way of gaining control, of being the one who pulled the strings, for a change."

"How did the girls react when they found out?" Anne had asked.

"The Baker girl didn't seem all that surprised. The other one refused to believe it. Said the boy was an agent of the Devil or some such nonsense. Both of them denied being on drugs. Although Lauren seemed out of it."

"And Leo?"

"Claimed he never meant any harm. It was all a lark. Yada yada yada."

"What do you make of the whole thing?"

There'd been a brief silence on the other end of the phone. "I don't know, Hardaway. The ME's doing an autopsy on the Whitehouse girl this morning. We may know more then."

What a horrible way to die, Anne thought now, as she drove through a string of nondescript beach towns. *Fighting for air while you were wrapped up like a mummy. Why had Pam entered the bay when she did? Because she'd seen the Devil in the sky? No,* Anne thought, trying to piece together the sequence of events. *The splashing had come first. The "Devil" didn't appear until twenty or thirty seconds later.* Anne assumed there was supposed to be some sort of ceremony, words chanted or spoken, some form of preparation. *Why hadn't Pam waited until her friends had arrived?*

Olivia Smith's house was in Loveladies, the fanciest, most exclusive part of Long Beach Island. There was no boardwalk. Just sand dunes peppered with beach grass and houses that snuggled up behind them. Olivia's house was right on the beach. Built on stilts, it had a modern, jaunty air—full of sweeping curves, bold angles, and sparkling glass. Brown cedar exterior, lots of sliding doors, a big deck facing the water.

As Anne climbed the steep set of stairs in front, she rehearsed what she planned to say if this was the right Olivia Smith. How Dr. Arlene just wanted to talk to Olivia, to make sure the girl was okay.

Anne hadn't told Dr. A where she was going. There was no sense getting her hopes up until Anne was absolutely sure. Besides, it was a delicate situation. Olivia had demanded money, and Anne didn't know why.

She'd tried calling the unlisted number a few times this morning. When she'd dialed she'd gotten a recording, music blasting in the background, and a girl's voice saying: "Speak at the beep. *Ciao.*" Anne considered leaving a message. But it seemed too abrupt and intrusive. She didn't want to frighten Olivia. And she didn't want Dr. Arlene bullying the girl. What she did want was for Dr. Arlene to get back on track with the parenting book. And hightail it back to New York.

Loveladies was only an hour from the Heights. If this was a wild-goose chase, it was a pleasant one, a relaxing drive down the shore.

Anne rang the bell and waited. She heard footsteps inside and after a few moments, the door swung open. The woman standing before her was tall and slender, with pale, anemic-looking skin and prominent cheekbones. Her black hair was streaked with gray, and she wore it back, held in place by a thin black velvet headband. There were no obvious signs of a drinking problem—no bloodshot eyes or tremors, no booze on the breath. But then Anne had known alcoholics who were quite composed, so skilled at masking their addiction that you'd never know anything was amiss.

"Yes?" the woman said pleasantly.

"Hi. My name's Anne Hardaway. I was hoping to speak with your daughter if she's around."

"She's out back," the woman said. "Won't you come in?"

Without further ado, she ushered Anne into a bright, airy living room furnished with an oversize sofa and love seat upholstered in a crisp blue-and-white-striped fabric. The wooden bookshelves and coffee table had been stained white, and ceramic vases in shades of coral and cream had been artfully arranged on the mantel. Every window faced the ocean. With the sun streaming in, it was like being on board an elegant boat.

"I'm Lorraine. Can I get you something to drink? Coffee? Soda?"

"No thanks."

There was something off about Lorraine Smith: a tightness in her smile, a sadness behind her eyes.

Through the glass doors, Anne could see a teenage girl lying on a chaise lounge on the deck. In her turquoise one-piece bathing suit, the girl was all legs. She had a long, swanlike neck, and her tan was deep and even.

"We were expecting you this afternoon," Lorraine Smith said apologetically. "But it'll only take her a minute to change." Lorraine rapped on the door with her knuckles. "Charlotte," she called out. "The interviewer is here."

The girl rose from the chaise and hastily slipped a long-sleeved denim shirt over her bathing suit.

"I think there's been some mistake," Anne protested.

"You're from Northwestern, aren't you?" Lorraine Smith said, as her daughter pulled the sliding doors open and stepped into the room. "Charlotte's heard very good things about your art history department. That's one of the reasons she's applying for early admission."

"Mom, I can tell her myself," said Charlotte petulantly. Then, turning to Anne, "We can talk in my room."

Anne said, "I should have explained. I'm not from Northwestern. I'm here to see Olivia."

At the mention of the girl's name, Lorraine Smith's face seemed to collapse in on itself. It looked as if she were in physical pain, as though someone had jabbed her hard with a long sharp needle.

"What?" she asked softly.

Charlotte bit down on her lower lip.

Anne was beginning to think she'd made a big mistake. Aloud, she said, "Does an Olivia Smith live here?"

"Mom," Charlotte said. It was only one word, but it echoed the pain in her mother's face.

"Go back outside," Lorraine told her. "I'll handle it."

Reluctantly, Charlotte edged toward the sliding doors and went back out on the deck, sitting stiffly in the chaise, her head bobbing tensely on her swanlike neck.

Lorraine closed the door firmly behind her. She placed one hand on her hip. "Now then, what's this all about?"

Anne cleared her throat. She felt foolish and uncomfortable. What had she been thinking, barging into a stranger's house on the basis of a phone number?

"I'm looking for a sixteen-year-old girl named Olivia Smith. I'm a friend of her birth mother."

"Oh," Lorraine whispered. She sat down heavily in the striped love seat. "Oh," she repeated, and Anne saw the sadness in her eyes deepen. "I always knew this day would come. I just thought . . ." She broke off and stared at Anne helplessly. Her hands were gripping the edge of the seat cushion so hard her knuckles had turned white.

Anne didn't know how to proceed. She should have let Dr. Arlene handle this, should have stayed out of it. She looked at the distraught woman sitting across from her, and said, "My friend would like to get in touch with Olivia. I could leave a phone number where she can be reached."

When Lorraine spoke, her voice was shaky and raw. "Olivia's dead. She was killed in a plane crash four months ago."

Anne was stunned. "I'm so sorry," she said quietly.

"It was a foggy night. Low visibility. A single-engine plane. The pilot lost control, and they crashed in the woods in north Jersey. My husband and Olivia were killed instantly."

Anne looked past Lorraine, out the window. The view reminded her of a David Hockney painting: a band of turquoise blue water, powdery sand, cloudless sky, the girl on the deck somehow isolated and remote.

She thought about what it must be like to lose people you loved so suddenly. To be cooking dinner or rearranging your hair or sipping a glass of Chardonnay on your beautiful, modern deck when the telephone rings and your world shatters into a thousand sharp-edged pieces.

Lorraine Smith still looked fragile, as though nothing were certain anymore, as though she still shouldered the unbearable burden of loss.

"Olivia knew she was adopted," Lorraine said slowly. "But she never tried to find her birth mother. She felt we were her true parents."

"How was Olivia adopted?"

"Through a lawyer in Chicago. He's dead now."

Anne watched the dark-haired girl on the deck, who was gazing at the distant blue horizon as if it were a promise. "And Charlotte?" she asked.

"Charlotte is my biological daughter. A year after I gave birth to her I learned I could no longer bear children. So we decided to adopt."

Lorraine got up and walked over to the fireplace. She moved one of the ceramic vases on the mantel an inch to the left so that it lined up perfectly with the others.

"What does Olivia's birth mother want exactly?" she asked, and Anne heard the edge in her voice.

"My friend is very well known in her field. Someone claiming to be your daughter contacted her a month ago, demanding money."

Lorraine looked simultaneously puzzled and angry. "That's outrageous," she exclaimed.

"Do you know anyone who would pull a stunt like this? A friend of Olivia's? Someone familiar with her past history?"

Lorraine thought a moment. "No. No one."

She perched on the arm of the sofa, then got up and crossed the room, resting her frame against a rattan chair with creamy white cushions. She reminded Anne of a small, nervous bird—a sparrow, maybe—alighting briefly and flitting off, never still. On the deck, Charlotte got up and walked toward the water. There was something self-conscious about the girl's gait, as if she were an actress exiting a scene. The noonday sun made the sand appear to glitter.

"How did you find us?" Lorraine said.

"I have a friend at the phone company who looked up

the address and phone number of an Olivia Smith. There was only one in Jersey."

Lorraine's mouth trembled. "The girls shared a phone. The phone line was in Olivia's name, and I never bothered to change it." She drummed her fingers lightly on the back of her chair. "So," she said. "What now?"

"I don't know. I'm sorry I've upset you. I should have called before I came over."

Lorraine shrugged sadly. "Not a day goes by that I don't think of Olivia. She was a great kid. Smart. Beautiful. Self-possessed. She was happy." A tear trickled slowly down Lorraine's cheek. "You can tell your friend she had a happy life."

"Would it be all right if she called you?"

"I guess so," she said hesitantly.

Lorraine continued to stare out the window. Charlotte had waded hip deep into the ocean. Suddenly, she dived under, vanishing beneath a towering wave. Anne could almost feel Lorraine Smith's anxiety level escalate. Lorraine seemed to be holding her breath as she scanned the choppy water. Waiting and praying for her daughter to emerge.

Chapter 21

*When you fall in love,
it's like you're sixteen
all over again.*

It was so hot outside that people on Main Street walked slower than usual, seeking out the shade of awnings and doorways. The sun glinted off the hoods of cars, baking the pavement, creating a hazy glare. Anne ran a few errands—picking up Diet Coke and rye bread at the Mini-Mart, buying a Blues Clues Colorform set for her goddaughter, taking film to be developed.

By the time she got home it was close to one o'clock. The heat in the house had become unbearable. Ceiling fans churned the air listlessly, and Anne threw open all the windows, as well. She looked longingly across the street, where a garden of striped umbrellas bloomed on the beach. She was supposed to be polishing her outline for Dr. A.—not tracking down adopted daughters. But she felt like playing hooky again.

Instead, she reached for the phone and dialed Delia's number. It rang sixteen times before Anne finally hung up. Delia might have stepped out for a bit. She'd stop by later, see how her friend was holding up. She logged on to her computer and checked her e-mail. Four people had messaged her with the names of various mail-order catalogs from which she could purchase all sorts of herbs and potions. Anne copied down the phone numbers for the catalogs and started making calls. But all of the companies were affiliated with Wicca and none carried jimsonweed, so she was back at square one.

After she'd finished making the last call, the phone rang. She picked up and heard Trasker's voice on the other end.

"Autopsy results on Pam are back."

Anne felt herself tense up. "Jimsonweed again?"

"No. There were traces in her system, but not enough to harm her. The official cause of death is drowning. It didn't help that she'd ingested another poisonous herb, which left her dazed and unable to swim to safety. The contents of her stomach revealed chicken soup, low-fat vanilla yogurt, a couple of Melba toasts, a half-dozen carrot sticks, and henbane. Believe it or not, henbane plants flourish in sandy spots, near the sea. The roots look a little like parsnip, producing blurred vision, giddiness, sleepiness, and eventually delirium and convulsions. Henbane flowers in July and August. We're rechecking gardens all over the Heights."

Anne inadvertently glanced out the window to where her own geraniums and impatiens were wilting in the noonday sun.

"How long does henbane take to work?"

"Anywhere from fifteen minutes to an hour. Listen, are you free for lunch? Why don't you meet me at Quilters, and I'll tell you what we've come up with so far."

"I'll be there in a few."

"Great."

Anne hung up and stared listlessly into space. Delirium. Convulsions. God. What a terrible way to die. Why would Pam subject herself to something like that?

Anne got out the witchcraft books Allegra Goodbody had lent her and looked up henbane. There it was. A staple of any witch's garden, along with belladonna, nightshade, hemlock, and a half-dozen other herbs. Anne studied a picture of a henbane plant. It grew as tall as one to two feet and had hairy leaves and funnel-shaped yellow flowers. Shouldn't be hard to spot in tiny Oceanside Heights. Jimsonweed was a little more common-looking, a bushy plant with large leaves and pretty white flowers that emitted a rank, narcotic-smelling odor.

An illustration opposite the plants showed a sharp-faced woman with wild hair passed out beneath a tree. The caption read: *It was common practice in the 16th century for witches to ingest poisonous plants, which cause an unquiet sleep, very like the sleep of drunkenness, except that it is deadly.*

Antique quilts adorned the mint green walls of Quilters, a restaurant on the ground floor of one of the Heights' historic inns. The food was served cafeteria-style. It was hearty, high-cholesterol fare—meat loaf smothered with gravy, lumpy mashed potatoes, shepherd's pie, beef stew. Anne adored it.

She loaded her Fiestaware plate with fried chicken,

macaroni and cheese, and pecan pie, and joined Trasker at a chipped, white Formica table situated under an Amish quilt with concentric red, green, and brown squares. The quilt next to it depicted a couple in an old-fashioned horse and buggy. Above it was the phrase: *We grow too soon old and too late smart.*

The sound of The Drifters singing "Under the Boardwalk" floated through Quilters. The music was a new touch. As were the reduced size of the portions. A New York lawyer had recently bought the place and failed to understand that what made it so special was large helpings at low prices.

"Can you believe it?" said Trasker. "Twelve bucks for lunch?" He gestured toward the pork chops, applesauce, and string beans on his tray. "Last year, this would have cost me six dollars, tops."

"I know," said Anne, digging into her macaroni, which, if truth be told, tasted chewier than usual. She glanced around the restaurant to see if Lauren Jensen was working today, but didn't see Lauren anywhere. "So tell me," she said to Trasker. "What have you found out?"

"For starters, Rich Podowski has become a regular chatterbox. He's trying to plea-bargain his sentence down, especially once he heard Abby died from jimsonweed, not Ecstasy. Apparently, Abby found out he was dealing drugs and threatened to blow the whistle on his operation. He'd been paying her a lot of money to keep quiet."

Anne listened attentively. It made sense now: Rich badgering Abby's friends, dropping by Anne's house and bad-mouthing his stepdaughter. He was desperate for information. He wanted to find out how much they knew.

"That still doesn't explain how Abby came to be holding Ecstasy in her hand the night she died."

"I know," Trasker said. "There's a lot about this case that still doesn't add up. But the big news is you were right to suggest running a pregnancy test on Abby. The ME retested some blood he'd taken during the autopsy. She was about six weeks along."

Anne felt her heart sink. She was hoping against hope it wasn't true. Although it could explain why Tracy wanted Abby to drop out of the coven and stop taking poisonous herbs, maybe even why Tracy wanted to drop out herself. Anne could see Tracy wanting to protect the baby, wishing someone had protected her. *Am I a traitor?* Tracy had written in her Book of Shadows. A traitor for dropping out, for turning her back on witchcraft. *What if Abby tells* that she's pregnant.

"How did you figure it out?" Trasker asked.

"The paper Abby wrote for summer school English. I reread *The Crucible*. One of the main characters is a teenage girl named Abigail Williams. She conjures spirits in the woods, accuses women she doesn't like of being witches, and brings about the witch-hunts. Abigail. Abby. It was a natural connection. But instead Abby chose to identify with Elizabeth Proctor, another character in the play, who happens to be pregnant. I thought it warranted checking out."

"Speaking of summer school," Trasker said, "there's something I think you should see." He removed a white envelope from the breast pocket of his blazer and slid it across the table.

She picked it up and opened it. Inside was a one-page typewritten letter from the principal of a private high school in Hightstown. She read it quickly and felt a queasiness in her stomach that she couldn't blame on the macaroni and cheese.

"Browning left this particular school off his résumé," Trasker said. "You can see why."

"How come this hasn't come to light before now?"

"Because Browning did his damndest to cover it up."

"Do you think he's the one who got Abby pregnant?"

"Could be. But that doesn't mean he killed her. We're back to suicide. And your friend Browning appears to be in the clear."

The last word seemed to echo in the air. *Clear, clear.* But nothing about Abby's death was clear. Nothing had been from the start.

"The contents of that letter is strictly between us," Trasker added. He looked down at his plate. "Since you've been seeing the guy, I thought you should know what you're getting yourself into."

She wanted to clear the air, to tell him that Browning meant nothing to her, that the only one she cared about was him.

Instead she said, "What about the henbane?"

"It works on the central nervous system, shutting it down and causing violent convulsions. All the parts of the plant are poisonous, though we're still trying to figure out how Pam consumed it. You could boil the roots and leaves in soup. That's one way. The chicken soup."

Anne shuddered. "Sounds like a horrible way to die."

He smiled then and looked at her with such concern, such caring in his deep brown eyes, that it took her breath away.

"Mark," she said softly.

It was only one word. But without thinking she'd invested it with emotion, with all the feelings she'd been having about him these past few months.

"What?" he said, his voice barely above a whisper.

"Do you feel it, too? Whatever it is that's between us."

There. She'd finally gone and said it. Although the fact that they were sitting in Quilters, surrounded by noisy tourists and elderly retirees, amid the clank of silverware and the smell of grease frying on the grill, made it a less romantic moment than she'd dreamed about.

She studied him nervously, her heart somersaulting in her chest, awaiting his reply. He looked stunned, absolutely incredulous. His eyes widened in surprise, and then he laughed so loudly and heartily that people sitting near them turned to stare.

"Oh, man," he said, chuckling.

It wasn't what she'd been expecting. *Okay*, she told herself. *This is the absolute last time I let my guard down with a man, the last time I risk telling the truth.*

But then Trasker reached across the table and took both her hands in his. "And all along," he said, "I thought you'd never go out with me."

"Why not?" she said, confused.

"Because I'm black."

She was so taken aback that it took her a moment to speak. "What does race have to do with anything?"

"Look around this room. Do you see any other black people?"

She didn't have to look. She knew he was the only one.

"You thought I was prejudiced?"

Now it was her turn to be amazed. Her mind skipped lightly over the past year. Had she ever said or done anything to indicate such a thing?

"Hey, this is the Jersey shore," Trasker said, with a laugh. "It gives new meaning to the word minority. I thought . . . Oh, forget about what I thought. It's not important anymore."

"What is?"

He was still holding her hands. His skin felt smooth and cool as porcelain.

"You. Me. Us."

Anne smiled. How could three little words sound so completely right?

They spent the next hour talking about their friendship, discussing all the miscues, misperceptions, and miscommunications that had kept them from getting together before now.

From time to time, Trasker reached over and touched her lightly on the hand or the cheek, as if to reassure himself that this was really happening. Each time he did she experienced a physical thrill that started in her fingertips and pulsated through her entire body. It was like being sixteen all over again, and it felt wonderful.

"So when did you first know?" she asked him.

The lunchtime crowd had thinned, and they practically had the place to themselves. A busboy had cleared their trays away and the two of them were sharing the remains of a large mint iced tea, saturated with sugar. The quilts on the wall fairly shimmered in the afternoon light. Anne thought they'd never looked lovelier.

"The night we drove down to Seaside Heights. We were walking along the boardwalk, remember? You were wearing a green sweater. It's my favorite, actually, because it brings out the color of your eyes."

She thought back to that April night. The wind was blowing hard off the ocean, and the boardwalk was packed. The air smelled of caramel popcorn and amusement-ride grease. Shrieks echoed from the Casino Pier as the giant roller coaster plunged downward. Pinball machines jangled in the arcades and the carousel organ played the same tune over and over. The red disc of a giant Ferris wheel floated like a harvest moon over the ocean. "We played skeeball," she said, remembering.

"And I tried to win the giant stuffed crab."

"I think the game was rigged."

He chuckled. "See, I knew there was a reason I liked you. No, seriously, I laughed so much that night. I had so much fun, and I remember at one point thinking, wow, this is so great. There's nowhere else in the world I'd rather be, no one else I'd rather be with." He paused to squeeze her hand again. "How about you? How long have you known?"

"Since the spring, I guess. It kind of sneaked up on me, little by little. I'd find myself thinking about you all the time—what cases you were working on, what you were doing, and hoping you'd drop by or call, so we could get together."

He smiled at her again, and it made her feel incredibly happy. "You know, you have beautiful teeth," she said.

"Yours aren't bad yourself, Hardaway."

He leaned across the table and kissed her lightly on the mouth. He smelled like mint and aftershave and summer—familiar and exotic at the same time. It left her wanting more, to taste more of him, to be swimming in his arms. She felt as though someone had pumped her full of helium, as though she were floating. She felt that giddy.

"What?" he said, with a warm, lazy smile.

"I'm really glad this is happening."

"Me too."

"You know, you could have given me a clue you were interested," she kidded him. "I thought you loved being on your own. Every time either one of us mentioned any-thing connected with dating, you made it seem like you'd rather be getting a root canal."

"Hey, what can I say?" he teased. "I have an image to protect. Practically everyone at work is married or has a steady partner, and the guys envy the way I can just pick up and go fishing anytime I please or take off for parts unknown. No ties. No serious attachments."

"No terms or conditions. No dashed expectations. Be-lieve me, I know the drill."

Trasker let out a mock sigh. "Are we crazy to ditch it?"

"You're forgetting the downside."

"Lonely nights. Old routines. When you see a really great movie by yourself and after it's over, you have no one to talk it over with."

"Uh huh."

She nearly told him about the spell she'd cast, but de-cided it was too ridiculous to share. There'd be time enough to reveal all the nutty things she'd done in the name of love.

He watched two women leave a tip and head for the door.

With a grin, he said, "You do realize in a little while it'll be all over town that we were making out here."

She shrugged. "So?"

"Have you ever dated a black guy before?"

She shook her head. "Have you gone out with white women?"

"Once. It didn't work out. We couldn't get past the race thing."

A sudden shadow crept across the face of her happi-ness.

"What happened?"

He put up his hand to fend off the question. "It was a long time ago. And she was nothing like you."

Trasker touched her cheek again, and her misgivings evaporated like smoke. He pushed his chair away from the table. "Much as I hate to, I have to get back to the office."

"Me too."

"Could I stop by later, after I get off work? It'll probably be after eleven."

"I'd like that."

As they walked to the door, he took hold of her hand. She felt that in the space of an hour her whole life had completely changed. She still couldn't get over it.

Stepping outside was like entering an oven. The air fairly shimmered with heat. "Wow," Anne said. "It's really hot out."

Trasker kissed her full on the lips. "Not as hot as it's going to get."

When Anne walked into The House of Blondes at a little after three, clusters of pink-smocked women were discussing the latest tragedy to befall the Heights. None of them had actually seen anything—not the "Devil" hovering over the bay, not Pam's wet, lifeless form—but Anne heard Estelle Grimes tell Tammy Sellers that poor Pammy hadn't been right in the head since she started dieting. Which prompted Francine Palatchnik, who was a member of Witch Finders, as well as every other club and civic group in town, to chime in that girls who played with fire were sure to get burned.

Monsieur Andre shot Francine a withering look that immediately shut her up. Two of the stylists tittered. A third was on the phone, rehashing the events of last night. Oblivious to the commotion swirling around her, Jolene

Baker lounged in a haircutting chair, smoking furiously and swigging coffee from a mug that said *Shopaholics Anonymous: Cash or Charge?* She glanced up when Anne walked over to her.

"You ready for that haircut yet?" she asked.

"Afraid not. Actually, I was looking for Melissa. Is she around?"

"You just missed her, hon. I sent her over to the pharmacy to pick up some extra cotton balls. Shipment's late." Jolene fanned herself with a beauty magazine. "Mel didn't want to come in today. But I'm shorthanded. And I think the best thing she can do right now is concentrate on work. That was part of the problem in the first place," Jolene announced loudly. "My daughter has too much free time." Jolene glanced toward the door and eased herself out of the chair. " 'Scuse me, Annie. My three o'clock just walked in."

Anne said good-bye and headed down Main Street to Advent Pharmacy, an old-fashioned drugstore and luncheonette, founded in the late 1930s. Not much had changed since then. The lighting was dim, the shelves crammed with all sorts of things—saucepans, Hummel figurines, picture frames, dish towels. The store stocked everything from suntan lotions to obscure little-known remedies for stomach ailments and sore throats. You could still get a root beer float at the soda fountain, and, two years ago, the egg creams were voted the best in the state by *New Jersey* magazine.

Anne found Melissa seated at the counter, her chin cupped in her hand, the cotton balls piled in a plastic bag at her feet. She was as pretty as ever, but she looked spent. There were faint circles under her eyes, and the tip of her nose was red.

"Hi," Anne said. "Your mom told me I could find you here."

"I'm all talked out," Melissa said listlessly.

"Then you can listen while I talk." Anne slid onto the adjoining maroon vinyl stool and ordered an iced coffee. "I guess you're aware by now that the police know about the jimsonweed and the henbane. They're running around town looking for deadly herbs in people's gardens, which we both know is a complete waste of time."

Melissa wound a piece of her thick blond hair around her finger and gave it a tug. It was a nervous schoolgirl gesture, and it reminded Anne of how young Melissa was, how young all the pseudo-witches were.

Anne took a sip of her drink, which was strong and sweet. "Tracy Graustark was in charge of getting the herbs," she continued. "Tracy ordered them through a catalog—that much can be traced—and divvied them up among the five of you."

Melissa stiffened, then wrapped her arms across her chest. Her expression was tense.

"What's the point of denying it?" Anne asked. "You told me yourself you and Tracy aren't close. Why protect her?"

"Lauren said . . ." Melissa blurted out.

"Go on," Anne said. "What exactly did Lauren tell you to do?"

Melissa bit down on her lower lip. She seemed to be making her mind up about something. "Lauren said we shouldn't tell anyone about the herbs," Melissa said shakily. "No matter what."

"Why not?"

"Because they're drugs. Dangerous drugs. We could get in big trouble."

Anne looked around the pharmacy. A couple of tourists were buying sunscreen and magazines. The old-fashioned ceiling fans whirred noisily.

"But you didn't take any of the herbs, right? How can you get in trouble for something you didn't do?"

Melissa gazed at Anne beseechingly. "I wish my mother believed that. She always thinks the worst of me."

"Try telling her the truth," Anne suggested, feeling like a cheap imitation of Dr. Arlene. "Explain that you were never really into witchcraft. That you just did it for kicks. You never took drugs. You never worshipped the Devil. Because you realized all along it was only Leo Farnsworth playing a part."

"How can you be sure I never took anything when my own mother won't believe me?"

"Because it's easier to be fooled by flashing lights and a magic show when you're tripping on hallucinogenic herbs. And you never were. Fooled, that is. Now why don't you tell me the name of the catalog Tracy ordered the herbs through?"

Melissa gave a little pout, which had probably made many a teenage boy dizzy with love. "It's called *The Dark Path*. They're based somewhere in Pennsylvania. Lancaster, I think. But you didn't hear it from me."

"Thanks."

Melissa got up from the counter. "Look, if I knew where Tracy was, I'd tell you. But I don't." She held up two fingers. "Scouts' honor."

Anne couldn't resist smiling. "Something tells me you were never a scout."

Chapter 22

*All kids lie at one time
or another. They don't
think in terms of right
and wrong, only about
how to avoid
getting caught.*

Douglas Browning was sitting on Anne's front steps eating a peach when she got home.

"Want one?" he asked, pulling a second peach out of a brown paper bag. "I'll wash it off for you."

He went over to the side of the house, turned on the spigot, and rinsed the peach with the garden hose.

She took the fruit from him, feeling the soft downy weight of it in her hand. She was sweating, her face flushed from the heat, her clothes clinging to her skin.

"What's up with your flowers?" He jerked his finger toward her drooping geraniums and petunias, her impatiens curling at the edges, their petals dry as paper. "Everything's wilted."

"I have a black thumb."

An hour ago, before lunch with Trasker, she would have invited Browning inside to escape the heat, offering him iced tea and flirty conversation. Now she studied him with detachment, as if he were practically a stranger—someone she'd sat next to on a train and chatted inconsequentially with for the time it took to get from Newark to Landsdown Park. Her utter lack of feeling for him took her by surprise.

She sat down on the far end of the step he was on, keeping her distance. The ocean was calm and still, the color of green sea glass, as though the water had been numbed by heat.

"I was wondering if you were free tonight," he said. "We could drive over to Red Bank. Have you ever been to the Downtown Café? They have terrific martinis and the jazz isn't bad."

"I'm not free."

Something in her tone made him glance up. "What's wrong?"

"Abby's autopsy report came back."

She wasn't supposed to be telling him the results. She was pretty sure of that. But she had to. She wanted to see the look on his face when she said it out loud.

She steeled herself, and began, "Abby was pregnant."

He lifted an eyebrow in an ironic way, as if to say what else is new? Then he saw Anne's face and dropped the cool facade.

"You think I'm responsible?" he said, sounding incredulous.

She realized it had been the first thing she'd thought of

when she'd suggested the medical examiner run the test.

He looked down at his peach, which was dripping onto his hand, and tossed it into the grass in front of Anne's house. "I thought you knew me better than that."

He didn't bother to keep the anger out of his voice, and Anne realized it had been there all along, just below the surface, like a patch of black ice you don't see until your car has skidded out of control. She wondered how long it would have taken until he turned the force of it on her.

"When you come right down to it," she said slowly, "we don't know each other well at all."

"I told you nothing happened between Abby and me. God. I thought you of all people . . ."

His jaw was set. His fists had clenched into knots.

"I know what happened in Hightstown," she said.

His face registered surprise. Then he glared at her. "The girl was lying. She was a tramp. She slept with half the school."

Anne's mother's voice echoed in her ears: *Where there's smoke, there's fire.* Even Dr. A. could have told her that. How could she have been so trusting? So incredibly naive? How had she tricked herself into believing anything Doug Browning had told her?

She thought back to last night: the sweet crush of roses; the lush, romantic garden; kissing in the moonlight. She was already outside the memory. It seemed like it had happened ages ago.

As if reading her thoughts, he said: "What about last night? You can't just turn your emotions on and off like a faucet."

He was yelling now. A couple walking by her house turned to stare.

She got up, still holding the warm peach, climbed the

porch steps, and went inside the house, locking the door behind her.

When she looked out the window, ten minutes later, he was still sitting there, hunched over, tight with rage.

Anne forced herself to concentrate on the parenting book. Working from the outline, she fleshed out the chapters as best she could, relying on the transcripts from Dr. Arlene's radio broadcasts and what scraps of information Dr. A. had provided during the past two weeks. Every few minutes, she did a word count on the computer. The book was supposed to have about 250 pages. It made her feel better to count the words, like she was making rough, slow, progress.

After another ten minutes, Browning had gotten up and left. His absence came as a relief. She wanted to stop thinking about everything: the witchcraft; the poison herbs; two girls dead, one still missing. She wanted to shut down that part of her brain and focus on her job, so she could finish the damn book, so Dr. Arlene would finally move out and life would return to normal.

The hours passed quickly. At some point, she went into the kitchen, nuked a plate of macaroni and cheese, poured herself a Diet Coke, then returned to the computer. She typed until her wrists began to ache, until the words on the screen grew blurry and she heard a key turn in the lock.

"I'm back," Dr. Arlene sang out.

"In here," Anne answered.

She both looked forward to and dreaded telling Dr. Arlene about her trip to Loveladies. Had she overstepped? Would Dr. A. be furious?

When Dr. Arlene appeared in the doorway, her cheeks

were flushed. Her eyes danced with excitement.

"I want you to take a look at this," Anne said, stalling. "I got a lot done on the book. I think we can . . ."

"Wait till you hear," Dr. Arlene interjected. "Olivia tried to contact me again. She called the radio station. She wants to meet me later tonight at a bar in Landsdown called Hanratty's. Do you know it?"

"Sure. But I don't think that's possible," Anne said slowly.

Dr. Arlene looked confused. So Anne reluctantly launched into an account of her morning visit to the Smiths.

Instead of getting angry, Dr. Arlene looked positively delighted. "Do you know what this means?" she said, when Anne had finished. "If the girl is dead, so is the story. The press won't be able to touch me. Of course," she amended hastily, as if hearing how callous she sounded, "how sad for Olivia's family. The mother must be devastated."

"It's a loss I don't think you ever fully recover from," Anne said, remembering as she spoke how Dr. A. appeared to have recovered just fine from the loss of her infant daughter.

Dr. A. said, "Whoever called the station instructed me to bring five thousand dollars in cash tonight."

"Which brings up an interesting question," Anne said. "If Olivia is your daughter and Olivia's dead, exactly who will be meeting you at Hanratty's tonight?"

"I'll be damned if I know."

Hanratty's was a dark, narrow hole-in-the-wall bar on a dark side street in Landsdown. It had been around for as long as anyone could remember and had survived and even prospered while an antique shop, a men's formal wear store, a dry cleaners, and a florist on the same block had gone out of business. A Rheingold sign in the big plate-glass window was the only form of decoration in what was otherwise a dingy, dimly lit storefront.

Dr. Arlene, dressed in a black designer pants suit and clutching her pocketbook to her chest as if someone was threatening to snatch it from her, looked distinctly out of place. Anne watched from her car as Dr. Arlene slunk into Hanratty's, a wide-brimmed hat shielding her face in an effort to maintain her anonymity.

Dr. A. took a seat by the plate-glass window and ordered a mixed drink, which she nursed slowly, taking baby sips. Anne noted with amusement that a drunk at the bar tried to pick Dr. A. up and was promptly rebuffed.

The person who'd phoned the station had instructed Dr. Arlene not to tell anyone about the meeting. Dr. A. would have gladly complied if Anne hadn't insisted on tagging along.

"You need some backup," Anne had told Dr. A. earlier.

"I just want to get it over with," the radio shrink had replied.

"But what if this is just the beginning? What if 'Olivia' decides she wants more money, or she exposes you anyway and gets her own book deal out of it? Don't you want to know who this girl is and where she lives? Don't you want to stop this before it goes any further?"

"I suppose you're right," Dr. Arlene had said. "If you get her off my back for good, I'll really owe you one."

Yes, you will, Anne had silently agreed. *Find a black-mailer, lose a houseguest.*

Now she sat in her car, her eyes trained on the entrance to the bar. Hanratty's was half-full. Music blared from a

jukebox. Bottles clinked. Cigarette smoke drifted up to
the ceiling. It was ten-thirty at night, and she'd been sitting in her car for an hour. Anne wondered if the girl, who
was an hour late, intended to show at all.

She was getting ready to go inside and talk Dr. A. into
leaving when she saw someone approach the shrink's
table—a teenager in a short, tight, flowered dress and
stiletto heels. She had on sunglasses and a hat with a brim
even wider than Dr. Arlene's. Her shoulder-length platinum blond hair flipped up at the ends.

Anne got out of the car and approached the bar, keeping an eye on the girl, who had sat down opposite Dr. Arlene. In her tight dress and high heels, the girl looked
cheap, low-rent. Anne couldn't picture her anywhere near
Loveladies or Lorraine Smith's modern glass beach
house.

Dr. Arlene removed an envelope from her bag and slid
it across the table. The girl leaned forward, crossing her
legs. Something clicked in Anne's brain. She started to
run. She had almost reached the entrance when Tracy
Graustark spotted her. Tracy pushed her chair back hurriedly and stood up. Then she grabbed the envelope,
which Anne happened to know contained a personal
check for a fraction of the amount Tracy had asked for,
and ran to the back of the bar. Anne ran after her, noticing
Dr. Arlene's mouth form an O of astonishment as she
raced by.

"Back door?" Anne called out to the bartender.

He jerked his thumb to the left and went back to pouring shots of whiskey. Anne was moving so fast that the
men knocking back drinks and staring up at the Phillies
game on TV were transformed into a noisy, testosterone-
fueled blur.

Anne yanked open the rear door of Hanratty's, which faced a deserted alley. The night air was fresh as a promise, instantly dissipating the smell of cigarettes and beer. A dozen different thoughts tumbled through her mind. But it all came back to why? She peered up and down the alley. No sign of Tracy. To the right was a high chain-link fence and a row of metal trash cans overflowing with garbage. She turned left, emerging from the alley into a dark, narrow street she'd never seen before.

More abandoned, graffiti-smeared storefronts. A shuttered liquor store. A Laundromat with a *For Rent* sign in the window. A shoe store whose plate-glass window had been partially knocked out. A defunct tattoo parlor called Tattoo Lou's.

Tattoo Lou's. Anne hadn't known there was a tattoo place in Landsdown. She approached it as quietly as she could. The windows were cloudy. Someone had knocked the O out of the word Lou on the sign. A broken streetlamp blinked, throwing off intermittent light.

Anne tried the front door and it swung open with a low, painful-sounding groan. She didn't bother calling Tracy's name. She knew it was futile, that if Tracy was inside she wouldn't answer. Anne felt along the wall, located the light switch, and found herself in a narrow, medium-size room with a peeling linoleum floor. A long counter extended the length of one side of the room. On the other side were four green vinyl chairs lined up in a row, facing four identical, rectangular mirrors and Formica cabinets with drawers that had been built into the wall. On top of the cabinets were some dirty-looking tools and what looked like injection needles.

Anne had never been in a tattoo parlor before. It reminded her a little of a beauty salon, except that the walls were covered with rows of dusty framed tattoos. There were thousands of them: flowers, fruit, animals, calligraphy, numbers, geometric designs, full-figured naked women, ships, bugs, reptiles, Native American motifs. A couple of posters showed photos of people with tattoos. One man was completely covered from head to foot; his features were indistinct and somehow inhuman, a sideshow freak staring defiantly out at the camera.

Anne noticed a narrow doorway in the back of the shop. She walked through it into a smaller windowless room containing a massage table covered with a sheet and a pillow. There was a mirror in here, too, plus a small wicker table and a three-tier shelf containing a box of tissues, a CD player, a couple of audiotapes, and a dusty plastic plant.

Anne went over to the far end of the room and yanked open the door of a small closet. Tracy Graustark was crouching on the floor. Her blond wig had slipped to one side and perched precariously on her head like a ratty mop. Her dress bunched around her knees. In her hand, she clutched a khaki-colored knapsack.

"Believe it or not," Anne said, "your aunt is going to be thrilled you're okay."

Tracy stood up slowly and stepped out of the closet. She looked frightened and tired. Her face seemed to have aged since the last time Anne had seen her. It was gaunt, worn-out, hollow-looking.

"How did you know it was me?" Tracy murmured.

"The wolf tattoo on your ankle. Delia told me you'd gotten it. I figured if you were serious about dropping the witchcraft, you'd try to have the tattoo removed."

Tracy shook her head sadly. "It costs too much money to have them taken off. Besides, this place is closed. I know the owner. He lets me crash here when I need to get away from things."

"What's with the needles in the other room?" Anne asked.

"Hookers crash here sometimes. Some of the girls are using. But I've never even tried it. Honest."

The fear in Tracy's eyes made Anne want to reach out and give the girl a reassuring hug. But she knew it would be the wrong move, like cozying up to a skittish fawn. Instead, she took the opposite tack.

"Nice clothes," she said. "Are they yours?"

"I kind of borrowed them from a thrift shop on Cookson Street," Tracy replied.

"Shoplifting. Extortion. You've been pretty busy lately, no?"

"I can explain about Olivia," Tracy said nervously. "I met her last summer at a party on Long Beach Island. We hit it off right away. She is . . . I mean she *was* this incredibly smart, pretty girl. And we had so much in common." Tracy's voice cracked. "We'd both lost our parents. We were both in a lot of pain. Olivia had found out she was adopted, and she'd managed to track down her birth mother. She was going to contact her. Just to see what her mother was like, so she wouldn't feel so . . ." Tracy stopped, searching for the right word.

"Lost?" Anne suggested.

"Yes," Tracy said gratefully. Tears welled up in her eyes. "Exactly."

"And then Olivia was killed in a plane crash."

"I read about it in the paper. It was so unfair."

"And you decided to capitalize on the tragedy?" Anne asked.

"No," Tracy protested. "I just wanted to get away from

here. That's all. Away from New Jersey. Away from Aunt Delia. That's why I contacted Dr. Arlene."

"But you didn't show up the first time."

"I chickened out. Then when Abby died, I needed money. And I didn't know how else to get it."

"The part about Olivia's parents being alcoholics. Was that true?"

"Her dad drank too much. At least that's what she said. I never met him."

Anne studied Tracy carefully. She wanted answers, but she knew she had to proceed with caution. She didn't want to risk losing the girl a second time.

"About Abby . . ." Anne began tentatively.

"Don't let the cops know where I am," Tracy pleaded. "They'll arrest me."

"It's time to stop hiding and tell the truth. If you do, nobody's going to blame you for Abby's death. I promise."

Tracy smiled bitterly. "You don't know what you're talking about."

"I know you didn't poison Abby with the jimsonweed you ordered from *The Dark Path* catalog. You wanted to protect her and her baby. Once you learned she was pregnant, you urged her to drop out of the coven, to stop taking herbs or else she might kill herself and her child."

Tracy stared at Anne in astonishment. She looked confused, like a pet who'd wandered too far from home.

Anne said, "You have the catalog with you, right?"

Tracy's eyes flew to her knapsack.

"It doesn't prove anything," Anne said. "Except that you were in charge of ordering herbs and potions for the coven."

"But everyone thinks I killed her," Tracy cried out, her

voice rising hysterically. "I know the police searched my house. I know someone saw me with Abby on the beach."

"You also know who killed her, don't you?"

Tracy buried her face in her hands. "Nobody's going to believe me," she sobbed.

Anne took a stab at edging closer to the truth. "Is that what he told you would happen? That you'd be blamed for Abby's death?"

"Yes," Tracy said. Tears trickled down her face in a slow, steady stream. The fight seemed to have drained out of her.

Everything happened fast after that. One moment, Anne was standing with Tracy in the back room of the tattoo parlor and the next moment, the lights had gone out and it was pitch-black in Tattoo Lou's.

"Oh, my God," Tracy whispered, her voice tight with panic. "He's here."

Chapter 23

Fear of the dark is a stage many children experience. Sometimes, a fanciful treatment works best. Brush the goblins from under the bed, shoo the monsters away, exorcise the witches and ghosts, say a chant to the moon to stay up in the sky.

 Anne could hear Tracy's frantic, raspy breathing and then a new noise—the unmistakable sound of approaching footsteps.

"Help me." Tracy's voice trembled with fear.

Anne stared into the darkness at the spot where the doorway should have been. She tried to remember the contours of the room—the position of the closet, tables, shelf. His footsteps louder now, almost upon them. The darkness heavy and complete, thick as a shroud. Anne stretched out her arms, felt her fingertips connect with the vinyl edge of the massage table.

She felt, rather than saw, Tracy rush by her, the air shifting ever so slightly, the scent of sweat and fear, the sound of heels skittering against the floor. Tracy let out a sharp, high-pitched scream. Then a heavy thud, just as Anne, still holding on to the table, propelled herself forward and ducked underneath it, bumping her head in the process. She crouched, willing herself to stay absolutely still, not daring to make the slightest telltale sound.

He was circling the room, stumbling into things. Anne winced as she felt him collide with the massage table, then veer away. She could hear him breathing, could sense his eyes searching her out in the darkness. She reached out cautiously with her right hand, brushed against one of Tracy's limbs—an arm, a leg?—and immediately recoiled.

He stopped moving, and Anne guessed he was to her right, by the closet. Her heart seemed to be thudding so loudly it would lead him straight to her. Her mouth had gone dry, her whole body was shaking. *One* . . . she counted silently.

She heard him come closer, then stop. He was gauging his next move, hunting for her, tracking his prey.

Two . . .

The massage table jerked violently, and she felt it lift up and away.

Three . . .

She darted out from beneath the table and aimed for the doorway, bumping her shoulder hard against the wall, recovering, blindly propelling herself across Tattoo Lou's, her hands outstretched like a sleepwalker's. She tripped over something bulky, banging her shins, and tumbled to the floor. It was not as dark in the main room. She could make out dim shapes, the outline of the chair she'd tripped over, the shadowy room reflected in a mirror on the wall. The door to the shop was about six feet away. Her heart surged in anticipation. She was going to make it.

She pivoted toward the entrance. But he moved quicker than she'd anticipated and was upon her in an instant. His arm curled around her throat, choking the breath out of her. Waves of panic engulfed her. She kicked and thrashed, bucking forward, trying to elude his grasp. Her hands scrabbling, knocking stuff over, encountering something cold and metallic.

A sharp, piercing pain in her lower back. His hand tightening against her throat as she screamed. The pain shot upward toward her neck. She felt something slick and wet on her skin and realized she'd been stabbed.

She fought to breathe. Bright spots of color danced in the darkness. The room was slipping away until only the pain remained, intense and raw, spreading like fire over her body. She raised her arm and jabbed him with the thing in her hand.

He grunted in surprise and loosened his grip, allowing her to jerk free. She heard something clatter on the linoleum. Pitching forward, she fell to the floor, gasping for breath. Her back hurt so much she could barely move, but she forced herself to crawl in the direction of the door. He'd begun to moan, making low guttural noises in his throat.

Come on, she willed herself, trying to block out the pain. *Faster.*

She grabbed the knife and stumbled to her feet, yanking the door open just as she felt his arms wrap around her knees, tackling her to the ground.

She was half in and half out of the tattoo parlor, her back throbbing now, her body achy and sore. She rolled onto her side, screaming wildly, and caught a glimpse of his face as she slashed at him with the knife, fending him off.

Brian Miller glared at her, then his grip loosened, and he closed his eyes.

She looked at him, sprawled there in the doorway. For one long moment—before she pressed her hand to her back and tried to stem the blood, before Dr. A. and the police appeared at the other end of the block, before she ran back inside to Tracy—she thought that he was dead.

"I should have put it together sooner," Anne said. "What struck me about Abby's 'suicide' from the beginning was how contrived the witchcraft elements were. The circle in the sand, the amber necklace, those runes I found, all arranged for effect."

"It's called overkill," Trasker replied. "Brian stacked the deck so it wouldn't look like murder—planting the Ecstasy on Abby, making it look like her English paper was a suicide note."

They were sitting on Anne's front porch at eight o'clock the next morning with a fresh box of Dunkin' Donuts between them. It was going to be another scorcher. Not a cloud in the sky and already seventy-six degrees, according to the radio. Harry the cat lounged at their feet, keeping his one eye firmly on the donuts.

Anne broke off a small piece and gave it to the cat. She winced as she bent over. She'd had to have twenty-seven stitches in her back. She was lucky, the emergency room doctor had said. The wound wasn't deep enough to cause organ damage or any permanent disability.

"How are you feeling?" Trasker asked.

Anne touched her bandaged back gingerly. "I'm still a little sore. I guess it could have been a lot worse."

"How's Tracy doing?"

"According to Delia, her condition's been upgraded from critical to stable."

Tracy Graustark had been stabbed once in the chest and was in the intensive care unit with a punctured right lung. Delia had told Anne she thought the worst was over and that Tracy would make a full recovery.

"Hey," Trasker said, gazing at Anne, "I know that look. It's your Monday morning quarterback face. Let yourself off the hook, okay? Or hang me up there next to you. I had Browning pegged as the father of Abby's baby, too. I never guessed it was Brian. I never suspected he was so worried about his football scholarship and pleasing his parents that he'd murder Abby when she threatened to keep the baby. And I certainly never thought he'd poison her by tripling the amount of jimsonweed in those funny hand-rolled cigarettes the girls were smoking. Jimsonweed that Tracy ordered from *The Bad Seed* catalog or whatever the heck it's called."

"*The Dark Path*. You know, I think another reason Brian used all those witchcraft touches, including nailing that heart to my door, was that he wanted us to link Leo to Abby's death."

Harry jumped up onto Trasker's lap, and Trasker gently stroked the fur between the cat's ears. "I thought those guys were friends."

"So did I. But now I realize Brian hoped to capitalize

on Leo's playing Devil. He resented Leo's friendship with Melissa. Bottom line: He wanted Melissa back, and Leo was standing in his way."

"Leo's gone back to California. Apparently, his parents were so troubled by his role in all of this that the entire family is going for counseling in the fall."

"Good. I really hope it helps."

"I think it might. He seemed pretty upset when I saw him at the sheriff's office." Trasker helped himself to a jelly donut and poured them both more iced tea. "Tracy wasn't able to talk much last night. Did she tell Delia how she knew Brian killed Abby?"

"She said they'd been sleeping together for weeks, but Brian insisted on keeping their relationship secret. I guess he was still hoping Melissa would come around, not realizing that Abby was deeply in love with him and even dreamed of marrying him. According to Tracy, Abby told him about the baby the day before she died. An abortion was out of the question. Both their families are religious, as are most people in town. Brian probably freaked out. His scholarship, his plans for the future, his tenuous relationship with his parents, were all on the verge of collapsing. He knew about the witchcraft and the herbs. And he saw his chance."

"Why would Abby risk damaging her unborn child's health by smoking jimsonweed?" Trasker mused.

"I think she was conflicted. She wanted Brian and saw she could use the baby as leverage; on the other hand, having a baby would seriously impact her life and ruin the golden girl image her mother had of her."

Anne stared out at the ocean, which was a pearly shade of gray, flecked with rippling whitecaps. The sand was smooth and powdery. A curtain of mist rose off the water, low and thin, like gauze. Her eyes slid back to Trasker.

"Abby had told Tracy she was meeting Brian right after the coven had finished its witchcraft ceremonies. But Tracy was worried. She knew how volatile and emotional Abby could be. She didn't want Abby to do anything reckless. After the *esbat*, she . . ."

"The what?" Trasker interrupted.

"The gathering of witches. After it was over, Tracy went home. Then she went back to the beach. She found Abby much the way I found her the following morning, lying in the sand with the circle traced around her, clutching the 'suicide' note. Only Tracy didn't believe that Abby had committed suicide. So she confronted Brian, who didn't seem the least bit surprised or upset by what had happened. Tracy told Delia he'd looked relieved. She guessed what Brian had done and threatened to turn him in to the police. He told her she couldn't prove a thing. He also said that if the cops suspected foul play, they'd look to Tracy first, since she was the one who procured the jimsonweed."

"That's when she ran away to Landsdown."

"Uh huh. Far enough to keep out of sight, but near enough to monitor what was going on at home." Anne finished the jelly donut she was eating and reached for a toasted coconut. Her injury had made her more ravenous than usual. She said, "I was pretty clueless not to realize Brian's been following me for the last two days. Hoping I'd lead him straight to Tracy, which is exactly what I did."

"Unintentionally," Trasker added. "By the way, he's going to be just fine. That needle you jabbed him with was rusty and filled with some pretty mean drugs, but the doctors told me he hasn't contracted HIV, and he's already come down from his high. His other wounds were superficial. He's admitted killing Pam. Said he knew the coven was meeting on the docks and got there early, hoping to learn whether Tracy had confided in Pam. He was frantic because he thought that Tracy had told Pam how and why Abby was killed."

"How did he even know they'd been in contact?"

"On the beach the other day, he heard Pam admit that she'd seen Tracy, that Pam was the intermediary between you and Tracy. He claims he never meant to hurt her: He walked up behind her. She got frightened and screamed. And he panicked and pushed her into the bay. Maybe if she hadn't been wearing that heavy sack and if she hadn't been disoriented from the henbane, she could have swum to safety."

The front door swung open suddenly, and Harry jumped off Trasker's lap. Dr. Arlene stepped out onto the porch. She was wearing a white silk tunic over black slacks and looked rested and content. "You guys want some coffee?" she asked. "I'm making myself a fresh pot."

"Sure," Trasker said.

"Why not?" Anne seconded.

Dr. Arlene was driving back to the city in a few hours. Not a moment too soon, Anne thought, savoring the idea of having her house all to herself again. No more wet towels piled on the bathroom floor. No more papers cluttering up the living room and designer food crammed on the refrigerator shelves. No more houseguests from hell—not this summer, anyway.

"I'll call Phil later today," Dr. A. told Anne, "to get us an extension on the book. How does an extra six months sound?"

"Like a blessing," Anne said, laughing.

"Leave it to me. Have I ever steered you wrong?"

"Now that you mention it . . ." Anne began.

"On second thought, don't answer that." Dr. A. started to go inside, then turned around. "Do you think I ought to rent a house down here for September? Maybe that cute little Queen Anne on Abbott?"

Anne felt her smile start to slip.

"Just kidding," Dr. Arlene announced. "Jersey's nice, but I'd rather be in Monaco. No offense."

"None taken," Anne said with relief, as Dr. A. went back inside the house.

Trasker said, "Oh, there's one other thing I forgot to tell you. We got a court order to search Noah Wright's house. The guy is a wacko. He was spying on the coven, taking pictures of the girls, collecting bits and pieces of their stuff. Turns out he operates an Internet porn site starring underage adolescents. I don't know if he was hoping to recruit our young friends or if he just got turned on by them. In any case, he's been brought up on charges and is sitting in jail."

"Wait till my next door neighbor finds out," Anne said with a smile. "Martha is going to have a fit."

"Speaking of Martha Cox, there's one thing I don't get."

"What's that?"

"Didn't you say the girls tried to give Martha migraines and it worked? How'd they manage that?"

Anne shrugged. "The craft works in mysterious ways." She thought of the love spell she'd cast. *An interesting man.* And now here he was, on her front porch, munching a chocolate donut. Maybe a little well-placed witchcraft wasn't such a terrible thing.

Trasker stood up. "That coffee's not going to be ready for a while. Meantime, what do you say to a walk on the beach?"

He held out his hand and she took it. The cat rubbed his back against Trasker's ankles and purred contentedly, looking up at Trasker with unbridled adoration. Now here was a first, Anne thought, as they walked slowly down the porch steps and across the street to where the ocean glittered in the early-morning sun. Harry actually warming up to someone—to a man, no less. Trasker draped his arm across her shoulder. He leaned in, brushing his lips across her cheek.

"What's that for?" she teased.

"Because we're finally together, and I'm so happy I feel like dancing."

To prove it, he did a little jig, kicking up his heels for good measure.

Anne stood on the boardwalk, threw her head back, and laughed so hard it hurt.

The Jersey Shore Mysteries by
Beth Sherman
Featuring Anne Hardaway

"Anne Hardaway is a delightful mix of humor,
pragmatism, and vulnerability."
Margaret Maron

THE DEVIL AND THE DEEP BLUE SEA
0-380-81605-9/$5.99 US/$7.99 Can

The late night satanic activities of bored teens in the God-fearing
New Jersey Shore community of Oceanside Heights seem more ditsy
than dangerous to ghostwriter-cum-sleuth Anne Hardaway—until
she stumbles upon the corpse of a young, would-be witch.

Also by Beth Sherman

DEATH'S A BEACH
0-380-73109-6/$5.99 US/$7.99 Can

DEATH AT HIGH TIDE
0-380-73108-8/$5.99 US/$7.99 Can

DEAD MAN'S FLOAT
0-380-73107-X/$5.99 US/$7.99 Can